FINNLEY WREN

HIS NOTIONS AND OPINIONS

T0284685

Partially funded by the Illinois Arts Council, a state agency.

www.dalkeyarchive.com
Victoria, TX / London / Dublin

Cover: Typography and layout Arnold Kotra
Composition by Jeffrey Higgins

Printed on permanent/durable acid-free paper

FINNLEY WREN

His *NOTIONS* and *OPINIONS* together with A HAPHAZARD HISTORY of his *Career* and *Amours* in these MOODY YEARS, as well as SUNDRY RHYMES, FABLES, DIATRIBES AND LITERARY MISDEMEANORS ❧

A NEW NOVEL IN A NEW MANNER BY PHILIP WYLIE

Published in 2015 A.D. by

DALKEY ARCHIVE PRESS

"De la manière dont on reçoit ses idées
dépend celle dont on se les rappelle."
—Denis Diderot.

"When your heart is sick your liver is
just around the corner."
—Arthur ("Bugs") Baer.

CONTENTS

PART I

FRIDAY AFTERNOON

THRUST from the bloody bowels of woman and driven into the black, perpetual hiding place called death—with little between but blood and women and solitude—" said Finnley Wren, drawing a line of the tablecloth with his knife—"sometimes I am so terrified of life that I come near putting an end to it as a boon to my dreadful little nerves. I have all kinds of nerves. Those in my scalp are for horror and, oddly enough, the ones for tragic love are in my belly. I wouldn't have slept tonight. Or—had I slept, it might have been worse. If the sleeve of care is only raveled—it can be mended; but when it is charred— why then, God help you—sleep brings nightmares. You've probably had the falling one. And the dark shape swiftly approaching. But have you had the slowly turning spiral? Or the expanding musical note? I doubt it. You are not tough enough to survive those dreams. And how that reference to charred sleeves sticks in my subconscious! Maybe I'm mad. Certainly I'm loquacious." He made a mark on my feelings with his eyes.

"Have a drink," I said.

"I will. I'll have several. I'm going to tell you the story of my life. It comes on me at odd times—that story. I told it last week to my secretary. The poor child had a grotesque cold. All my secretaries are subject to colds. But she insisted that I come over to her apartment for the day's dictation. Interesting girl—interesting and indispensable. As hard and shiny as chitin outside, but filled with something warm and sweet and probably cloying.

[3]

"Anyway, I ran through it all. From the first cry on the snow-crusted steppes of North Dakota to the present Manhattan heebie-jeebies. I could perceive the tenor of that saga from the beginning: I was a periwinkle, a pearly nautilus, an opalescent cockleshell on the black and white breakers of life. No surcease. No Nirvana. Nothing but here and there the inpulling arms of women warm and lush. I went on, setting up a perpetual shame in my conscience, until I was holding her hand, and then I departed abruptly. I had a Bromo-Seltzer for my hangover and I bought a bottle of Listerine. I took a mouthful of it against her rheum. The cork came out in my pocket on the elevated train going up town and I arrived at the office smelling like a dispensary.

"That illustration of hardship in a world of things is unintentional. History and introspection were my keynotes. I want neither sympathy nor assistance for my autobiography. I will merely ease it into a mind where the compression is less great. What's your name?"

"Wylie," I said. "Philip Wylie."

He ruminated. "Heard it somewhere. But you're going to be the victim of a graceless incuriosity. I want to talk about myself. You have the eye of an audience and the manner of a loiterer. My name is Wren. Finnley Wren."

I nodded. "I read it on the letter you destroyed as I sat down."

"That letter." He revolved the letter and certain obviously painful connotations in his brain. "It was from a lawyer." He smiled. "I was born on the first of January in nineteen hundred."

The man came in a sleigh, driving over the stiff, moon-blue drifts as if wolves were behind him. He stood on the porch beating his mittened hands together.

Light slanted into his face. "Doctor?" he asked.

Dr. Wren was inside. The room was overhot, fœtid. A woman in it moaned softly.

"His foot," the man said. "Green."

The Doctor looked at the woman and began rolling down his cuffs. "How far?"

"Six—seven miles."

The Doctor put on his waistcoat, his coat, and a massive envelope of fur. He turned to his wife. "I'll be back—in time."

She stared at the aspirant patterns on the wall and said, "Hurry." He paused, wondering whether she was speeding his errand or imploring him to return swiftly. Mrs. Thomas came from the kitchen with a pan of water. She put it down, thrust out her underlip and blew her hair.

"Yes," Doctor Wren said. He bent over his wife. "In any case—it's a natural function. Think of the Fiji Islanders."

He left her to think of the Fiji Islanders. He worried more about the effect of this departure on her attitude toward his work than he did about her condition. She was rugged. He despised frail women.

He followed the man into the parlor of the farmhouse. He inhaled slightly. "Gangrene," he murmured.

A woman with eyes like oysters and a huge, meaningless body moved across the floor, gulping. The Doctor dropped his heavy bag. "You should have sent for me when it first happened."

She began to cry.

There was another woman in the room. She was silent.

The man said, "He got it caught—in the corn sheller."

"You told me that before." Dr. Wren turned up his sleeves again. Their lower edges, after the last turn, looked rusty. He wanted to shout, "How in the name of God did you get your foot in the corn sheller?" But he said nothing. He pulled back the blanket, unwound the rags, and regarded what had been a human foot.

Presently he lifted his face. "Do you think you could—?" he said to the man.

"Sure," the man replied. The bright chimney of the oil lamp appeared and vanished, appeared and vanished behind him.

"Boiling water. Lots of it."

He walked into the kitchen and cleared off the large, scarred table. Then he went to the pump and began to wash. The snorting stream was icy. He filled a basin and put it on the stove. The porcine woman brought sheets. She shivered, whimpered, sweat. The other woman collected all the lamps in the house except the one in the parlor where a pair of tremendous hands unraveled a blanket patiently and persistently.

When the doctor started home behind a reluctant horse the man at his side was quite drunk. Nevertheless, he drove mutely.

The runners and the harness squeaked.

Miniature snowstorms sifted and tinkled across vast alabaster breasts—breasts empty of nurture and unsullied by nipples.

A white halo froze around the doctor's mouth upon his collar and his mustache.

The careless immensity of stars grew less distinct.

Suddenly it was morning.

The doctor opened his front door apprehensively. Mrs. Thomas held a finger to her lips. He walked slowly to the bed. His wife slept; in her arms a baby blinked and whimpered.

He sat down heavily and the ice on him began to melt. Mrs. Thomas made "boy" with her lips.

He had not inquired.

"I'm in the advertising business," Wren said. "I'm partner in a relatively large firm."

He looked at his watch.

[6]

He put more water in his highball.

He hummed the music which the orchestra was playing.

He stared at the legs of the girl at the next table.

"Last year I made sixty-three thousand nine hundred and fourteen dollars and eighty-one cents. Twice as much as my father made. Ten times as much as any of my more distant progenitors have made as far back as Christopher, at least, on my father's side, and on my mother's as far as records go, including John Milton.

"Thus," he continued, waving hands on which the fingers were long wands, "we briefly introduce and dispatch my illustrious forebears. If, accidentally, I mention them again, I shall remember to apologize.

"My father—is a fraud."

Dr. Gordon Wren
sat on the bench in front of his locker at the Country Club. Afternoon sunlight shone on his bald crown. A mild perspiration trickled into his Vandyke and merged with the particles of dead skin beneath the beard's glossy surface. Gray hair, like frayed manilla rope neatly combed, dominated the composition of the austere ornament.

His face was fleshy. A certain shrewdness of his pale olive eyes still favored his presumption of hypnotic and masterful powers. There was, indeed, fresh enough chemistry in his irises to reflect considerable light. But muddy-colored sacs lay along his cheek bones; his liver-spotted hands quivered as he withdrew a woolen sock; he panted slowly and without evident cause.

Hairs grew from his nostrils. Hairs climbed up his inbent chest. His eyebrows were horizontal hedges of hair.

From below his ribs his naked paunch swelled out, variously empurpled by meshes of broken blood vessels and flaunting an

[7]

antique, evilly-incised scar that was like a drawing on an over-blown balloon.

His genitalia dangled. His thighs were like porridge. His calves were spindly. His feet were large and flat. From between two of his cramped toes there jutted up a small pale sail of deceased epidermis and the air creeping along the floor blew upon that sail and became indelicate.

Over him were the presences, the mementos, and the promises of pimples, cuts, scabs, scars, mosquito bites, hives, felons, blood blisters, bunions, ingrown nails and hangnails, dandruff, boils, bruises, strains, breaks, sprains, warts, small tumors, wens, burns, vaccinations, piles, blackheads, and the evidences of a variety of ailments of which arthritis was the most readily diagnosable.

Dr. Wren was sixty-one
a monument to use.

He walked forward, balancing his belly with his blanched buttocks and he stood beneath the shower. The water dribbled warmly over him.

He dropped his soap, belched when he bent to pick it up, and whistled absently as he discarded in his mind eleven of the strokes he had made on the golf links that afternoon.

The vice president of the Orange Park Bank and Trust Company, which subsequently failed and paid back three cents on the dollar to hundreds of millionaire Orange Park widows and multimillionaire North Orange Park orphans, spoke from the adjacent shower where he was steaming his navel.

"That you, Wren?"

"Hello there, neighbor."

"How'd the game go?"

"You know that little rough spot they've left in the middle of the twelfth fairway? I dropped my drive into it. Blew up a bit after that. I'm going to speak to the greens committee about a course where a hard, straight ball is penalized."

"Think you should," the vice president replied, quickly

stemming one of Dr. Wren's renowned recapitulations of his day's play. "Saw a piece about your son in the *Saturday Evening Post* yesterday."

Wren's mind budged disappointedly to a contemplation of his eldest offspring. He had read the article three times. "Heard there was something about Finnley in the *Post*."

The other man chuckled. "I wouldn't be so modest if I had a family like that. What are the rest of them doing?"

"Tom's home. Vi is getting ready for a concert. I forget just when it is."

"Great kids," the vice president repeated heartily. "Wonderful thing, these American youngsters. In spite of all you hear to the contrary, they're as straight as a die and as clean as a whistle. Smart as whips, too. Tom called on Verna a few nights ago. Great sight to see a young giant like Tom with a sweet, good girl like Verna. I envy this generation. And I know it through and through. Give you a lift?"

"No—thanks," the doctor replied.

He decided not to take a cold shower. He decided that open pores would be beneficial. He went back to his locker, donned a moldered jock strap, a tight girdle, frayed B.V.D.'s, and, over the unsavory ensemble, a well-cut tweed suit. The shoulders of the suit were heavily padded to relieve him of the burden of good carriage. His girdle was reinforced by a belt and a tight vest.

He massaged his Vandyke and anointed it with a sharply perfumed oil. He set his pince-nez on his large nose.

He ascended to the clubroom, sleek and aromatic—a fine figure of a man.

He remembered that someone had called doctors the "dauntless duelists of grim Death" and as he stepped conspicuously and confidently forward, deep in reverie, he meditated that the inventor of the magic epithet was a poet.

In his automobile, he poured out power with a delicate adjustment of his toe. The mechanism moved forward, shining and sibilant. On both sides of the road autumn displayed its grandiose funeral for summer. Birds swam in the spangled sky.

Dr. Wren sniffled and wished he had taken the cold shower.

When he came to his home, he read the notes his nurse had left for him. He saw a copy of the *Saturday Evening Post* and acted upon an idle urge to telephone his son. But Finnley was not at home. He was in a speakeasy, with me.

The doctor moved importantly to the living rooms of his house. Tom, hearing him approach, hastily pulled down Verna's skirts.

Wren and I looked into our glasses with an almost sad reluctance to drink. We were realizing in our separate manners that, when the process was well under way, anticipation of it would depart, and since alcohol is no refuge from the hot tides of life but only seems as if it might be, we dwelt on the seeming, while we listened to words and watched our flickering thoughts.

now, said the man with the girl at the next table, we have learned better, we know that to inhibit those impulses is to commit a slow, emotional suicide. that is psychology.

the girl breathed and nodded.

look at the old maid, the man continued. there is the perfect example of what happens. let me tell you, evelyn, let me warn you

"I could weep," Wren said, "at the pitiful exigencies of sex and the handicaps put upon them by our society. That girl understands he wants her. Why doesn't she say yes or no? Psychology! Good God, what wretched aphrodisiacs we've got ourselves around to using."

Somebody came in through the door and for a moment I saw the street and the lights outside. Manhattan had put on the black hat of night. Automobiles went whizzing through its streets like bright-eyed bugs through the cacophony and the crowds and the colors and the signs making their jerky circuits through the talcum powder and the horse manure past the skyscrapers and the cheap cigar stores. Ragtime night, rape night, penny candy night.

Caused, I reflected, by the trivial fact that our face of the planet was looking away from the sun and into the sickening abyss of the firmament.

"i am crying, a man said, leaning on our table and suiting his "actions to his words, because of the failure of the republican "form of government. imagine the idiocy of Jefferson. con- "ceive of the stupidity of Solon and Clisthenes. i grant you "that the theories of oligarchy and hereditary right are un- "sound. but—representative government, my friends! who "could be so blind as to want all men to have the power to gov- "ern? who could embrace the notion that the best govern- "ment could be manufactured by the worst people acting "equally with the wisest? who? fools. all fools. ten "trillion fools come to make my vote meaningless, my voice "soundless, my brain useless, my education valueless. do you "wonder at my tears?"

"No," said Wren.

i went down to St. James infirmary, a girl began to sing. The orchestra tootled along behind her, sweetly miserable.

"I will tell you," Wren went on, "about the end of my adolescence. It is the second episode."

The music faded and blurred into another song. A song less skillfully played. A song made sweet by misty memory.

"Dardanella."

[11]

Round and round a ballroom moved the bright dresses of two hundred girls passing first a line of young men and then a row of seated matrons and dowagers who looked on through two prunes each. Among them, Jessica danced.

She was seventeen. She danced close to her partner, loving him a little while she was in his arms. Her radiant brain was peopled by desires which stepped into her eyes and pulled the corners of her mouth. She ached with beauty so contagious it infected all those young, young men around her. Without the vaccination of experience, without the immunity of age, they fell ill beneath her eyes, Delilah eyes, and her half-embraced virginity. She looked as if she would presently burst open, like a rose.

She had been Finnley's sweetheart for five years.

Finnley was going to leave for college on the following day.

He stood in the immemorial line of stags watching her and wishing that his suit were better cut, his shoes finer, his shirt more elegant.

The air in the room was feverish.

The contact of so many people made impossibilities out of his desperately clutched dreams.

Night. Stars. Automobile headlights licking up puddles of darkness on the road ahead. Jessica kissing, kissing, kissing, twisting in his arms.

The first time he had touched her under trees that were like women in huge skirts standing on their heads. Sitting on somebody's tombstone.

He liked that. It fitted neatly into his incautious cynicism —as so many things did.

Evenings beside the fire at her home when her father and mother had gone to bed and they sat with their heads together on the floor.

Little-by-little year-by-year edging toward a physical knowledge of each other.

He cut in.

"Let's talk," Jessica said.

They walked into another night and found Dr. Wren's car. They sat in it.

He put his arm over her frail and fragrant shoulders. But he knew, even then, that love was flying away and the rose was about to open not for him. He knew it before his fingers stuck upon the diamond.

A little crystal which a negro had dug from blue African mud and a Dutchman in Antwerp had ground into a regular polyhedron.

Jessica cried.

"Jeff," she said.

Finnley found himself nodding as if his head were on a spring and the rest of him immobile.

"He's a nice boy."

"You don't have to say that."

"But he is."

"You can say he's only a car salesman and never finished high school and is—is funny-looking."

Finnley meditated. Jeff was funny-looking. And he was not. "When did it happen?"

"Well—I've always known him."

"Sure."

"He's independent. He has a house. And—and—I can't wait forever. I can't. I can't wait any longer. And you'd only hate me if I stopped waiting with you. Four years—and after that maybe four more while you got started. Finnley. Why! I'd be twenty-five. Practically ancient."

He put his foot up on the windshield. "That is true."

"It's terrible," she continued. "I love you so. But I can't wait. And Jeff is nice. He's so good to me."

A car swung around a corner and vanished. He rubbed his back where perspiration was running down and tickling him.

"Good orchestra they have tonight." He dug the words into himself.

"Aren't you going to say anything else?"

"I hope not," he replied with incredible wisdom.

"Will you kiss me—just once more?"

"Maybe. It's funny. I suddenly got the idea as I drove over here to the dance that something was going to happen to you and me. I knew it. Not a black cat had crossed my path. I hadn't walked under a ladder or spilled salt or broken a mirror, but I knew it. I couldn't see lights very well and I couldn't remember what I had eaten for supper. Now I remember perfectly. Lamb. Roast lamb and wax beans. Potatoes and blancmange. And the lights are excessively bright."

"Don't talk like that!"

"Why not? I can hardly recall a time in my life when my conversation has been less hysterical."

"That's just the trouble with it."

They began to smoke cigarettes. "Tell me," Finnley said, "did he make love to you? Is that why—?"

Jessica did a terrible thing. She answered. "Not yet—but I promised him—tonight. Oh—Finnley—I'm so scared."

Finnley stood on top of the precipice and watched the sun rise. He could see his car beside the road in the valley far below. He thought how the sun must roar. He looked across Orange Park and Newark to the shrouded spicules of Manhattan. All the cities of the world lay before him in ruins. He kicked a stone over the cliff and observed its descent, pretending that it was himself.

He wondered how long he had stood there without moving. He wondered why he had come there.

It was the worst possible place to spend that morning.

For there, a hundred times, he had taken Jessica. Across the path and behind the road was a natural pavilion where ferns grew in the thick pine needles, where, in June, ladyslippers lifted their bloated blooms and all around lay a pink snow of azalea, and where, in the fall, partridge berries stretched strings of red beads and wild grapes hung pungent and full. Thither, with a woolly rug from the car, they had gone for many an unnumbering of the hours.

That delicious dell was scarcely three hundred yards from where he stood looking down on the collapsed, unconquered cities, but he did not dare go near it.

Then suddenly, as the sun was becoming warm and the first blandishments of day were filled with bird-songs, he heard voices.

He knew hideously whose voices they were.

He contemplated throwing himself over the cliff.

He climbed into a tangle of sumac and bull briar.

Jeff and Jessica walked to the rail along the precipice and surveyed the dazzling empire, the steel fairyland beneath them.

"It was wonderful," she sighed.

"You're a peach," Jeff answered.

There was no more ache in her voice. The rose was open and one could already imagine the dropping of the petals—a tragedy unthinkable on the previous evening.

Jeff's voice was mundane, slack, weak, ritualistic.

Finnley shivered in his bushes as if rattlesnakes were crawling on him.

It was another night.

A summer night.

Finnley recited a poem of his own composition:

> *"Life is but a passing spasm*
> *In an aggregate of cells;*

Kiss me, pretty protoplasm,
While your osculation dwells
Glucose-sweet, no enzyme action
Or love-lytic can reduce
Our relations to a fraction
Of hereditary use.
Nuclear rejuvenation
Melts the auricle of stoic:
Love requires a balanced ration—
Let our food be holozoic;
Let us live with all our senses
While anabolism lets us—
Till—with metaplastic fences
Some katabolism gets us,
Till, potential strength, retreating,
Leaves us at extinction's chasm;
And, since time is rather fleeting,
Kiss me, pretty protoplasm."

Dutch Goodwin came from the telephone. "Betty said she would be over—and that she'd bring her cousin. But remember—I get Betty, because you were too lazy to call."

"Sure," Finnley replied. "What is the cousin like?"

"We can go to my house," Finnley said to her. "It's only a couple of blocks—and there's no one at home. All away on a vacation."

The girl swallowed some of her gin and ginger ale. "What if they come back?"

"They won't. They're two hundred miles away. By the way, what's your name? I can't just call you—Betty's cousin."

"Libby."

"How old are you?"

"Nineteen. Why?"

"What's your father's middle name?"

"Don't kid me."

Finnley drank. "How about it? Just you and me? We can't sit here on Dutch Goodwin's front porch and neck all night, can we?"

The girl smiled with her dark, bovine eyes and shook her head. "I don't know you very well, though."

"You will," he answered. "And you'll like me."

"Yeah?"

Dutch stopped the phonograph. "What?"

"I said, Libby and I are going over to my house."

"Oh."

"Tell Betty, will you? Where is she?"

"In the bathroom. Sure."

"Have Betty call her mother and say she and Libby are staying with some friends in Orange Park. She's done it before."

"I will."

They lifted one of the slanting cellar doors and went down the irregular steps. He put his arm around her waist when he led her to the first floor.

"Hope you don't mind the dark. Lights turned off."

"No," Libby said. "I like it."

He peered into the ink and made out the specters of furniture. The inside of the house was stale and sweltering. They went to the second floor and then the third. The girl sat down on the edge of a bed. "What's in here?" she asked.

"Books. A desk. Chairs. Pictures. A banner on the wall. I'm in college, you know. The job I have in New York this summer is only temporary. I go back in a month."

"And Dutch is in college, too?"

"Yes. Dartmouth."

"What if your father came home from his vacation?"

Finnley laughed. "At one in the morning? He won't. But it would be tough if he did. He doesn't know I've ever had a drink—or held hands with a girl."

He opened the windows and peered over the panorama of Orange Park as it was described by Mazda bulbs.

"I hadn't ought to do this," she said slowly and without conviction.

"Why not?"

"I don't know. You college fellows—come and go. You only want to get girls in bed."

"Is there anything wrong in that? Don't you like it?"

There was a long silence in the room. Then rustling. He turned away from the windows. "What are you doing?"

"Undressing."

Finnley suddenly burned from head to foot. His mind was clogged by a picture of the girl—her voluptuous figure, her thick, crimson lips, her lazy black eyes, the deep softness he had found in her. What did it matter that she made grammatical errors, that her father worked for day wages, that her clothes were cheap and tasteless? What did anything matter except the ecstatic crescendos of sweetness and passion upon which the brain of all men and women remains fixed and toward which they move so charily?

He could see nothing in the room.

He clung dizzily to the window sill.

Her shoes dropped on the floor.

"Well, sweetheart?" she said.

He moved. "You wait. We—we don't want to surprise ourselves with children, do we?"

"I was going to speak about that," she replied.

He found her melon-like contours in the sable heat of the room. Rhythms were hammering inside him. He turned her

[18]

head from the pillow. He felt the spill of her hair over him.
He pushed his mouth against her mouth.

He looked at morning.

Soothed, contented, alive and luxurious. The girl's body
was the color of honey. Again the pulses of that past darkness
stirred in him. She opened her eyes and looked at him with
profound affection and gratitude. When she had scrutinized
him for a moment and understood his mood she said sleepily,
"Not—now—sweetheart. It's light."

"I like the light better."

She shut her eyes and moved herself close against him. "Me,
too," she whispered tremulously. "Gee—you're something."

Afterward she cried a little. "I don't know why," she said.
Then the dream burst.

A bus thundered outside the house. The hot new day became
real. They began brushing their teeth and scrambling into
their clothes. In her mind, already, belts were pulling the
wheels of machines around and around amid a crushing din.
In his, a piece of cheap paper thrust into a typewriter was gathering upon itself a warning about the dangers of colonic infec-
tion and an insinuation of the curative powers of yeast.

When she was dressed, he looked at her, and wondered.

He hoisted her aboard a trolley car and then ran for a commuters' train as if he were trying to escape from himself.

He had almost forgotten her when she telephoned.

Vi was playing morbidly on the piano.

Tom was passing a football with a friend in the back yard.

"I must see you," she said. "It's absolutely necessary."

Fright went into him like a pitchfork. "Say when and
where," he answered.

"In the park on Wayne and Orange Street. Right by the point where they meet. At nine tonight."

He hung up.

Dr. Wren came from the garage and nodded vaguely to him. "Hello, son."

"But I couldn't have," he protested. "It's impossible."

"You can feel it," Libby said in quiet horror. She put his hand on her belly. It bulged solidly.

He wanted to be angry but he could be only afraid. "I tell you, Libby, I couldn't. For one thing I know I couldn't. And for another it was only six weeks ago and babies don't get so you can feel them—like that—in six weeks."

She sat down tiredly on a park bench. "You did, though," she said.

Trolley cars banged and shrieked along the street. People passed them—lucky people who were not faced with the dilemma of pregnancy, who did not have dull girls calling them the fathers of their unborn children.

"You aren't going to try to tell me now that you never had anything to do with anyone except me, are you?" he asked.

"I never did." In her shivering dread, she believed herself.

"You know that I know you did." He felt vulgar, mean, base. He hated her for making him feel that way. Even his customary gracefulness of speech had deserted him and he was reduced to bickering.

"No," she said.

"Why don't you go to a doctor—and have it—taken away?"

"I went to one," she answered. "He said it was too late."

"Then—that lets me out." He wished he had said it more studiously, more nobly.

"No. You did it."

He thought of his family. Suppose this fact of his private life came to the ears of his father?

Wren was *stern* and *sadistic.*

Wren was a *deacon* in a *church.*

Wren lived by the *proprieties* and *conventions.*

And his mother.

Finnley did not have the courage to think of his mother. The time was at hand to act forcefully.

He turned to Libby. "Look here, Libby. If you'd come to me and said someone had gotten you in trouble, I'd have helped you. But I won't stand being stuck with a mess like this. You go to the man who did it and tell him. That's all I'll say or do about it."

She stared at his dark excellence. "Anyway, it's too late to matter, now. How about taking me out riding? We could have a lot of fun—because there wouldn't be anything to be afraid of."

Her words jarred him. His mind became an uproar. Desire and memory burst and spurted inside him. He saw himself temporarily drowning his fear in a welter of lust. And his quickly prejudiced reason whispered that after another locked association she might be more amenable to reason.

"I—" he said, taking her hand—"I—"

He dropped it. He recoiled. The fear returned. "Libby, you're a pretty rotten girl," he said. "Get the right man—and tell that to him."

He walked away.

Libby sat on the bench and cried. What he had said was true. There was another man. A youngster. And before him there had been others. The stirring life within her was due to the younger man. But she coveted Finnley. All through the weeks when she had not seen him her mind had been fastened upon him, her appetite had sucked on memories of him, and when this crisis had descended she had denied its origin and made it into a claim upon him.

Now as he walked away she wept because she felt that he had betrayed her.

When he came back and said bitterly, "You know it is not my fault," and then, in terror, "I warn you not to connect my name with this," she only resolved the harder to catch and hold him by it.

Finnley drove his father's car through the rancid night, unable to cope with the monstrousness of the situation.

Remembering the agony of those hours, Wren shuddered and ordered another drink. I had my glass filled. The orchestra played a new and unfamiliar song, easing the undertones of our memories.

"Plenty of dreadful things had happened to me before that sloe-eyed Jezebel pinned her pregnancy upon me," he said thoughtfully. "I was tough and possibly I had a sense of humor. But a plethora of horrors in one's life does not make fresh apparitions more endurable. The burnt child dreads the fire. And, by the way, if I should get very drunk do what you can to check these references to burning, will you?

"I digress. I would like to picture the stupidity and tyranny of my father accurately for you. I haven't time. His hypocrisies are those of every self-satisfied and self-centered man. But it will be impossible to make you see the difficulty of telling him what I eventually had to tell. As for my mother—she was a saint in the pickle of his bile. A sarcoma devoured her years ago, but I believe she was already numb, even to that.

"In looking back, I see there is no blame—as we generally do in looking back. I was afraid of my father. I had a normal terror of public opinion. I was sensitive. I hated suffering.

"As for Libby—her problem was simple. She had been a

passionate and youngly matured girl. Seduction was inevitable. Her home life was nasty—her mother was a compound of bitch and behemoth, as I subsequently discovered. Her father was a wizened nincompoop. When she became pregnant she picked me out because of my social superiority and because, I daresay, of my not unattractive sexual capacity.

"She was in love with me to the extent of her ability to love. She had the intellectual trick of being able under the pressure of need to convince herself immutably of a lie—a property of a great many female minds. From the day she decided to make me her victim she believed I was really culpable. A regiment of clinical facts could not have altered her opinion. It is a kind of insanity—or, rather—a lack of mentality, I presume.

"My fears are easy to comprehend. I can still taste their burn and their variety. My subtler reactions are less easy to explain. I held myself morally wrong in the whole matter because, as I said, I had made love to that girl in the most vehement and pleasant ways I could design. The possibility of a possibility that I might have been the father of a child of hers if another man had not beaten me to paternity weighed upon me. I could not take the attitude, quite, that, as in my other amours, I had avoided the danger as sedulously as possible, and was therefore guiltless. I was without compunction concerning any of those other and uncomplicated affairs. But, since Libby was pregnant, and I had—do you see?"

"Perfectly," I replied.

He seemed relieved. "And in the same circumstances, you—"

"I would have been harder, I think," I answered. "Since you were sure of your innocence, you should have insisted upon it. The girl was wrong."

"Of course," Wren answered. "Well—in a way—I did. The whole matter became rather spectacular, however."

A week had passed and Finnley had heard no more from Libby. It was a week of anxiety, filled with the usual alarms at the ringing of telephone bells, the droppings of the stomach at unexpected knocks on the door, the discomforts of awakening into each new day, and the resolutions to live chastely forever if this occurrence should prove to be of no further consequence.

On a quiet autumn afternoon some ten days before the time when Finnley was due to depart for his sophomore year at college, an answered knock at the door brought him face to face with four strange men.

They asked Finnley his name, and when he responded, they walked directly into the house. They had hard faces. They were dressed in cheap clothes, obviously their best. Finnley saw that one of them was in every particular the image of Libby. There was nobody in the house.

They asked him to take them to a place where they could talk.

He conducted them to the music room and closed the sliding doors. He offered them cigarettes, which they refused. They stood, looking at him. He believed that he was going to be horsewhipped.

One of the men took out an automatic pistol.

"We are the brothers of Libby Maretti," he said. "We came here to talk to you."

He looked at the gun uncomfortably and then pointed it at Finnley.

"Our sister," said another of the men, "is going to have a baby."

A third added, "She claims it is yours."

The last one said, "Is it?"

Finnley found himself looking at the gun and thinking. He thought of a number of things. He realized that not for a

[24]

golden million dollars could he have risen to his feet. He wondered if his family would come home and find him dead. He believed they would. The last notion cleared his mind. He began to talk in a high, fantastic voice.

He said, "No. I am not the father of Libby's child."

"Prove it," one of them muttered sullenly.

He collected air into his lungs. "Well—I will. How far along is she?"

They looked at each other.

Finnley shrugged. "I'll tell you. About five months. And I never saw your sister in my life until seven weeks ago."

"She says it's yours," the brother who looked like Libby replied. "And she ought to know."

"What are you going to do about it?"

"Plenty." One of the men stood closer to Finnley.

"All right." Finnley bit his lip. "I can't stop you. But I'm not the father of that child. And your sister probably can't tell you who the father is. Now—do what you want to."

The man who was holding the pistol became tense, jerked his arm, and accidentally pulled the trigger. The top of the weapon flew open and revealed that it contained a package of cigarettes.

Finnley began to laugh.

The men looked at him, at the furnishings of the room, and at each other. One of them opened the door and they started to go.

"You'll hear from us," they said.

The atmosphere seemed to contract around Finnley. He went outdoors. The gap between himself and the passers-by was so great that they might have been Martians. Houses seemed vast, vague and ominous. Next door on the right, the Wilsons brick-evergreens-and-big-collie. Then, Paintors white-clapboard-gay-pergolas-arbors-and-cats. Then, Meekles can-vas-and-chocolate-scrollwork-porch-and-Verna. On the left, Falcon Arms Apartments sandstone-and-overdecoration.

He found Dutch packing, his white shirt open, his tie pulled down, his curly blond hair dangling on his broad forehead.

"You look as if God had trampled on you personally, Fin."

"He has."

Dutch sat on his bed, lighted a cigarette, and listened.

He began to pack again.

"You'll do it?" Finnley asked anxiously.

"This afternoon."

Finnley waited. Dutch telephoned just before supper.

"Betty said that it was young Bud Davis, probably. Bill's brother."

"Thanks, boy. Well—have a good year. Wah-hoo-wah."

"Wah-hoo-wah," Dutch replied in a childish voice.

"What on earth is the matter with you these days?" Finnley's mother asked, as he groped among strips of yellow carrot.

Bill telephoned. His voice was funereal. "Listen, Fin— I've got to see you. Got to. Go to the movies with me?"

"I know what it's about," Finnley said hopefully.

Bill looked at him. Good old Bill Davis. Some fifty thou-sand years ago they had spent part of a glamorous youth to-gether in the Adirondacks. Now they were old ghouls shuf-fling among meatless ghosts. Finnley switched off the motor of the car.

"You do?"

When Finnley looked at him, he saw that he was crying. His mouth was painfully contracted. Tears ran down his cheeks. "Bud told me today. Good God, Fin—I'd never dreamed of anything like that. I've kept my ideals—about women. But I couldn't imagine—Bud. Gee—these high school kids must be rotten."

Finnley waited a long time, then said, "The thing is—Bud is to blame. Not me."

Words came out of Bill like ashes. He twisted inside his top-coat. "He's only sixteen, Fin. He's almost crazy. I expect any minute that he'll kill himself. And if he doesn't—and if the old man finds out—he'll probably kill him anyway. They're at home now—the old man reading his Bible and Bud upstairs in bed—sick. He said he was sick—anyway."

"Your father wouldn't—"

"He might. He has a terrible temper. He almost killed a colored man once. Found him in the barn with a colored girl—"

Finnley shook. "Still—what about me? It wasn't my fault. It was Bud's."

"That's why she went to you. She told Bud—a—a long time ago."

"How long?" The question was asked quickly.

Bill turned his face away. "Sorry, Fin. I can't tell you."

"You mean—you're going to let them pin it on me?"

The world moved a vast distance through space. "You're morally as much to blame as my kid brother," Bill replied. "You're twenty. You can stand it. He can't. You're tough. He's practically a child. I—I sort of hoped you'd agree to take the blame—because you and I have been such good friends—for so long." Bill could say no more at that moment.

"Well." Finnley meditated. "Well. How do you imagine

my own family will feel? Dad's business here depends on his reputation. And if people began to whisper the story around —I'm sure it would get around—why—"

Bill turned fiercely. "Listen. Bud and I have stood together against our old man all our lives. The lickings you got when you were young don't even compare with what happened to us. I know what dad would do to Bud. Why don't you just admit it—and then—go away somewhere? Change your name?"

Finnley was shocked. His roots were deep in the places where he had set them. "It isn't so horrible a crime," he said. "And it isn't the first time it has happened. Not even in this beautiful and moral little suburb."

"All right, then. You take the blame. I've already told that girl that if she mentions Bud's name to anyone I'll kill her. And now I'm saying it to you." He leered crazily at Finnley. "If Bud's name is connected with her in any way, I'll wait for you on the street and shoot you."

"With that rifle I gave you when we went camping together, I suppose," Finnley said.

"I swear I will."

Finnley spread out his hands. His soul was glacial. "Well— you better clean it and load it. I don't know what I'll do. And there are so many people who want to shoot me these days that the best advice I can give you would be to get your execution in early or it won't take." He started the car.

The lawyer peered unhappily at the young man before him. "I carried out my investigation, Wren," he said. "The case has several bad features. In the first place, the girl is under age. Seventeen. So that affidavits from the various boys would not clear you. She could send every one of you to prison for twenty years, if she wanted to."

"She told me she was nineteen," Finnley said.

"She lied, then. In the second place, if she wishes, she can, by court trial, compel anyone she names and proves a possible father to pay for her confinement and the support of the child for fourteen years. That would be a better course than to be tried for carnal abuse of a minor."

It took Finnley a long time to say, "what." "What do you advise?"

"I'm sorry, Wren—but this is not the sort of thing I can handle. You'll have to get someone else. I suggest you hire one of the largest firms in the state—for the effect of their name."

"I—" Finnley said. "I—"

Dr. Wren looked at him peevishly. "What, son? I'm in a hurry."

"I have something to tell you—that will probably upset your whole life."

"Eh?"

Finnley ran his voice like a Victrola needle over the bare facts. The doctor lighted a cigar. He was perfectly composed. Finnley was standing at the window in the waiting room with his shoulders hunched.

The doctor spoke. "You say, son, that you are not the child's father?"

"I am not."

"Very well. We'll fight them, then. In court, if necessary. Anywhere."

Finnley fainted dead away.

Finnley Wren versus the town of Springville.

Charge: Bastardy.

A small courtroom split by a railing. A bank of jurymen. A judge behind a long bar. A crowd of strange people. Libby, pale and hollow-eyed, bulging. Reporters.

Finnley's lawyer whispered to him. "We will probably fail here. It's her home town. The jurymen are local taxpayers and friends of the family. But we will appeal. When the child is born, we will have expert witnesses present. Then— the decision of this court will be reversed."

Finnley tapped his shoe on the floor. The gavel struck.

we will show, said the lawyer for the town, how this sleek, smooth, insidious rich man's son defiled and despoiled this poor, charming, defenseless minor

we will show, said finnley's lawyer, that this girl has been leading a fast, loose life for at least two years. we will show that she has been with child for about six months. we will prove that our client met her about three months ago, making his paternity manifestly impossible

and the towels were bloody, said libby's mother. i am sure it was the eighteenth of august because that is my sister's wedding anniversary and i had come home from

the fœtal heart is beating, said a rotund doctor in defense of finnley. the position of the uterus makes it impossible that impregnation occurred later than

i have here, intoned a chiropractor for libby, a copy of a medical book published in budapest in 1883 and translated in 1894 by doctor john oglebaugh which details an account of a three months' pregnancy in which all the symptoms just described were present, thus proving that the condition of the plaintiff is quite possible in the time that has elapsed since her meeting of the defendant

i object, said finnley's lawyer, to forty-year old, antiquated, european quackery offered as clinical evidence

objection overruled, said the judge

[30]

mr. wren, please take the stand

finnley looked at a whirlpool of faces, at the delighted jury, at the strangers. his father was not there. his father's sup-port had been confined to one statement that they would fight and to the provision of money necessary for the lawyers. he touched the bible and swore to tell the truth. bill was not there. dutch was at dartmouth. nobody was there except enemies and emotional cannibals

i met libby at a party, he began

libby sat on the stand, black and indomitable and poured out soft lies. he promised to marry me. he told me it would be all right. he said he loved me

Finnley stood on the porch of the courthouse. The jury was out.

A reporter approached him. "I'm from the *New York Gazette*. Looks as if you were going to get it."

"You don't intend to put anything about this in your damned tabloid, do you?"

"If it goes against you—plenty. Plenty, brother. It'll be a hot story. Your father is a pretty big shot in Orange Park."

Finnley wondered how often and how powerfully he could feel the world drop from under him before he ceased to feel. "But I'm not the father of her child. As soon as it is born—it will be obvious. I tried to get the case put off till then—but the town where she lives rushed it through."

The reporter nodded. "Sure. I believe you. You can tell what that girl is at fifty yards."

"Then why print anything?"

"If the court decides you are guilty—what is the opinion of a leg man? It's a story. All that love stuff. You don't look that sappy."

"It's all lying."

"Of course. But she says it's true—and that's copy."

"I suppose you realize that it will ruin the lives of about ten people if you do print it?"

"Too bad," the reporter answered. "Too bad you weren't a fairy."

There wasn't anyone in the room. Not anyone who cared. Not anyone who especially wanted to see him freed. Not anyone who was interested in justice. If his father had come with him. Or a friend. But they hid, tonight, because scandal was walking in public with beady eyes and dripping jaws. The magnificence of his father's first words had died to feeble repercussions in those last days.

He wondered. Was it because of Jessica, Jessica, Jessica, beautiful Jessica who could not wait? Was it because of the torment of those rosy-fingered mornings afterward? Was it because nature is omnipotent and morality vain? Or because the fate of man lies in some sinister Sibyl's stirring leaves, dreadful and unchanging? Was this stupid social scene, this capture by Lilliputians, acceptable to an intelligent man?

The jury filed in.

Guilty.

He heard something about the granting of an appeal. He turned over the thousand dollar Liberty bond with which his father had provided him.

He watched Libby and her mother sweep victoriously from the courtroom.

He was in the night again. Alone. He drove as if he were

in a cortège. The car squeaked over the bunion cobblestones.
A dead moon teetered in the sky.
Thirty dollars for confinement.
Five dollars a week for fourteen years.
Appeal.
And the newspapers.
He found his father in the pain-laden aroma of his inner
office, and beside his father, Mrs. Wren, wretched and white.
He told them.

DOCTOR'S SON APPEALS ILLEGITIMACY VERDICT
DENIES HE LOVED UNWED MOTHER
PETTING PARTY ENDS IN COURT
EMINENT PHYSICIAN'S SON ACCUSED
TURNS HIS BACK ON UNWANTED STORK
SUBURBAN ROMEO SENTENCED
COLLEGE STUDENT'S ROMANCE SOURS
GOOD TIME CHARLIE NICKED BY JURY

*Finnley Wren, eldest son of Dr. Gordon Wren of Orange
Park, was convicted of bastardy in Springville, pending appeal.
The home of a well-known Orange Park physician and surgeon,
vacant during the month of August, was the scene of the love
nest of a formerly well-liked and respected high school student
of that town. Once Captain of the Orange Park track team,
leader of the school orchestra, class poet and valedictorian,
Finnley Wren, son of a prominent local physician, was brought
into court in Springville last night and charged with being the
father of the unborn child of Libby Maretti, seventeen year old
daughter of a factory employee.*

There were newspapers all over the house when Finnley came downstairs. As he passed his mother's room, he could hear her sobs. Vi patted him on the back and went on toward the bathroom in a kimono. Tom regarded him with subdued gravity and said nothing.

But, oddly enough, Finnley was almost happy. He noticed that the autumn sun was blazing. There were birds on the back lawn around the jet patch where trash was burned. Crisp leaves rode the wind. Somebody was playing a Victrola in the house next door. After he had left the second floor and descended to the first, he began to whistle the melody floating through an open window.

"All that night," Wren said, leaning toward me, "I had slept soundly. My wits had jumped into a perspective of the thing. I was no longer frightened. Nothing more could happen to me. The world was having its revenge, its succulent fun, at my expense. But it couldn't touch me. The brothers had not shot at me. Bud's offspring would never challenge him. In those pent, silent weeks I had suffered enough for my uneasy conscience. More, I daresay, than the girl would suffer in childbirth. It seemed to me that civilized parents would have understood, that society should not demand any great price for blunders of that sort even from the guilty, that any further reference to it would be exclusively on the part of hypocrites.

"I felt even a trifle heroic. I still do. I had taken another man's punishment. Of course, many other factors than generosity and heroism had prompted me to do so. But the case was settled, ultimate vindication was certain, and, as I said, I enjoyed the sunshine once again.

"At my breakfast table I found a reporter who had climbed

in the dining room window and terrorized the maid into giving him coffee while he waited. I treated him with elaborate politeness and told him to print anything his fancy suggested.

"As I went out the front door for an exploratory stroll a news photographer with a camera set up on my porch snapped my picture. I decided forthwith that I was in a capricious and an active mood. I slowly and carefully gathered together the legs of the tripod and clubbed the camera on the broad railing. I remember that the lens rolled out in one piece. The photographer had made no effort to interfere but suddenly he hit me in the face and ran. I chased him down the street, block after block. I could run a great deal faster than he, and every time I caught up with him I kicked him so hard that he was lifted clear of the ground. Finally, on the main street, he hopped a bus.

"I returned home, panting and quite exhilarated.

"But I never could understand that and I expect I never shall. Chemistry is not enough, and conscience is not enough. I have a clear idea of why everyone does everything, and at the same time I haven't the faintest idea in the world. I see my genteel old popsy-wopsy this very day playing his objectionable golf— he's a picker-up-of-tees-before-you-drive—and going home to his trade; open a little wider, Mrs. Pleeplepitz; this is going to hurt a good deal, Marcia—how the old man rolls that little sentence into a rivet for your spinal cord; now, my friend, brace yourself, because what I'm going to tell you, while it may seem hard, is what we all have to be told sooner or later—another of his religiously demoniac nifties; swabs and scalpels—you'd think he'd get some sense, but he doesn't—not even about his own profession. He hasn't read a medical journal in fifteen years although they jam a score of shelves, but he'll tie you on a table and haul out your guts for a thousand dollars with the blandest equanimity. You'd think he'd learn something about people— but he's just mechanical releases; I touched off one when I poured out my confession that day. And my mother, God rest her soul, worked on another set of strings, as we all do. She was a quiet sufferer. She suffered a great deal, and she complained in the quietest voice imaginable. Her 'oh's' and 'ah's' always indicated inscrutable misery.

"*Chemistry* isn't enough. *Conscience* isn't. I cannot understand why I loved my mother. And the sciences explain her no better than they describe me. She never once in her life really admitted the cause of her wretchedness. She suffered because my father was brutal and lazy, cruel and unimaginative, selfish and overbearingly righteous. Never did I hear my father admit he was wrong. When he was trapped— and we occasionally bothered to catch him out of indignation or spite—he used a spiritual bludgeon to free himself.

"In the end, my mother turned the trick. I happened to be present at the time. She vomited a mass of granular stuff on the bathroom linoleum. 'Coffee grounds,' she said in her meek, unmelodious voice. I knew what that meant. So did she. So would Vi or Tom have known. The dinner conversation at our home was, for eighteen years, decorated with diagnostic symptoms and surgical anecdote.

"Father examined her at the hospital and they came home together the next day. They sat at opposite ends of the table and we sat along the sides. 'Your mother,' my father said, 'has a well developed cancer of the stomach. Dr. Elpet and I agreed that surgery would be futile and we are afraid—' he wiped his mouth with his napkin—'that she will not be with us long.' Mother sat there—lined face, stringy hair, bumpy house dress—and turned a ghastly color. Father wiped his mouth again. I could have crucified him, and sung as I hammered in the nails.

"When she died—I wasn't at home, thank God—and she managed although father bravely restricted the morphine—

father said she was a good woman and prayed for her soul in church on the following Wednesday.

"You can understand, possibly, why I fainted with relief rather than gratitude when he agreed to fight Libby, and why I never regarded him highly for the deed. Chemistry, conscience, strings. It was a purely professional reaction.

"Ah—well.

"He felt the gesture was noble. But it whiffed back putrid in his nostrils soon enough. He detected its odor in time to check himself from accompanying me to court and making an extroverted ass of himself there.

"My little incomprehensible exhilaration of the morning following the trial lasted for some time afterward. The whole matter became funny. In Orange Park, a town where scores of debs make frequent visits to cousins named Curette, I received publicity enough to balance a decade of everybody's fornications.

"People entered my life in vast numbers. An unnamed individual called me on the telephone to tell me that the current issue of the *New York Gazette* was particularly atrocious in its references to me. As I had been twiddling with Beethoven all afternoon, I went downtown to a news dealer and asked for a copy. He said that he was sold out and surmised that I wanted to read about that bastard Finnley Wren. I said I had requested the sheet for some such purpose. He shook his fist and replied that he wished God in His justice would send that fellow into his store for one minute. He was big and mad, so I went discreetly into the sunset without aiding God and justice.

"I ran into Alice Dunfelt shopping with her mother in McKeogh's grocery store. The beauty of her yellow hair among the apples, bananas, dead meat and bright lights attracted me. I spoke to her, and her mother came about simpering. But quite suddenly two hatpins jumped out of Mrs. Dunfelt's eyeballs and she snatched Alice into the shelter of the family Buick

[37]

out on the curb. Now, Alice was a hefty-hipped, bucktoothed girl of no great cerebral aspect, but she was a true nymphomaniac and had been a crawler into ventilators of the high school study hall since her sixteenth birthday. I imagine she had had what my legal experience with Libby had taught me was carnal knowledge of as many males as the last two centuries of her grandmothers. Moreover, I saw no harm in it. She liked to be pawed and mauled, she didn't seem to have Libby's unfortunate fertility, and the boys were all clean, young Americans. But it must have seemed odd to her, as it did to me, when her mother pulled down the curtains of the car before she drove away.

"That night at home while I maundered over Bach and thought about the photographer and the newsdealer and Mrs. Dunfelt, an intimate little group of about thirty or thirty-five men from the church called upon me. In a misguided period of my adolescence I had been extremely religious. Even today, I am a glib hymn-singer and Bible-quoter. And although I had been absent from the fold for some three or four years, to the apoplectic annoyance of my father, it seems that there still remained in the till, vaults, or register of the Orange Park Methodist Episcopal Church a chit or item known as a letter. As sheep emeritus I had attracted no especial attention, but now, as the McCormick of the wild oat crop, the boys romped over and put Kliegs on my soul.

"The phrase they used has always been ants to my nerves. They said that they wanted to work with me in prayer. There was one old goat in particular, a Mr. K. John Purvis; seventy-five if a day and unable completely to close his mouth since sixty, I should imagine; a salivator with, otherwise, complete glandular desiccation excepting, I presently realized, one other endocrine. I was about to jump out of an open window into the shrubbery when the lift and exhalation of the morning carried me into this new public manifestation.

"They talked to me for a while, sitting and standing in a circle. They said, first, that my case was so unusual that they felt I should be prohibited from attending church until it was seen that I had repented and reformed. I let that piece of Christianity pass unchallenged. Then one of them turned out the lights and they began to pray. That, too, I permitted, and if God listened he certainly heard my sins lavishly and repetitively described. They warmed themselves by the effort. They turned on the lights again, and made another digression from church policy.

"K. John Purvis, oversecreting furiously, told me that it was not customary in the Methodist Episcopal Church to have or to make use of the confessional, but that since my transgression weighed so heavily upon them it presumably depressed me even more and doubtless a confession would relieve me—a full, stark, absolute confession, leaving out no detail however obscene or lewd lest it torture me afterward. His words, I think, although rather more expertly arranged.

"I really felt sorry for them during the space of a minute or more. I felt sorry because I knew their wives. Then I became indignant—or possibly I tired of their mumbo-jumbo. I was casting about for a quick, neat out when a miracle of *starch fermentation* took place.

"I perceived it in the making, in the offing, so to speak. At the time I had no concept of its magnitude and glory. But I suggested, pacing the thing perfectly, that we pray again first and I confess afterward. The lights were nimbly doused and we knelt.

"In some discomfort I made my prologue. As I spoke, I realized that the opportunity was unique, magnificent. I chose a skillfully strained posture.

"Now, I do not know how loud the trumpet of Gabriel will blow or how enduring that blast will be, but I assure you I can tell you the stunning effect it will have.   I let the echo die among my stony guests.   I rose.   I switched on the lights.

" 'My answer, gentlemen,' I said, 'comes from deep within me.' "

I put my handkerchief back in my pocket and looked at Wren.   He had an extraordinarily long and mobile countenance of which every feature was vivid in color and pronounced in shape.   He was a contradiction in bodily and facial characteristics, seeming at once to be saturnine and introverted, athletic and vaguely ordinary.   He was manifestly sensitive, forward, and reckless.   His mouth was firm, wide, sharp-cornered, and almost as expressive as his black, imponderable eyes.   His nostrils arched out like those of a timid animal but the nose above them was like the beak of an Eighteenth Century reformer.   His hair was coarse and like polished coal.   It did not curl but it curved, falling over his high forehead almost to the point where a permanent frown brought beetling ebon brows together.   He had the largest and the most tactile hands I have ever seen.   When, eventually, he stood up, he proved to be an inch or more over six feet in height, broad-shouldered, narrow-hipped, and big-footed.   I saw him later under a shower.   He was powerfully muscled, although very lean; he had large joints; and, as a final inconsistency, his copious pubic hair was brick red.

His voice was an even baritone which rose easily in excitement.   His delivery and loquacity were amazing.   Words poured in a brilliant stream from him, not only without effort on his part, but apparently so far behind the maelstrom or merry-go-round of his thoughts that, as he talked, remote flashes and smolderings in his eyes suggested an imagination charging ahead of speech and investigating scores of murky corners and bright pageants his tongue was too laggard to report.

His style of address changed with his mood and his subject. When talking to what he called the "pedestrians of life" and its "ornamental morons" he was grossly careless of diction and verbiage. On the other hand, in the presence of literate persons, he adopted a kind of conversation that was, perhaps, a mockery of the classics, although at times it had the range and selectivity of very fine prose. Into its frequent beauty he flung sooner or later, the brashest slang or else he intermixed it with scientific and technological terms often strained to an unfamiliar meaning. His vocabulary was immense and accessible. But he could, on occasion, vie with any of that school of novelists who spring from frozen soil, and conjure up a remembered deed or emotion in words so passionately compressed that they emerge small, hard and individually alive.

He spoke about it.

"I have given you," he said, tasting the middle part of his second highball, "the brief detail of my birth, and the crass termination of my youth. The gap between was ordinary. I shall, however, illuminate it from time to time. We moved to Orange Park from North Dakota for a reason precisely the reverse of the one my father gave. He said it was his duty to go to a populous center where his services would be more needed—although no doubt the compensation would be smaller. At ten I had already peered into the crooked mirror in which he saw himself often enough to understand that racy little rationalization.

"To go on. And, by the way, you'll have to bear with my desultory sentence sculpture as I do go on: at an early age I retreated into books and there I assimilated an admiration of the language—uncritical but sincere. Today I secretly pride myself on as easy and resounding an evacuation of words as any of my contemporaries."

"i am crying, said the drunken iconoclast who had inter-
"rupted us previously, because of the american legion, legion-
"heirs. do you perceive the pun? in the first place, most of
"them were drafted into our recent army and their attitudes are
"spurious. in the second place, while we tried to make heroes
"of them they have turned themselves into mercenaries. we
"now perceive that the huns were menaced not by brave patriots
"who wished to protect their homes but by hired help. greedy
"hired help. what a day! what a race! what a horrid exam-
"ple of republicanism! the bonus! there was a time when
"the gentlefolk who had thrust out bayonets to their enemies
"did not afterward extend tin cups to their countrymen. i am
"ashamed of my brothers."

"It was necessary for me to leave Orange Park," Wren continued. "I did so with reluctance. The private ecstasy which
had followed my trial was of a quite enduring nature. Once I
had survived the inleaking torture of the weeks preceding it, I
rebounded into heights which gave me wide vision. I watched
my mother mourn and weep because of the dogmas which infested her—unable to love her then, unable to sympathize or
tender an apology. I regarded the growth in my father of distaste for myself with indifference. For Vi I felt some compunction; she had given up a concert engagement in Newark
to protect her person from eyes which would identify herself
with me. Tom emerged but once from his young majesty. He
mumbled to me that the world was filled with slime and that,
in so far as he was concerned, he was distinctly pleased with my
conduct.

"I sat in my father's house. I slept in my own bedroom in
the precise spot where I had slept with Libby. I ate at the

family table. I listened while my mother told me that although the sacrifice would be hard on her, she was sure I would be happier in some other place, and while my father enumerated the patients he had lost through my copulation. I walked on the streets and proffered greetings which went unanswered by scores of my erstwhile friends.

"One generous episode marked that eccentric period."

Finnley sat in the music room pouring his hands on the keys of the grand piano. From across the hall came the clatter of supper dishes being removed. Violet entered the chamber and sat down beside her brother. He was conscious of her outline beside him: soft profile, rounded shoulders, and the braid of dull gold hair above her brow. She reached out hands very much like his own and joined in his skillful imagery.

By and by he realized that she was crying.

He stopped playing and she continued.

"You know," she said, after she had finished the piece, "you could play much better than I play—if you wished."

"I haven't your patience."

"But you have—the rest of it. The very thing that made you—"

"Toss that wench?"

"Please—Finnley!"

"Bunk, my dear sister. Apple sauce. No brief for that. No proof. Millions—I daresay billions of expert bedfellows never heard of Beethoven or Bach. And, Vi, on the other side of your mistaken picture of art, is the beauty of such lambent virginity as yours. You can't explain that away."

She turned to face him and looked down. "Tell me, Finnley —is it very much—"

"Very much what?"

"Fun?"

"In anticipation, Vi. I'll tell you more when you're eighteen. Now—play me that sonata again."

She commenced to weep silently and as she wept, she played. Before she finished, she left the piano and left the room and Finnley sat in its questioning silence until the doorbell rang.

The maid ushered a tall, ruddy man through the sliding doors.

"I'm David Hewitt," the tall man said. "I don't know you, Finnley, but your father has been taking care of my family for years."

"Sit down," Finnley replied, wondering what idiocy would emerge from so strong-seeming a man.

"I'm President of the Guarantee National and Merchants' Trust Bank—in New York."

"I've heard father mention your name."

eighteen holes with dave hewitt, the millionaire, you know

"I can't stay. I'm glad you were at home. I wanted to leave a letter with you. You'll open it after I leave."

He shook Finnley's hand, bent upon him a most profound stare, said, "I thought so," and departed.

Finnley opened the letter.

"Dear Wren:—

"In the main office of my bank I have deposited to your credit ten thousand dollars. Fight that girl through the courts till you win. And don't give an inch to Orange Park. Consider the money a loan, if you like.

"Sincerely yours,

"David Hewitt."

"Gestures?" Wren murmured. *"Gestures.* A good many have been made in this world. Ten thousand dollars was a gesture to him. My case in the newspapers doubtless stirred such poignancies in him as no one could appreciate—except

me. He wanted to help. Unquestionably he knew the foibles of my father and did not wish to see a human being destroyed for lack of money. It was a little thing for Hewitt to do—a scribbling with his pen, a short ride in his limousine.

"It broke me up. It tore me to pieces. I left home on the next day.

"I never touched the money—but it stood in my credit until long after the Court of Appeals had thrown out my case. You see—five months and eighteen days from the day I first met Libby she went to the hospital and had a normal baby. The impossibility of my parenthood was automatically determined. Her case collapsed. . . .

"I used to get statements from the bank, however. Even in Paris.

"After Hewitt had gone, I made a tour of the house."

Finnley put coal on the furnace fire. The wood crosspiece of the shovel handle had been broken away, leaving a bare iron core which smudged his palm with rust. It was an old shovel with bent sides and an upcurled edge. He leaned on it after he had slammed the door of the fire box.

The cellar was filled with memories. Dust-coated memories.

Outside the large anthracite bin was a heap of ungleaming soft coal which lay on the floor in lumps. This coal gave vitality and warmth to the rooms upstairs. It burned throughout the winter in fireplaces, illuminating Finnley's face when he studied or read, Vi's hair, his mother's placid garments. Beside it was the crate in which last year's radio had arrived, waiting for some unguessed use, and a heap of barrel staves, and a jumble of branches brought in from the back yard.

Against the whitewashed wall a rusting sled with a movable steering bar reminded him of laughter on sparkling hillsides and cold and slush and ice and poinsettias, of sleigh-bells and heavy coats, of valentines and hot schoolrooms, of snow falling. Beside the sled was a maze of window screens which ricocheted his imagination to slamming doors and flies and blue water and trees washing themselves in the wind.

He prodded darker corners with his eyes and discovered other heaps, drab, meaningful, stricken—a door with a broken pane, a bedpan, aged cartons from which issued glaciers of jam jars, a brass bedstead glittering morosely, jugs, a pile of bricks, and, beyond them inscrutably ticking, gas and electric meters.

He went up the wooden stairs and switched out the nude and dusty bulb which had revealed those deceased possessions.

The kitchen smelled like hot bread. Its windows were steamed. Cleanliness and use were at war in it, with the former momentarily triumphant. His eye ran along the unmatched dishes in the glass china closet, stopped at the bent silver cup on which his first teeth had been cut, and moved to the gas range, so carefully noting the flecks on its enamel that they might have been objectives on a military map. He peered out upon the back porch. Ash and garbage cans stood like portly sentinels beside the steps. A battery of exhausted brooms and mops leaned against the rail.

The motor of the electric refrigerator whirred suddenly.

He left the kitchen.

The dining room wall paper had upon it brown trees and behind each clump of three a house with a light burning in it. The quartered oak buffet and the round-ended extension table had come from North Dakota and an unforgettable youth. But the asbestos logs in the fireplace were indigenous to the house itself, emitting stink and nothing else.

He stepped into the living room.

Its hideousness was an insult.

He had heard it called beautiful and charming and attractive and well-appointed by a hundred women. But it remained the horrid soul of the house.

Oriental rugs lay upon the yellowish floor at random angles to each other. In two corners there were permanent bookcases filled with sets. In a third corner was a brick fireplace and in the fourth, windows and a built-in seat where chintz-covered cushions waged illegitimate war with the rugs and the blue windmills on the walls. A chair, a vast thing of opulent black leather set on runners, squatted in front of one set of bookcases. Beside the window seat was a spindle-legged walnut desk, and in front of the fire, a brown divan backed against a long table. Into this mess a chandelier hung down. Each of its globes was the clapper of a salmon glass bell. It was suspended by chains from a brass abscess that grew out of the silver-white ceiling paper.

Finnley had wanted the living room to be beautiful, but it was not.

He moved into the front hall where more oriental rugs lay on the waxed parquet. He saw his reflection in a long, mahogany-framed mirror. He saw his rubbers and his coat and the stairs leading to the second floor and the small knob on the closet door where his father's golf clubs slumped beside Vi's forgotten hockey sticks.

Almost incredulously, he peered beyond and into the music room. The Winged Venus on her white pedestal flew toward a big fern that had brown death at the tip of each frond. The piano waited for the millennium, a dim, crimson elephant in the shadows. A madonna looked at the Rembrandt group around the horses. Over the whole hung a solemn asphyxiation.

Finnley shuddered.

He could hear a metronome ticking in there. He could hear a boy and a girl protesting as they drummed out monotonous exercises.

He did not open the door to his father's offices. He knew what was beyond them.

Beyond them was pain and intolerance and vanity mixed with insufficiently shiny instruments and a closet of bottles and stupidity and terrifying tables and a nurse with acne and telephones that looked dirty and quintillions of pills.

There was some kindness in the cellar of the Wrens' house, but none on the first floor.

He escaped slowly up the front stairs.

In spite of the fact that the second floor of the Wren home was functional, being consecrated first to rest, second to habilimentation, third to hygiene and fourth to reproduction, there lay in and upon every aspect of those human utilities the marks of decoration or else of concealment, as if sleep could be best accomplished among faded patterns and twisted gewgaws, dressing behind once roseate screens and in closets, bathing back of a curtain and copulation in a black pocket of sheets, so that even a pitying God could not rescue the weary in the first instance from eye-catchers of lace spreads, folded Navajo blankets, pink rugs strewn with yellow trumpet flowers, blue and white china boys and girls in Dutch costumes sitting on overwrought mantelpieces, bureaus whose bellies had for no conceivable reason zigzag cross sections and an artificial grain as pronounced as the marks in wet combed hair, stools and tables upon which scroll saws had figure-skated, rococo door knobs, panels painted with birds in salad hues, and lamps fashioned as if from a half-wit's memory of the headdresses of all ages, while in the next instance, dressing, as if it were unrelated to sleeping, and all its appurtenances from shoe trees to suspenders, were manifested only in closets that had no windows, and smelled like Y.M.C.A. gymnasia or behind the gaudy camouflage of angled uprights bearing pastoral scenes and embroidered silk, in the third instance chests, locks and drapes once collectively violated exposed the bathroom's epitome of slovenliness in ringed glasses, clotted tub drains, desiccations of paste on toothbrushes, medicine on glass shelves and suds on the floor, in the gray rancidity of rags hanging on once bright elbows beneath the washbowl, in fecal spray and foul-faint ordors, in squeezed tubes, empty bottles, rusted razor blades, sodden soap, sour sponges, spilled powders, small bandages used and half lost, finely cracked porcelain, water-blistered varnish, oozing plumbing, verdigris, aged mirrors, and the furtive presence of cockroaches, and in the final instance with no effort at even tawdry blandishment if the conventional design around the trade-mark of a douche bag be accepted, a passionate hiding of love-making and the ugly little contrivances invented to curb its normal course upon remote shelves and in the backs of drawers so that, in all, the Wrens might lie in beauty when they slept and for the rest, tend their bodies as near to oblivion as possible.

From the second floor, Finnley moved to his own quarters and he saw them as a recapitulation of the chambers in which the rest of his family lived.

He peered dejectedly into the attic. The chilly pyramid beneath its beams surprised him, as the cellar had, with the nostalgia he was seeking as a foretaste of going away. Piled against the walls were remembered magazines and in an ancient trunk which he finally opened were clothes he had worn long ago. A blue coat with brass buttons, a small, staunch coat— and leggings with the knees scuffed through. He found, beneath a hammock and a lidless suitcase, his schoolbooks. His fingers still knew the touch of the brown paper covers; his eyes recognized his own hand in the irregularity which spelled his name across the front of each; his memory, running along the lines of print, portrayed the backs of little girls' heads and the mouths of cross teachers, the sight of chalk, swelled inkwells bubbling on desk-tops and the sound of spitballs on sun-baked window blinds. He smiled and sighed. He had found what he was seeking.

Children's voices sang, "Oh, beautiful for spacious skies," and solemnly pledged allegiance to the flag. Boys thwacked their baseball mits. Youth skipped down the perpetually dim halls of learning.

Finnley lay on the floor with his hands locked behind his head and an old quilt covering him. The uplift of the past days, which most of his acquaintances would have called perverse, burned somewhere within him. He knew he was going to leave his home: he stirred with the same deep feeling that must be in the fledgling as it steps out on the branch, in the chrysalis as wings burgeon upon it—delight and doubt, magic and melancholy. His brain felt yeasty, moved by secret, internal processes, and strangely alert. The inventory of ugliness which he had just made no longer disappointed him. Instead, it became a basis for a philosophy of art: surely the hideous impedimenta of the middle classes were the best arguments for culture and taste. His emotions bathed in the loveliness and the sadness of lost years.

Into this his mother walked, bearing patient fatigue on her back like an invisible knapsack.

"Finnley! What on earth are you doing in the attic?"

"Lying on the floor."

"You'll catch cold." She stood over him, the hem of her modeless dress six inches from his eyes.

Finnley rose and folded the quilt. "It was pleasant in here."

She looked at him. "Honestly, Finnley, I believe you've lost your mind. Seriously, I do. I've thought so ever since—all this began to happen. You're not the little boy I used to know."

He smiled. "Did you expect me to remain that? Really, mother, I couldn't help growing up. I would have avoided it if I could."

"So would I. It's horrible—horrible—"

He put his arm around her waist. "Only because we make it so. Or, at least, partly because of that." A thought flicked through his mind. "Tell me, mother—isn't it true that you've never been really happy since you were a child?"

"Happy?" She pronounced a word that had no meaning. "Why—your father and I are happy most of the time."

"I don't mean that. I mean gay—irresponsible—full of internal music and dancing."

She shook her head slowly and into her eyes came dull reminiscence. "That goes away—when you grow up."

"You mean—when you marry?"

"It's part of growing up."

He walked his mother through the barren door to the third floor hall.

"I don't know you any more," she said.

He did not answer.

"You're planning something," she continued.

"Yes. I'm planning to go away."

He felt her stiffen inside her shoddy corset. "Away?"

"You'll have Vi and Tom still—and I've become the black sheep of the Wren family—as well as the ogre of Orange Park. Father is getting stomach ulcers from looking at me—"

"Your father is a strong man and a good man. He can bear the wrong you've done him."

Sympathy ebbed in him temporarily. "Just what wrong have I done father, by the way?"

She sighed disapprovingly. "I don't have to speak of it, do I, Finnley?"

"Not unless you want me to know. I don't intend to be mean. But in the first place, I maintain I did nothing wrong. In the second, I avow that anyone who fastens my behavior on my father is a fool, a scandalmonger, and a decidedly low person."

"That's taking the easy way out," she replied.

They started downstairs in step, Finnley still holding his mother. Her straggling, brown hair smelled of curling irons.

[51]

There was a spot of rice powder on her nose. Because Dr. Wren was privately out of sympathy with all cosmetics, she powdered herself by a quick, secretive motion which always left a tell-tale spot. It was like her indulgences of her children—so furtive that she was usually caught in them and reproved by the unerring paterfamilias.

At the bottom of the steps she said, "Where are you planning to go?" Her voice was so calm, so collected, that he knew many things from it: the sorrow and resignation it concealed, the fatalism, the ascension from querulousness and hysteria.

He did not know where he was going.

"France," he said.

After he had spoken, he did know.

Ordinarily he would have expected his mother to say, "But it's so far away and the people there are so dirty and immoral." Now, she said something else. She said, "I have a little money I've saved from the house accounts. I was going to surprise your father—"

They went into her room. Finnley pulled his tie hard around the lump in his throat. "You don't want me to go away, do you?" he said. "If it weren't for father—"

"His work is the most important thing in my life." After she had said that, she began to sob. She threw herself face down on the bed.

He sat beside her. "I know. What I've done doesn't matter to you. You know how I felt—and why. You've always known. You've always hated my father—somewhere—inside you—despised him. God knows why you've gone on—marriage vows—religion—dignity—I guess I do know after all. Us. Vi and Tom and me. All the pleasure you've ever had for twenty years and more has come from witnessing our fun—and not telling father that you've enjoyed it. He doesn't want you to be happy—because he's not happy himself. And he is not happy because he is a hypocrite, a liar, a braggart, a bully,

[52]

a cheap sport, a coward, a dullard, a weakling and a cad. And because he has a conscience somewhere that knows those things—a virulent conscience that lives in the dark. I know—mother."

To that rather inadequate and indefinite outburst his mother nodded once. She sobbed harder.

From the floor below came the doctor's voice in artificial cheer. "Ahoy there!" Finnley wondered what he wanted—for only personal desire could have produced the phrase, so merry and so flat. "One less mouth to feed tonight, mother. And perhaps some good fairy will drive down to the tailor's with my dinner clothes and wait while they're being pressed. Had a hard day, today."

Finnley came down to the hall. His father was still peering up the stairway, on his face the smile intended for the obedient Mrs. Wren.

"I'll go to the tailor with your God-damned tuxedo," Finnley said, his voice carrying the same false enthusiasm as his father's.

"Splendid, son. But see here—I don't like profanity. Won't have it in my house. And I mean that! Well—I'll run up for a splash in the tub while you're gone. Having dinner with the Carters—you know—the Fifth Avenue silk people."

"Let's shove off," Wren said.

We paid our check and went out.

He took my arm and bent over me as we negotiated a long midtown block, a blazing stretch of Broadway, and part of a second, darker side-street. He continued to talk, but the noise drowned out some of his words while still more foundered in the dancing faces, the plowing elbows, and the gushing light. When we reached the restaurant to which he had been conducting me, he assured me that what he had said was unimportant. I remembered fragments.

except for that one nod my mother never admitted in any direct way that she was conscious of father's flaws peccadillos shortcomings and vices

a man smelling of garlic

why i said france nobody knows but when i said it i knew it was correct and besides i'd had only a year of college and there was still sedimentary desire for formal learning in me which i imagined would be disintegrated at the beaux arts or somewhere

an elbow

three hundred and sixteen dollars to my amazement and she gave it to me in cash

a hydrant

the old man was so relieved to hear that i was going that he coughed up fifty bucks

vi told me that she had some friends not connected with the family who would lend her enough for my passage back if i cabled her and gave her a couple of days

tom put all his best socks in my bags

a blazing cataract from a hosiery advertisement

so i had more money than i needed for a ticket by far and on top of that i got a job

just as i was buying a ticket i saw a brochure which said that there were two orchestras on the ship and i asked about the chances of playing in one of them

the fellow told me that he believed there was a vacancy for a good jazz pianist

i played across the meridians and saved all my funds

a glaring canopy and a group of men staring at lithographs of burlesque girls

the first night out a woman came to the ballroom and sat alone looking at me most of the time she was about thirty-five i thought although i found out later that she was forty-one

she had smooth black hair and black eyes

after she stared at me for a whole evening i went to bed and found the ancient restlessness stirring—she was handsome as the devil and exquisitely dressed and she could not have said in words any more clearly that it was her intention to sleep with me before we reached havre or bordeaux or wherever the god-damned ship was going

noblesse oblige

i got out of bed again that night and went to the after part of the boat deck where i was sure she would be

she said, i'm old enough to be your mother and wise enough to be your great-grandmother but i am also passionate enough to be your mistress for an evening and that is what i would like to be

she was

i afterward married her daughter

In a small sub-basement dining room fitted with a dozen tables and a walnut buffet we were obsequiously conducted to a corner by a Frenchman. He arched his brows, smiled incessantly, and presently brought us two bacardi cocktails. We were the only guests in the establishment due to the depression rather than its dowdiness, I should imagine, because the wines and liquors were genuine, the food delicious, and the prices modest.

Wren repeated his statement as soon as he had tasted the cocktail.

"I subsequently married her daughter.

"Perhaps it seems odd to you—overcivilized, decadent, or pseudo-incestuous. I shall pause on that theme. But first we must examine the time-correlatives. Genevieve Jones was full

[55]

of lust and wit. On the night when I first saw her, she was alone. Her husband was playing poker in the bar. Hope, her daughter, was asleep. Ricardo Jones—a given name his eccentric mother had relished—enjoyed spasms of great devotion to his gorgeous wife and uncomfortable intervals during which he completely forgot her and sank himself in business, golf, aviation, horticulture, catboats, Homer, modern art or philately.

"Those intervals brought out nocturnal and feline characteristics in Genevieve.

"To that we add my own situation." Wren grinned. "At the time I should have described it as desolate. No one could have been more homesick than I as I sat at the ship's miserable piano and banged out 'Hindustan' and 'Swanee' and 'Dardanella.' There I was, with a few hundred dollars in travelers' checks in my pocket, three box-pleated suits in my cabin, a rather tasteful collection of haberdashery, a few books and—it seemed to me—nothing else but my skin and the emotions it barely contained.

"I need scarcely say at this time that my libido was generally overheated. I would have made love to any willing woman—a condition not abnormal in an adolescent young man as precocious and predatory (according to accepted standards) as myself.

"I thought that Jessica had forever dashed the possibility of monogamous living. I fancied myself in the rôle of pariah and social outcast. Strong silence, in fact, had been the keynote of my morale as I watched the Statue of Liberty fade in the fumes of commerce. Genuine self-pity had rolled up from my soul to join the smoke that poured from the liner's funnel as we steamed under early evening starlight. My mind made a roll call of my afflictions.

"For another man's folly you have been punished.

"You have left a home in which

your father is a greedy tyrant
your mother is a piteous martyr
your sister is a professional introvert
your brother is an immature replica of yourself
your friends are deserters.

"You have waved the flags and shot off the seventeen guns and stolidly departed from a devastated life.

"I lamented the interruption of my days at Yale as if I had been deprived of a passport to heaven—and yet—the truth was that I detested almost every aspect of campus life. I was somewhat older than most of my classmates when I entered Yale— due to a long invalidism incurred at a rather immodest railroad wreck which I attended and for which I must add in all fairness to our citizens I received a medal—so that my age, together with my struggle between individualistic needs and a desire to conform, led me quickly into a distaste for all undergraduate interests and attitudes.

"Yet as I stood at twenty-one on the deck of that ship, and as I hunched over its piano, I remember distinctly looking into a blasted youth. It was a magnificent feeling. It made me light-headed about the future. I had suffered all and emerged scarred but undaunted. I really believed that I had become a stoic and lost the power to feel keenly.

"Mrs. Jones shook that belief rather violently in a few minutes in my cabin that night.

"I fell insanely in love with her. I tried to prevent her from returning to her own cabin and if she had not had a sense of humor and considerable eloquence, I might have been the cause of vast embarrassment to her.

"When she had gone I cried and laughed and grew bloated with glory. I put on a lavender necktie to match the colors of dawn and went out on the deck to wait for it. In spite of cold and dampness, in spite of the grunting proximity of seamen hosing the decks, I carried out my intention. Eventually the sun came up, and, since I had never before been at sea, the spectacle of its vermilion dish across the gaudy water raised my nuttiness to the nth pitch. I imagined myself waiting for the woman's husband to die, or being shot by him, or following them to places such as Naples and Cairo. She had said nothing about coming to my cabin again, but she had left— absent-mindedly, as I learned later—a rather delicate undergarment on my pillow. It was, as I basked in the Fata Morgana dawn, stuffed inside my shirt and no doubt it saved me from catching a bad cold in the chest.

"However, as I was sinking into something more like delirium than sleep, Genevieve Jones' daughter was brushing her teeth in preparation for a new and different day of her life."

At noon Finnley appeared among the passengers, angry at having wasted five precious hours in sleep and ready to buy a passage from the purser in order to avoid further procrastination in the ship's orchestra.

He found Genevieve Jones sitting alone in a deck chair, her hat bound down by a veil. The motions of that veil in the wind were poetry to him then, although in retrospect it seemed incredible that she had worn any sort of veil. He sat down beside her with what he imagined as an alluring and romantic motion of limbs. She raised her eyes from her book.

"Hello, Finnley," she said. There was something in her voice that stunned him.

"I was up all night—waiting for the dawn," he answered in sepulchral tones.

"That was silly of you. It was chilly last night."

"It didn't matter—"

She sighed and set the book on her lap. "Listen, Finnley. Before my husband and daughter come back from a lap around the deck. What I did last night I very seldom do. I am sure I will not do it again for years. I haven't the slightest idea why I did it—except that I felt juvenile and you looked so dark and starved. Today you don't. Today you look as if you had katzenjammer. I think you are a very nice child, and I'd like you to be friendly with myself and my husband and especially my daughter, but unless you promise me not to moon and not to make private speeches and—in fact—to forget that I am anything but a middle-aged tourist—I won't let you see me at all."

Finnley's soul plunged in the spark-shot dark for the proper phrase. He decided on one and pronounced it. "I quite understand my inadequacies and I assure you that my acquaintanceship is at your disposal."

Mrs. Jones bit her lip and hastened back to her book with a quiet, "I *knew* you'd understand." The words before her meant nothing, however, as she found herself reflecting how pleasant it would be to badger Ricardo into giving her a few weeks alone in Venice and meeting Finnley surreptitiously in, say, Marseilles.

Finnley made a magnificent bow over her and walked to a position above the propellers. There, with tears in his eyes and fingernails biting into the rail, he wondered if one could dive onto the propeller in such a way that it would cut one to pieces and how it would feel to swim, swim, swim until one drowned and how painful the first visceral sawing of shark-teeth would be.

A steward told him that it was time to go to the dining room.

He played during the lunch hour without looking toward the passengers.

[59]

At five o'clock he found a place between two lifeboats where he could be alone with his sorrow. He had eaten nothing since the previous evening. Emptiness intensified his sentiments. He realized that he was destined to lead a life of tragedy. He foresaw that every woman he truly loved would desert him sooner or later and every woman with whom he trifled ("And I fear," Wren murmured, "that I expressed it to myself as 'trifled'—or possibly, 'dallied.'") would wreak dire and unnatural vengeances upon him. His career was ruined. He would go through life uneducated. Society would never hold a position for him. In fact, the sooner disease overtook him, the better.

But by and by, as the sun shone on the round, level sea and the wind blew upon him, as his experiments with bitter laughter reached his own ears with an ambiguous note, and as his appetite asserted itself, Finnley commenced to chuckle. In less than twenty-four hours he had run the gamut of a love affair from wonderment and heat to acidity and amusement. He was genuinely amused at himself. He held out his hands and feet and laughed at them and away went everything but a minor embarrassment. He took a cigarette from his pocket and smoked it.

A girl said, "Hello," to him.

"The instant I saw her," Wren continued thoughtfully, "a strange thing occurred to me; I recalled Genevieve Jones' complexion. There were definite signs of age in it. I wasn't revolted—no one could have been revolted by her—but I was delicately amazed at myself."

The girl was feminine and very sweet despite the short skirts, bobbed hair and conscientious rakishness of the early American flapper. She was a dark girl, not very tall, with a rapturous mouth and oblique, private ways of presenting herself even to strangers which were both charming and imaginative.

She sat down in front of Finnley, crossed her legs, and said, "There was a porpoise yesterday, but I'm afraid it's gone."

He nodded. "I find them like that. Quite unreliable. It's part of their fascination. But I can recommend the waves. We had several fine ones an hour ago. It's a pity you missed them. The color of tourmalines."

"Of course," the girl continued, edging a little closer to him, "there are two kinds of tourmalines."

"I referred, naturally, to the South American variety."

The girl yawned. "I've been sleeping all afternoon."

"So I noticed. In your dress."

"Is it so badly mussed?"

"Just a little. On one side. And there are fingerprints on your cheek."

"I usually take off my dress before I go to sleep," the girl replied. "But I wasn't able to do it today. I wanted my state-room door open and mother made me choose between that and a dress. So I went to sleep in my dress." She leaned forward and stared at him, her deep eyes wide open. "I trust I'm not offending an habitual peeping Tom."

"No offense."

She shook her head several times. Her hair was as dark as his own and faintly perfumed. "Shall we get married?" she said.

"Or shall we walk around the deck?"

"Or both?"

"Are you very hard to marry?" Finnley peered back at her anxiously and their faces almost touched.

"Dreadfully. There are the Sirens. And there is the Cyclops."

[61]

"Did you get A in Ancient History, too?"

"B plus."

"And how will I recognize these hazards?"

"The siren is my mother. Young men who see both of us fall in love with her. As if she were a plum pudding and I were a raisin."

"I see," Finnley replied with sudden comprehension. "And the Cyclops?"

"My father. Can you play golf? Did you ever collect postage stamps? Are you terrified by little men with bass voices? Do you get seasick? Do you believe that progress depends on national advertising?"

"He'll be a cinch."

"To the deck, then."

Finnley pulled her to her feet.

"But I'm not so sure about my mother," she said, as they started to walk.

He glanced toward the sea and down at her. "You come to my middle rib, approximately. Have no fear on that score. Consider, in fact, that the Sirens have been passed successfully."

"Oh!" the girl said. "I understand. We couldn't find her at all—that is—I couldn't. Father never looks. Maybe he knows better. Maybe he likes to say, 'Confounded nuisance' all evening and wants an excuse. And that's why you were laughing at yourself."

"You will be a pest around the house, Patricia."

"Hope."

"That's rather beautiful."

"Well?"

"Finnley Wren."

"Yes—I know."

"How soon were you intending to marry me?" Finnley was pleased with his composure.

"In about a year. It will take that long to convince my father that you are a great advertising man."

"I'll have to go in the advertising business?"

"Naturally. You see, I'm his only child."

"It follows. But I'm afraid"—Finnley suddenly chilled as if this reconnaissance had not been a game—"it's impossible."

Her quick turn of the head was alarmed. "You aren't—"

"No."

She laughed. "Insanity in your family?"

"No. You see—I'm going abroad to drink myself to death."

"They say it's revolting toward the end. I'll save you."

"No."

"When did you decide to do that?"

"Just this minute."

"Any particular reason?"

"A very good one."

"Better tell me. Because I'll think up an alibi for mother and father more easily if you don't just spring it on all of us at once."

They marched along the promenade deck, past rows of chairs in which extravagantly homely people sat reading books.

"I come from Orange Park," Finnley said.

"I live in Westchester. What of it? Where you live is like where a roulette ball lands. Besides, it's nice in Orange Park. Lots of shrubbery."

"We keep it for burglars to hide behind. We feel sorry for the hard lives they live."

"And so—?"

"I went to Yale last year."

"Father hates college men. He beats them at golf. I do hope you play well."

"Very well. I was a caddy. Understand—I come from a family that is sure it is on the right side of the railroad tracks. My father is a doctor. He is a miserable one."

"Not an osteopath, I hope?"

"No."

"Mother hates osteopaths. She had her back sprained by one, once."

"What I was getting at is that I was a caddy because my father didn't want me to get into mischief when school was out, and he believed every young lad should learn the value of money, so I never had any except what I earned."

"Did it work?"

"You mean—did I learn the value of money? I did. I used to steal it from the church collection plate and other sources. Not having any when my farseeing parent could easily have kept me in small funds gave me, I should say, an even exaggerated idea of the value of money."

Hope bent her head in agreement and hugged his arm. "Now—since I have such a clear picture of your home life— the matter of drinking yourself to death. Did you steal a great deal of money and get asked to put it back?"

"No."

"Why be stubborn? Why hide the truth from your bride? I can't be shocked—not when I'm on guard anyway. You are obviously running away from something."

"I like ships. I play in the orchestra—by the way. I should first unmask that fact."

"Father will approve of that. I can hear him say, 'If he had to go abroad—although America is the place for youngsters— why, he justified it partly anway by paying his own fare.' " She took his hand and looked at it. "Piano?"

"Piano."

"It will be pleasant in the long winter evenings."

"You will love it," Finnley answered in simple tones. "Now. About the other matter. I was accused by an unmarried girl of being the father of her unborn child. It turned out that I couldn't have been. Matter of the calendar only, however.

[64]

So I slung my mousetrap over my white horse and galloped off. I had to. Behind me was the outraged press and a company of stone-throwers with long arms and big muscles."

She had turned away from him as he spoke. She drew him to the rail and looked down in the water. He felt her shoulders tremble slightly and with great alarm he began to speak. "I'm —frightfully—sorry. I'll tear along—"

But she wasn't crying. When she faced him again he saw to his amazement that she was convulsed with laughter. Long afterward it seemed strange to him that he had expected to find her weeping. He stared at her with indignation.

"Well?"

She stopped laughing. She pointed her finger at him. "I know you. I know all about you. You are a friend of a girl named Esther Vickers, aren't you? You were in love with her for a week once, and she is still fond of you. How could you get excited about anybody so obvious? Even for a week? Esther's my cousin. And did your little scandal in the newspapers cause a riot in my family! My! Father and mother are very liberal, you know. They are leaders in a eugenic movement. They were so mad at Orange Park, that they almost came over and shot up the town. They used to bring the papers home every evening and get so enraged over the martyring of what they called a normal young man that I heard nothing but your name all last month. Mother pointed you out. Dear me. It's going to be so easy to marry you now that it will be positively dull."

"I'm sure it will be," he said, feeling outwitted, impotent and enraged.

"My! You have a funny expression! Grin, or ogle or something, but don't leer."

Finnley fumbled with his emotions. Hope took his arm again and turned him around.

"This is my father," she said casually. "Father—this is the man I am going to marry."

Ricardo Jones squinted. "You have a large smudge on your nose," he said.

"His name is Mr. Wren. Finnley Wren. He's the young man who was in that Orange Park trial last month."

Jones hurled his unlighted cigar over the rail and stalked away without replying.

Finnley remembered the days and the nights by skies and music and the sense associations related to Hope. Polished blue skies and ultramarine horizons toward which one looked vainly and eternally for a glimpse of curvature. Endless rhythms and perpetual gliding bright and black costumes above sliding shoes. A perfumed woolen scarf blown against his face. Disjointed Cassiopeia and the Dipper brimful of frigid infinity. Aquatic mountains frothing with rage, and song on the lips of the pimple man the hair oil man the boy with the big feet. A voice, low, dulcet, whispering in his ear about the people who live on the moon and the great ship crawling across the Atlantic, about trees in spring, girls with wooden legs, maple-nut sundaes, an absent-minded postman, and the probable meaning of runes.

"I found myself," Wren said, as he dipped a spoon into his petite marmite, "standing on the God-damned gangplank holding the hands of Hope and her mother and staring at a self-consciously picturesque city from the seaside.

"Hope's father, whom I had conscientiously licked every day at shuffleboard, was behind us, hugging a steamer rug around his shoulders, eyeing me with the cold malice of a habitual spike-biter.

"Everyone said good-bye.

[66]

"We chuffed around a little material relative to meeting in Paris. They went on, waving.

"Hope had tears in her eyes but she kept them from falling by such grimaces as I have seldom seen.

"And that was that.

"Hope loved me.

"I loved Hope.

"We didn't know what to do about it.

"We were young.

"The poignancies rolled over me. I'm subject to poignancies and all the allied emotions. Weltschmertz—I get. Nostalgia. Loneliness. Yearning. My ecstasies all verge on the shuddering sort—but in the sad-sweet and bitter-sweet categories, I'm a mass of raw ganglia. A distant locomotive whistle can make me weep—for no tangible reason. The smell of burning leaves can rend the material of my soul. There is a fur I do not dare put against my cheek.

"And when they pulled up the anchor that day they pulled up arteries in me.

"Of course, there are limits to the capacity for feeling, and when I reach them I am automatically transubstantiated. I maintain my soul in cold immobility, as if I had frozen it in a block of ice, and the real world becomes a dream—faint, fragrant memories in the making.

"Emotional fatigue generates its own anæsthesia. Prolonged confusion creates sanctuary. Frustration is the very substance of self-effacement.

"My difficulties ran round and round in my head like a carousel mounted with bleeding horses.

"A shade elaborate. But I had a hell of a time.

"Her father found me an unfailing source of annoyance, boredom, clumsiness, and gaucherie. I struggled to be agreeable and invariably took attitudes at direct variance with his complicated convictions. I mouthed bushels of platitudes and inanities in an overweaning effort at adult conversation. I accidentally knocked cigars out of his mouth, hats off his head, and once I untied his shoe and scratched his ankle under a steamer rug, imagining idiotically that it was Hope's extremity with which I toyed.

"Genevieve retreated into a deep dignity which covered, I subsequently realized, a great deal of fear.

"And little Hope, after our flippant and really admirable first meeting, fought pitifully against awakened feeling. She didn't want, then, to love anyone. She wanted gaiety and adventure. Fun. It wasn't fun to be in love with me in those painful nineteen-twenties.

"As my eyes turned inward they were revolted by what I had hitherto considered my golden youth. It seemed tawdry and snide. I took wave after wave of purity on the chin and I will say now, once and forever, that if I could relive the dream and drizzle of my days, I would endeavor to keep my love-life noble and confine its early experimentation to something as preordained, as clean and clinical as a Childs restaurant.

"Oddly enough mother nature, queen of the human hothouse, alcohol, and mischance destroyed that brief reform.

"After I reached Paris, I heard nothing from Hope. My messages and missives to England were returned with tax stamps attached. Winter came. Snow fell.

"I had never so much as approached any of the colleges or universities.

"I went broke."

for no good reason he stood outside the madeleine his face so pinched and haggard, his posture so indrawn and wretched that he might have been part of the nocturnal throng of all the world's tubercular, poverty-stricken addicts of evil. he moved his bright insensate eyes along the light-spattered street from

which the wind sucked itself to make room for winds yet colder
and more penetrating.   a small badge of ice hung on the tail
of his threadbare coat as if the gelid puddles under his feet had
reached up and pinned it there.   his hands were in his pockets
and the gloves that had covered them lay on the floor of a dingy,
distant, night-hung bistro.   an old woman shivered up the steps
of the stone cathedral.   rumors of dinner-bound traffic came
to his ears from the remote planet which he haunted.   christ-
mas bells tintinnabulated and his white, immemorial breath stood
out against a world adorned by red and green, against a multi-
tude of smiles and sentiments, against a falling down from
god's great pillow:
 through his brain ran the word hope
    like a rat in a garret
the angels shook the pillows harder and threw them at each
other until the down of their wings was also dislodged and fell
to earth in loving, freezing memory of the birth of jesus.
 he moved from the pale pillars pointing heavenward.
 he thought that the pagan gods were better for having been
born in the spring.
 he coughed dust out of his lungs.
 through one of the outdoor hallways of civilization he went:
aching aimlessness;
passionate obscurity;
grief—
the masterpiece of his juvenilia
 he wondered for a little while what had become of the months,
the two months, the precious months, the months which had
dissolved in his palm
 and wondering, he reckoned to his mind a giddy wall paper
with a moving pattern, a cracked and sweating water pitcher,
and ten thousand streets that led to nowhere in paris
 out of paris
 paris

when he wanted to howl the wind did it for him
when he wanted to weep the rain fell
when his chill was most insupportable the ground froze.
finnley stopped
and stood in the ten thousand and first street as if the other
thoroughfares had been part of a necessary pilgrimage
8574.3 joggle over trolley track.   left at fountain
he found himself beside a door with his ear toward it
you've got to cross that lonesome valley
inside that door a black gabriel sang
he opened it.
j'ai faim, he said to the man at the door.
je joue très bien au piano.

They led Finnley to the piano.   Simultaneously he earned his supper and thawed his hands.   For the first time in an indefinite nether epoch he understood human voices.   Around him people dined and talked.   He accompanied the Negro who had discovered the lonesome valley, and as notes, voice, wine smells and dish sounds mingled with warmth and tobacco smoke he found the lost thread that held his body in the world's web.

"I played in that dive for nine weeks," Wren said, slicing through the red middle of his fillet.   "There were rooms upstairs and girls.   For incidental atmosphere I refer you to the motion pictures, where you will notice particularly that I had a glass of beer on the top of the piano and a half-smoked jaune on the side.   They paid me a small salary.

"It is difficult for me to remember now just what I did.   The period telescopes into itself and becomes a long twenty-four hours in which it may be supposed that I rose at ten or eleven and walked along the wintry Seine, partook of a three franc lunch on the left bank, sat inside the Dome or the Rotonde and talked to a number of persons who afterward became celebrities, rode to my honky-tonk on a bus, banged the piano for my growing clientele until midnight and slept either at my cheap hotel, or in the rooms upstairs with evanescent-faced girls who spoke a chattering argot, and developed clammy, cloying passions for me that generally went unconsummated.

"One night when I reached my decaying dominion a gendarme was waiting for me.

"Hope's family had sent him.

"Winter water had turned my French shoes into yellow plaster, but I still had a fine New Haven tweed suit. My overcoat was no longer a luxury in gray herringbone, my hat looked stained and beaten, like the Latin Quarter, but my haberdashery was presentable and I had new gloves.

"I wrote down the name of their hotel on a five franc note. I found it today when I was ruminating my treasures. A gem of sentiment. The gendarme had an indelible pencil and the words, 'George V' are blurred by tears and trembling.

"Ricardo Jones met me in the lobby and threw his cigar halfway across the room.

" 'You look like the devil,' he said. 'Damn pining fools. Drink. Left bank revolutionists. Whores. Are you venereal?' "

" 'No,' I replied.

" 'Tubercular? You look it.' "

" 'No.'

" 'Sit.'

"We dropped ourselves into a crimson plush divan under a tree in a brass pot. I always get dizzy in large French hotels because of the labyrinths of glass and gilt gewgawgery. That day I was positively sick. I hadn't eaten well and I'd drunk too much and the room whirled around me like Nausea unveiling herself. Hope's father was the only focal point—gimlet eyes above his foghorn voice.

" 'I give up,' he said to me disgustedly. 'I was a tough bird once. I'm plucked. We took her to England. I must say frankly that I think you are a nitwit and a buffoon. Unfortunately, Hope doesn't. First she lost seventeen pounds. We had to hire a man to keep her from cable offices and telephones and a private detective to send back your mail. I steamed it open and read it all. Your talent for turning girls' heads is second only to your giant ability to turn the stomachs of mature men. Your poetry was especially foul. Then she got hysterical. We had specialists around in droves. Hotel got to be like a mortuary. Sad bastards with big hands. Then Genevieve went to work on me. My wife—is efficient and persistent. Did I say I was stubborn? For four months I have been Napoleon, Machiavelli and Disraeli in one. Hope went to bed—permanently. Her mother went to bed. By Jesus, I had to go to bed myself in the end. I must say, I have never really hated before in my life. Young man, you have touched emotional depths in me that I did not know I possessed.

" 'I have had dreams about you. I have seen you on racks and rails and in buckets of boiling oil. Poor compensation for my waking hours. Yesterday I gave up. I routed them all from bed and brought them to Paris. They got well while they were dressing.

" 'I put the police on your trail. I was delighted to find that you had been acting in a way that reminded me strongly of my women-folk. Delighted. Harlots for heartbreak. You have the moral fiber of a scorpion. I asked you to come here to accept my surrender.'

"I was so bewildered and weak and ashamed," Wren said, "that I commenced to cry. He looked at me and muttered a sour, 'Splendid.'

"That suddenly made me mad. I got up. He asked me where I was going. I gave him some stony, little-boy answer.

He took me by the shoulder and led me to a bar. We had a drink and I got still madder."

The pre-dinner hour in a bright café. Outside, the faded, early spring sky. Wren and Ricardo Jones sat across from each other in a small booth with highballs on the table before them. For three minutes they locked mutually insolent eyes and neither glanced away.

"I tell you," Jones said at last, "what. Those letters—I shan't mention them again—showed a certain skill with words. A feeling for them. I'll pay your passage home. I'll give you a job in my company. It's advertising, in case you don't know. If, in a year, the crabs haven't eaten you, we'll talk over a marriage with my daughter. Providing, too, of course—Hope hasn't come to her senses in the meantime. Hope's a fool—but she has a fine background. She comes from the Scotch Bruces who were one of the soundest royal families—"

Finnley sipped his highball very slowly, his eyes still on Jones. Finally he gathered himself together and spoke.

"I didn't mean to bring this up again," Wren said, smiling at me. "You'll forgive the reference? It's an intrinsic part of the story.

He put down his glass.

"Look here, Jones." He thought momentarily. "I'm a lineal descendant of John Milton and of Christopher Wren. I'm as well born as you are. I'm as well informed and I have as good a mind. I have ten times as good a body and a thousand times as fine a disposition. I have chased around with a lot of women. They like me for all the above reasons and several others. Men like me. If I wanted to ask for money, my family would send it. If I wanted a job, I could get one. I happened to fall in love with your daughter. If it's of any interest to you, I may say that I never even kissed her. I was in no hurry to do so. On the other hand, if it is of any interest to you, I kissed your wife and I kissed her hard and all meaning went out of it in a few hours. I could be a great advertising man, a great pianist, a great author and a great gigolo.

"Don't interrupt me. I've listened patiently to what you think of me. I agree with you in one sense only: I've been afraid of you—otherwise I would have left the boat in England—and fear of you has made my behavior with you stupid. I'm not afraid of you any longer. I think you're a charlatan and a martinet and a hypocrite and a son-of-a-bitch. I am going to do what I should have done long ago. I am going to marry your daughter immediately, and decide what course to take afterward. If you wish to prevent me by thugs and injunctions and arrest, you can. Temporarily. But in the end, I'll marry her. And I'll express my resentment of any interference by knocking you down every time I see you in the future, and I assure you I shall go out of my way to catch glimpses of you."

Wren stopped talking. He was seized by swirling debility and for a moment lost track of his antagonist.

Jones slowly took a cigar from his pocket. He bit off its end. He lighted it. He gulped.

He began to laugh.

He flooded the room with Gargantuan blasts of laughter. People stood up and craned their necks to see him. Waiters frowned. Finnley eyed him through thinning haze and abruptly he grinned.

Jones got up and came around to his side of the booth. He pounded Finnley on the back until he coughed.

"By God," Jones roared. "By God! Why didn't you say that four months ago! I thought you were a lollipop. A chicken-gutted jackass. By God!"

Finnley continued to grin at him in dazed incredulity. He tried to pick up his glass with vague and mechanical embarrassment. Jones hit his back so hard that the highball splashed on the floor.

"Nobody has called me those names since I was ten years old," Jones thundered. "Martinet! Hell! Charlatan! Stupendous! Hypocrite! Immense! Son-of-a-bitch! Get up, you God-damned lily! Let's go and see Hope!"

"Hope and I were married in Paris that spring," Wren said wistfully. "I'd like to describe our nuptials to you. But I'd rather—just remember them. She was an angel—that girl. A slightly crazy angel without tinsel. I never quite believed she was my wife in all the long time we spent together.

"Her father habitually bolstered himself with indignations, but he believed them. He was intricate and willful, but he was genuine. I loved that man. I still do. I love Genevieve. And—" he shrugged.

"One of his flamboyant prejudices was against foreign languages. I found out, the day after he had summoned me to the hotel, that a competitor of his was gourmandizing Parisian advertising accounts for American magazines. A Park Avenue sissy named Blakely was harvesting them over apéritifs. So I went out, with my school French bawdy-house polished, and took him over. I brought old Jones a platterful of contracts.

"God sat right on my shoulders. Everything went the way it does in storybooks. In six weeks I had the prettiest girl in Paris, and money to burn. We sat up all night and danced and listened to music and rode through the Bois in carriages. The horse chestnuts blossomed. We bought a wire-hair named

[75]

Mr. Smith. We rallied through the department stores and drank beer on warm afternoons at sidewalk cafés.

"In June we came back to America. Ricardo and Genevieve gave us a house in Westchester for a wedding present. I commuted every day to the offices on Fifth Avenue at Forty-sixth Street. Hot weather came. From our front porch you could see the Hudson. Behind our house was a lake artificialized into a swimming pool. We had a cream-colored roadster and the best delphiniums in the state—"

Wren looked at his watch. "Good Lord!" he said. "We better start."

"Start?"

"Certainly. For the Dwyers'."

"Dwyers'?"

"Of course. That's where we're going over the week-end. Didn't I tell you?"

"You failed to mention it."

He stared at me. "But you'll go? You see—I've only begun the story of my life. Only touched the hem here and there." He smiled anxiously. "You're married. You see—I've identified you. And I've met your wife. Beautiful girl, too. You'll have to tell her that it's impossible to spend Saturday and Sunday with her."

"It's impossible to tell her," I answered. "She's on her way to Bermuda for a week."

"Wylie," he said, "you're colossal. Rather—your wife is. And what were you going to do?"

"I'd left my bag at the check room in Grand Central. I was on my way to my place in East River to plant some tulip bulbs. I missed a train. Went over to Angelo's for a drink to pass time."

Wren looked reverently toward the ceiling. "Sometimes," he murmured, "I believe. We'll have a brandy and a taxi. Where's East River?"

"Above New Haven."

"We'll run up on Sunday and plant the bulbs. I am a gardener of the primordial variety. On to the Dwyers', then, stopping at my apartment first."

We sat in a cab. "Who are the Dwyers?" I asked.

Wren beat on the window. "Faster," he bawled. "Does it matter? Does it matter? You'll like them. I have to take a bath and pack. I was out last night in the rain. My necktie ran all over my chest. I changed my clothes, but I didn't bathe. I forget why. I am blue from my nave to my chaps and I had been unseamed." We whirled into Broadway and he leaned out the window. He waved and yelled. "See that girl? That's my secretary. Remember? The one to whom I told the Maxfield Parrish version of my life?" He wound up the window. "Lots of people I'd rather not see. Not all of them really there."

We stopped in front of a brownstone house on Tenth Street. Wren took a ring of keys from his pocket and let himself into a somber, ornate reception hall. An ancient man with grimy eyes sat in front of a telephone switchboard. He gave Wren an expression of unimaginative disapproval. We crossed the room and climbed into an elevator. Wren pressed a button and we started up. When the elevator stopped we stepped into a hall. He opened another door and we were out on a roof, surrounded by leafless vegetation, tiles, dead fountains, and faced by a large, brick penthouse. He unlocked its door and found a light switch.

Radiance filled a square hall with gray walls around which silver gulls coasted. Wren took my coat and hat. We progressed through an arch and he touched another switch.

Twenty lamps cast their tinted auras on the central room of a modernistic, duplex apartment. It was a handsome, startling place. A chrome-railed staircase and balcony swept from and overhung the chamber itself which was thickly carpeted in sea gray. Low chairs and divans geometrically overstuffed were interspersed with delicate furnishings of steel and canvas and glass. On the walls were a few unframed, violent-colored canvases. In one corner was a black piano, angular and yet ethereal, which described the entire room in that the spirit of its design tended toward the beauty of mathematics rather than toward comfort.

My eye fell as if by deliberate direction upon one of the portraits: A slender, red-headed woman with greenish eyes and a demoniac mouth standing naked in the half-crouch of a Javanese dancer.

"My last duchess," Wren said, staring at the picture. "This apartment is—or was—her soul. Please excuse me while I bathe and pack. You'll find liquor behind the middle panel on that wall. The rose in the vase on the niche above opens it. You pick the rose and it slides. Fifteen—twenty minutes—"

He went up the stairs.

Left to myself, I stood for some time in the center of the chamber. Since I am a rather rare fellow on my own account, sensitive and logically imaginative, with a flair for investigation and human research, I reacted to the Wren penthouse as powerfully as I have to any dwelling in which I have ever been. My mind probed it and cast up shadows of its inhabitants and their characters.

Wren's classic carelessness had been abolished from the place. His love of color and novelty were there, but they had been machined into a system. His piano, for example, was not an instrument of melody, but a tool. His lust for isolated grandeurs was certainly represented. However, the red woman was in that room. Whether she had been his wife or his mistress, I did not know.

But she was there—stern, sterile, masochistic, unrequited and relentless. Beautiful as perfect apparatus is beautiful. Orgiastic. Vain.

On my right side was a door, and presently I opened it. Other lamps immediately shed light on a chamber bizarre because it was almost bare. A flat couch, glass-covered bookcases, a desk and a chair together with the lamps and a curtained window in front of the desk represented its entire content. I drew the curtain and, although it was only five or six stories above the street, the window behind it framed the spangled skyscrapers of central New York with the toytown shaft of the Empire State Building precisely bisecting the view.

There was a typewriter on the desk and beside it a heap of dog-eared manuscripts, disheveled, unsorted, clipped together impermanently. In the typewriter was a sheet of paper on which a title had been X'd out. I discerned the lettering underneath: FIVE LITTLE PEPPERS IN HELL.

I picked up one of the manuscripts and sat down on the couch with it. I read the following:

AN EPISTLE TO THE THESSALONIANS

Comerade Nikolai Dimitri Eisenstein, the renowned Leninist incendiary and pickpocket, having heisted the keister of Mrs. Benjamin Bissel, housewife, of 1594 East Orchid Street, the Bronx, reviewed its meager interior as he stood beneath the elevated on Sixth Avenue. He was quite unaware of the lacy pattern described on the trolley track by the sun in conjunction with the elevated ties until the phenomenon was blotted out, some say rudely, some say politely and gradually.

We will now drop Comerade Nikolai Dimitri Eisenstein.

[79]

The cause of the shadow which fell over the whole city of New York and many other cities besides on that halcyon July morning was an obstruction of Old Sol in the form of a giant one thousand miles high.

The giant, appearing from no one knows where and unannounced by the world's observatories which, at the time, were jammed with hawk-eyed astronomers whose data tabulated in light years about matters of less consequence than the visitor to our planet was always available while on this pertinent matter their information was nil, dropped rapidly from a strategic position behind the moon. As he entered the gravitational sphere of earth's influence he picked up our rotary motion so that his descent upon the sea was not accompanied by embarrassing tidal waves. Indeed, he stepped onto the waters of the Atlantic so circumspectly that the lay notion he had jumped through space was absurd.

The lower two hundred miles of him penetrated our atmosphere between eleven-six and eleven-twenty A.M., Eastern Standard Time, and came to rest on the sea about an hour later, as he manifestly appreciated the danger of stamping upon the water.

However, his advent caused trouble enough, in spite of his elaborate caution. The sea rose in a slow surge which drenched the populous fringes of New York Bay and the lower portion of the Hudson River. His descending feet set in motion currents of air that roared and twisted over New York, Long Island, New Jersey and Connecticut, causing property damage later totaled by the Associated Press at one hundred and seventeen millions, loss of life to eighty-three persons and accidents of varying seriousness to a number estimated at two hundred and twelve.

A minor earthquake was reported from the seismographs of several stations, the most remote of them located at Butte, Montana, and one Torrence Bemis cabled an interesting story to the *New York Telegram* headed, "Malaise among Inhabitants of Mombasa, Kenya, Africa," with time corrections.

These geological eccentricities, however, were mere twaddle and fluff in comparison to the effect of the giant and his appearance upon mankind in general. No complete record will ever be made. Witness, for example, the following: at a time as recently removed from the incident as the present, no less than seven hundred and three volumes have been published relating to the monstrous man and ranging in scope from Glover's authoritative *Economic Consequences of the Giant's Visitation* to *Love in Giant Land*, by Jacqueline Chiffon, an opus from the typewriter of a young Cleveland woman so saturated with sentimentality, so saccharine, and so illiterate that one Amos Golf, after reading it, went stark mad (to his infinite glory) and assassinated not only Miss Chiffon but the eleven other most famous American lady authors.

Twenty-six religions were founded during the stay of the giant or are now identified with his sojourn. Bouncerism, originating in Georgia, attempted to drive away the giant, claimed sole credit for his departure (which is widely believed to have been voluntary) and now holds as its major tenet the prevention of further visits. The devotees of Bouncerism pray in pig Latin while jumping up and down in each others' arms. The Arrivalists, now segregated in Toledo, live in metal shacks, wear only garments woven of human beard hair, and celebrate July 19th as Giantmas. The Church of the Holy Nut, venerating a brown seed thirty-seven feet long which fell from the giant's person and is assumed to be a spore from the stranger's world believe that their deity was Christ in his Second Coming. Legal process was necessary to keep the members of the Church of the Holy Nut from worshiping Him by blowing up mountains—a form of veneration doubtless appropriate, but unduly hazardous to the skeptical, of whom there were luckily hundreds of millions.

And so it went. While a draft blew over the cities of New Jersey—cities named by persons with minds as poisoned as the imagination of their architects (Belcher has listed them in his "Inverse Lyrics": Hackensack, Trenton, Newark, Hoboken, Red Bank, Jersey City, Weehawken, Nutley, Ten Eyck, New Brunswick, Paterson, Camden, Perth Amboy, Boonton, Elizabeth, etc., ad naus.) and while the waters rose in the shipping focus of the world—the necks of the western hemisphere bent upward to behold the wonder in the sky. Millions were frightened. Millions sought for methods of turning the phenomenon into cash. Millions ignored the giant.

Fields and housetops were at a premium.

Telescopes swung from their patient routines.

Scientists hopped to long distance telephones.

The War Department drew in a lungful of air and bleated it out in its usual vain ignorance.

The President's lunch was spoiled.

But one fact—or perhaps it was a condition—dominated all others. Nobody—nobody in Hoboken and nobody in New York, nobody in Washington and nobody in Europe knew what in hell to do.

Standing in the Atlantic Ocean, southeast of New York, was a giant one thousand miles high.

Incredible.

Ominous.

Unprecedented.

[81]

Indubitable.

There he was.

The sun beat upon him.

The sea laved the soles of his shoes.

His trouser cuffs, seen longitudinally through the earth's atmosphere, disappeared in haze. But the higher portions of him reëmerged. His head, a thousand miles out in space, was boldly visible. Through telescopes mounted on the loftier summits, even his expression could be observed. It was speculative, absorbed, and yet bland. He had gray eyes (which shone like moons in the late afternoon sun) and chestnut-colored hair which revealed a distinct tendency to curl. Lowell Wertzberg, of Ohio Wesleyan, located at Delaware, Ohio, was first to report the mole on his left cheek. His age was promptly put at thirty-five—although when an editor of an evening paper asked, "Thirty-five what?" no answer was forthcoming.

During the afternoon following his arrival the giant was seen to blink seven times. The process required about fifteen minutes (15 min. 36.9006 sec. average for 24 winks—Ed.). His head turned downward sixteen degrees between noon and four P.M. His arms swung forward eighty miles (Westcliffe and Leadbecker) and his eyebrows lifted seven thousand six hundred and five meters (Finch). The most proximate position of the sole of his left shoe was accurately determined by the United States Coast Guard and afterward substantiated by the Geodetic Survey at one hundred and eleven miles east southeast of Sandy Hook.

Photographs taken by Binnel at seven-fifty show that the sun had set on his lower extremities, but his face was vividly illuminated and, in fact, it became clearer as terrestrial darkness increased. Equally interesting are Gukel's lens studies of the moon partially eclipsed by the giant's buttocks, Gukel's credit being shared by the enterprising University of Southern Illinois.

Before nightfall on that memorable First Day, Lieutenant Charles Windbuck had returned from his epochal flight to the giant's toe. Although subsequent observations demonstrated that the monster moved with a slowness which suggested either consideration of the human beings below or, more probably, a desire to avoid setting fire to his clothing by atmospheric friction, Windbuck's flight was regarded at the time as a heroic venture.

"I discovered," Windbuck said that night over the radio to an audience of millions, "that the material of the giant's shoe is granular and resembles at close range a rough, conglomerate cliff. The sole of the shoe itself, although submerged in the Atlantic, rises to such a height from the water that its upper edge was above the ceiling of my airplane. A few dead fish floated around the shoe, which appeared to be motionless. I cannot describe the feeling I had staring at the precipice which had dropped into the sea, or looking eastward where the giant's shadow stretched over the broad ocean."

On the night of July nineteenth to twentieth the uproar caused by the strange visit had spread over the globe. Hindus and Brahmins were praying as shriekingly as Presbyterians, and only remote Australian Bushmen shared tranquillity with a few Senegalese, Eskimos, and the like.

The morning of the twentieth, hot and cloudless in Eastern U. S., was marked by a partial evacuation of the seaboard, a Stock Exchange panic, the declaration of martial law, and innumerable other mass reactions.

Professor Grover Rigg, with a corps of university volunteers, endeavored to communicate with the giant by laying out thousands of yards of white muslin on the fields south of Princeton in varying mathematical configurations. Nothing happened. A fighting fleet consisting of six battleships, four submarines, three cruisers, twelve destroyers, four blimps and the dirigible *Akron* moved out to the toe, stripped for action. Nothing happened. A Gloucester fisherman approached the right shoe and detached some of its material with axes and an acetylene torch brought for the purpose. Still nothing happened.

General Trumpley Clutt made before the House of Congress his celebrated "survival of the fittest" address, parts of which were published on the front pages of every American daily. "The man," said the general, "is human, obviously hostile, patently an enemy scout. We must declare war on him, gentlemen. We must annihilate him. Otherwise he will return whence he came and carry the news that we are a defenseless rabble. He will bring back a host of his fellows and we shall be doomed."

His speech was greeted by a tumult. When Representative Smith of Connecticut stood up afterward and said, briefly, "How are we to annihilate him? What shall we do with a carcass weighing billions of tons?" he was booed down by the members of the House, who make it a rule to prefer any idiocy, so long as it is noisome, to the most obvious common sense.

The result of Clutt's bombast was the immediate formation of eighteen committees and commissions.

On the morning of the twenty-first it was perceived that the giant was bending at the waist, knees, and hips. His shadow slipped sidewise across eastern U. S., moving out of Ohio entirely. The afternoon newspapers carried the banner, "GIANT SQUATTING."

And squat he did, all during the hectic night that followed. At dawn he was within seventy-four miles of the surface of the sea at certain hitherto unapproached points. Otherwise his behavior was innocuous.

War was declared on him twelve hours later, as his hands swung forward. Clutts and an expeditionary force spent the night mining his shoe with eighty tons of high explosive. It was detonated at daybreak on the twenty-third.

With the explosion, vast chunks of the giant's shoe were ripped away, but when an animated drawing showing the relative amount of damage done was displayed in the New York newsreel theaters later in the day, public confidence in our military strength and resourcefulness diminished. The damage to the shoe was equivalent to the bite of a very small ant on a number twelve hiking boot. There was a brief wave of ridicule launched against Clutt. Editors pointed out that the giant could scarcely be called a military scout, as he wore not a uniform, but tweeds of the most informal sort. Clutts retorted that he would shoot any puppy who wrote a line about him and asked what scouts were presumed to wear in the giant's homeland.

Thus the whole controversey was soon at loggerheads.

During the night of the twenty-fourth, the giant put his fingertips down in New Jersey and New York and leaned forward on them.

Small cities and towns were wiped out. Thousands upon thousands were slain. Hundreds of millions of dollars' worth of property damage was done.

Higgle's report that the material resembling pudding or cobble stone retrieved by the Gloucester fisherman was cell tissue, interested few. His assertion that the possession of those vastly magnified, dry leather cells would advance the study of biology, physics, and chemistry farther than all the research in those subjects hitherto conducted, fell on deaf ears. Ryelin's amazing "Initial Remarks" referring to his inspection of material taken from one of the mighty, inverted canyons which were the whorls and patterns in the skin of the giant's fingers appeared in but two or three newspapers.

On the twenty-fifth, the giant stood up again. Nearly every cabinet in the world had collapsed. Half the people on the eastern coast of the United States had fled to the interior. Crime and lawlessness had surpassed the powers of the military authorities and there had been several mutinies among the troops closest to the giant.

General Trumpley Clutt had committed suicide.

It rained, generally, on the twenty-sixth and the blotting out of the shape in the sky had a salubrious effect on the population of the eastern states. This effect was lost, however, when it was observed as the storm cleared that the giant was standing on his right foot and had drawn back his left.

What happened after that appalls the most sanguine and capacious imagination. The giant stood for three hours like a football player about to kick a goal. Then his majestic toe descended in a slow arc. It connected with the earth at Fire Island. It rushed northward at a speed of forty-three miles an hour and scuffed out of existence the five Boroughs of New York, the cities of New Jersey, the Hudson River Valley and much of the region between it and the Connecticut River, leaving behind a smooth channel of polished rock and stacking up in a line between the Adirondack Mountains and Augusta, Maine, the surface material thus collected which included not only the forests, fields, farms, slums and skyscrapers of the region, but the corpses of eighteen million persons and which made a range of loosely integrated mountains rising at their highest elevation to fifty-six thousand four hundred and eight feet. By some absurd mischance the steel steeple of the Empire State Building protruded from the highest escarpment of the unnatural range.

After that devastating act, the giant departed. He seemed to float away into space, gathering speed as he went. He wore on his face a faintly annoyed expression, such as might be found on the countenance of a man who had come upon an anthill and kicked it out of existence.

Daçoit, however, and other Europeans, agree that the scientific knowledge of molecular and atomic structure and of cell function derived from a consideration of the skin and leather snippings are worth more than the lives lost and the property destroyed.

Who knows?

Having finished this remarkable fable, and realizing that Wren was not yet ready to join me, I turned to the second manuscript. This, also, I perused. It was entitled EPISTLE TO THE GALATIANS and read as follows:

EPISTLE TO THE GALATIANS

Burton Bellinger bit a cracker while his test tube boiled and hummed the opening strains of Schubert's "Serenade." He was very happy, as why should he not be, for, out of the boiling and sundry other laboratory maneuvers was destined to come the greatest discovery of modern science, which he had already discounted in anticipation.

[85]

This *discovery*—it might better be termed a *biological invention*—was nothing less than a form of *serum, potion* or *hellbroth* calculated to destroy every pathogenic bacterium in the human body. A neatly contrived fluid, all in all, which would insure to *geniuses* and *fools, heliologists* and *harlots* immortality and youth modified only by a long postponed katabolism and such mishaps as automobile accidents and drownings.

Fine for *syphilis* and *scarlet fever,* useless for *suicide* and *subway collisions,* Burton Bellinger's Subcutaneous Bitters offered to all mankind an end of *ailments, illnesses, maladies* and *diseases* without number. Three seconds quenched most of any Braunian movement and turned your ordinary microscopic slide into a frozen panorama.

Bellinger swallowed his cracker and reviewed with pleasure the onrushing fame which would be his. He saw fortunes driven in golden vans to his modest home, and chests of *medals.* He imagined walls papered with sheepskins bearing *honorary degrees,* and something in the way of a large mountain on which his name and face would be so deeply graven that geologists would quarrel about the millennia required to erode the last vestiges of it.

For a cold, a pimple, ringworm and a suspicion of gonorrhea he took the first dose on the afternoon of his expectant boiling.

The concoction tasted like unsweetened *chocolate.* Injected intramuscularly, it smarted. But in twenty-eight minutes his cold was noticeably better. By morning the pimple was gone, the ringworm only a faint memory, his secret worry dispelled, and his saliva, upon microscopic examination, was matched in purity by his teeth scrapings.

Realizing clearly that he was the greatest man ever to bedeck the human race, he started for the Rockefeller Institute in a Ford.

He was dressed in old clothes. He had not shaved for three days. He had not slept a wink during the previous night.

It was while he drove in the traffic stream through the Holland Tunnel that he noticed an unpreconceived effect of his invention.

Quite rapidly, he was turning *green.*

At first he attributed this unpleasantness to the lighting of the place. Then, rather hysterically, he meditated the possibility of error in his calculations, of a novel vertigo, of separate poisoning. But he had never felt better in his life.

When he emerged from the Tunnel, people stared at him in horror. He parked the Ford on Canal Street, went into a second-hand furniture store (to the dismay of the clerk), and surveyed himself in the mirror of an old bureau.

His skin was a villainous *pea* green. His eyes were *moss* green, except for the pupils, which stared back with the *dark sheen* of spruce needles. His hair was an *inharmonious Nile* green.

Pricking his earlobe (the clerk rushed out for a police officer) he was surprised by a drop of bright, *verdant* blood.

He went to the Rockefeller Institute anyway and was sent to Bellevue for observation. There, in a space of forty-three days, he rectified the misconceptions of the scientists who had illtreated him. He repeatedly lanced himself with pus-laden scalpels. He misconducted himself with a young lady as beautiful as she was venereal. He vaccinated himself with hydrophobia, tetanus, Asiatic cholera, spinal meningitis, and various other infectious maladies. In the end, having escaped any *harm* whatever from these dangerous pastimes, he boiled up a new mass of his Intravenous Bitters, gave the formula to science, and resigned himself to the fate of being forever both antiseptic as molten quartz and a morbid *green* in color.

The world did not take kindly to Bellinger's Jade Omnicure. People did not like to be well as much as they did not like to be green. They preferred a touch of private *tuberculosis* to a drenching of flagrant *verdancy*. Moreover, those individuals who, swollen and empurpled by peritonitis, elected to take the dose on an indisputable *death-bed*, were immediately restored to health but subsequently shunned by their fellows. These "greenies" were avoided because their color suggested to the popular mind past diseases so revolting as to make any further contact undesirable—although the "greenies" were ten times more healthful and a trillion times as germfree as those who turned away disapproving faces and edged sidewise from them in trolley cars.

Perfect health was available to everyone on earth for a cost of *one and three-tenths of a cent* each, but since it included a change in the hue of the mortal envelope, the price might well have been measured in pounds of radium.

When a "greenie" walked unhappily on the street, shopgirls could be heard to titter, "How would you like to kiss him!" or—"I know what *he* inherited from his father!"

This state of *affairs*

"Well?"

I looked up and saw Wren standing in the doorway, smiling. To my perpetual regret, I was never able to finish the story of Bellinger's Jade Omnicure. I have always wondered what happened to Bellinger and whether or not humanity was turned green in the end by a fiat, and what the Pope had to say about it (I am sure Wren would not have forgotten the Pope) and how green photographed in Hollywood and a great many other things.

Wren certainly did not enlighten me. He dismissed the Epistles with but the briefest comment. "When I come home from work sick of advertising toothpaste for things it will not benefit and of trying to sell automobiles that have generically weak rear ends—when my gorge rises at being compelled to use a new razor blade every other day although I know a blade can be made for a dime that will last a year—when all the flim-flammery and idiocy and stupidity of our system wells up to putrify my sensibilities as it has those of almost everyone else— I write another Epistle. I have about a hundred and ten of them. They are my sublimation."

He looked at his watch. "Let's go."

We took a cab and rode to the Grand Central Station without speaking. I watched the lights drift past us in an after-dinner stupor and my mind made me uncomfortable with the tedious pursuit of parallels. In this affair, I thought of literature, of Lady Macbeth's sleepless dark hours, of Joyce's night town, and of Proust contemplating a world as if through the side of a goldfish bowl. All this bored me excessively, but I could not throw it off.

Wren was asleep when we reached the station. I woke him and we dived into the bright, glamorous unreality of the half-subterranean station. A porter with a scar on his face which he voluntarily told us came from shrapnel carried my bag to a dormant train with yellow-lighted vitals.

Wren was asleep again before we rumbled out of the station. An edge of cold air blew on my elbow which was propped against the window sill. I peered into the third stories of a hundred homes—dim squares of squalor where people sat or stood listening to radios and waiting with tin eyes for God knows what implacable and fifth-rate destinies.

When I turned to Wren I was somewhat shocked. Awake, his face was a bold oil painting. Asleep, it was an etching. Strength, fecundity, imagination were still there, but added to them were pallors, horrors, tribulations, pities, revulsions, frustrations, fatigues, and such sadness that the conductor, his shoulders hunched and his incongruous belly littered with minute, silly alphabets punched out of tickets, stood over him for several seconds shaking his head.

Once, I saw him stir in his slumber and thrust away from his unseeing eyes something so formidable that automatically I began to nerve myself for the experience of hearing out the story of his life.

I felt a little relief when the train moved faster and Wren settled to a sounder sleep. It occurred to me that this sort of somnolence was foreign to his disposition and, further, that he had been up all through the previous night.

For what reason, I wondered.

What grisly sight did that reluctant hand endeavor to repel?

What streets had he walked? What grief had racked him? What unnatural strain had been put upon him? What lesions had he found in our sickly civilization?

And what hope?

For Wren, even in a haunted sleep, was the substance of hope, hope itself, intelligence, idealism, courage, will.

I looked out at the railroad jewelry. A train moving in the opposite direction made me flinch. Cyclopean eye. Red breath. Burning bowels. A tail of human souls run together by velocity into a long, pale-faced oaf.

At New Haven on a chilly station platform, we descended. Wren took my arm and propelled me through a tunnel and up a ramp to a bus. It moved forward like a Morris chair on long springs carrying, besides ourselves, a fat old lady in a silk dress, an antique Yankee who could not quite bend himself into the unholstery and sat like a dried lizard, his beady eyes discountenancing this unavoidable luxury, and a young, drunken millhand who, at intervals, raised his head as if it were a clock-works mechanism and in the most melancholy of voices shouted, "piss-ant."

Not understanding Wren's reasons for this murky hadj, and unable to inquire, as he was sleeping for the third time, I bounced torpidly in my seat and stared out the window. We moved through a garish shopping center and into a manufacturing district—a grimy Sheol where arclights on the pale, insane side of lavender cast shadows among darker shadows. Then another, meaner store district, crawling with signs, labels, cans, meats, posters and stultified people. Soon we swam lugubriously into the country. I saw the Dipper and Cassiopeia's Chair lying on the sky—two permanent and feeble tributes to Greek imagery.

I smelled new air, nocturnal, autumnal.

The bus bumbled on a smooth road. I caught sight of a kerosene lamp in a window. I heard a dog bark.

A million years passed.

We stepped into the night beside a garage. We hired a man named Pete to transport us to the Dwyer residence.

We were in an open car. I saw the place where the Sound was, although I could not see the water. Then we stood on the porch of a vast white house, holding our luggage in our hands. Wren rang a doorbell.

"Finnley!" someone yelled, and a dozen people ran into the Victorian hall where we stood.

Men and women of various ages—all vivacious—all a little drunk—four of the women young and beautiful. Finnley grinned at them and indicated them one by one. "Mr. Don Whittington," he said to me, "Rachel Whittington, Jerry Whittington, Paul Whittington, Cynthia Whittington, Les Whittington, Tom Whittington." I began to shake hands with them, astonished at the variety and number of the Whittington family. I understood when he continued, "Dorothy Whittington, Brooke Whittington, Hans Whittington, John Banner Whittington, Martha Whittington, Estelle Whittington." He waved his hand at me. "Dick Whittington," he concluded.

They shook our hands, took our coats and hats, carried away our suitcases, and led us into a spacious living room where a fire was burning.

For a moment they swarmed around Finnley—tenderly, I thought. Several of the girls looked at him with love in their eyes. The men chuckled and wrung his hand again.

And, on the staircase, through French doors, I spied the man whom we had seen weeping earlier in the evening. It did not surprise me to find him there—at that time.

"i am crying, he said in a low, monotonous voice, because of "the feminist movement. was there ever a more preposterous "misconstruction of biological aspirations?"

He swayed, caught the banister, rocked back on his heels, and continued in a solemn, impressive tone.

"*with ribald indignation i observe that all our ladies, conscious* "*of their brains, are leaving their particular domains and, filled* "*with purpose difficult to swerve, with strident voice, and* "*military verve, are giving up their seats on subway trains and* "*wearing garments cut in lines and planes which camouflage* "*the appetizing curve.*

"*all nature rises in dismayed rebellion when women purge* "*their uteruses sterile and claim their minds are fertile; every* "*hellion exhibiting herself in male apparel will some day slake* "*her lust on dirty pictures, since normal men cannot survive* "*these strictures.*"

He nodded his head slowly three times and fell face forward, narrowly missing one of the Whittington cats.

PART II

FRIDAY NIGHT

OME of us sat in chairs, some sat on the floor, and some occupied two obese divans. I guessed immediately that Don and Martha Whittington were Dwyers and that Cynthia was their daughter. The father and mother were tweedy and academic. His red hair was gray streaked; his manner of speech was both merry and meticulous. Martha's name must once have been Marthe, for she spoke with a faint French accent, and Cynthia was what Martha had been long ago: dark, svelte, desiring.

We were served highballs in glasses upon which Mother Goose animals tippled at enameled bars. The fire had been expertly arranged to hiss, snap and flicker without any lapse into gross combustion. Outside, the sea's indefatigable cavalry attacked rock and sand, while the wind moaned over the chimneytops and through æolian trees.

Wren sat in a wing-back chaise longue and when an interval occurred in the conversation he brought attention to himself by murmuring, "It's nice here," and after a time, "I was telling Whittington the story of my life."

I saw Don and Martha glance at each other. Cynthia said: "Why let us interrupt it? Brooke has told us all about Wall Street and October, nineteen-twenty-nine. Graceful but incompetent lies. And Les has been bursting to go into his act. You know the one. Chemistry. Always begins, 'Yes, in another hundred years—' and shambles along till you're asleep. The story of your life couldn't be duller. In fact—" she hesitated painfully.

Wren smiled at her. "The narrative impulse in me is recur-

rent. Probably I hope to solve my riddles by public introspection. It's the only sort I can tolerate. True introspection
is insufferable. You can lie awake all night trying to discover
exactly why you failed to set up diamonds in the dummy and
make your six no trump—or why you stuck your finger in
the blood of a man you murdered, for that matter, I suppose.
I'd just as soon tell you all the story of my life.

"It's ordinary." He paused and stared at the fire. "Ordinary." He repeated the word as if he doubted it. "Middle
class. Typical." He shrugged. "I have a theory which
makes me a liar. I want to go into it some time. It's a theory
that the middle classes are anything but ordinary—that they're
less predictable and less monotonous than the classes below and
above them. But we do get a ferocious machining at the start."

"School?" Les murmured.

At the same time, Paul spoke rather sharply. "Family."

"Both," Wren answered. "I was thinking of school."

I glanced at Don. His pipe jutted from his mouth at right
angles and he was grinning. He interrupted the conversation
because I was looking at him, I think. He seemed to feel that
I required a definition of his expression.

"Surely," he said, "in a world governed by child minds for
children, you aren't going to attack the educational system.
It's a—" he remembered the word—"set-up."

"Why not?" Wren answered. "Attack it in the big gen-
eralities we all love to use so well and resent in others. Just
consider, Don, what your profession commences pumping into
the human ape, aged six."

He rubbed his hand across his eyes. "Consider a morning
in May—"

A morning in May when the dreams that precede awakening
are sweet with the fragrance of blossoms, when the sun looks

first upon the dew damp earth, when the birds sing. When the bright birds—oriole, bunting and tanager—move through the emerald shadows like free-willed flowers. The trout and the turtle lie in the glassy suspension of their limited, limpid universe. Pigs stand in stolid affection. Dogs marvel and hens gaze one-eyed at the ineradicable green on the ground. The soil in the vegetable gardens is perfumed and dark with moisture, a pattern of parallel seedlings; and around the houses perennial borders (sharp sheared from the verdant puberty of the lawn) ache with bouquets of unbroached buds, with the starry leaves of delphinium, the red succulence of peonies, the stiff angularity of lilies, and the fanfare of broad leaves destined to rocket into hollyhocks.

There are blooms by the brook, yellow and blue, where the spiral tips of the ferns hesitate in masochistic ecstasy before giving themselves to the sun. The erectile tissue of all nature lies here stretched and lush, postponing as long as possible orgasm under the caresses of myriad cloying compulsions.

The greenness, the sweetness, the stillness, the fronds, the branches, and all the invisible melodies, the dew and the bud mist of woodlands, the wing-paths, the cobwebs, the empires of puddle sand pools, the bent pressure of earth-bursting herbs— all these have an hour of primordial magic before they are puked on by man.

By man with his milk wagon clatter, by man with his horrible trains and his autos, his belching and farting, oblivious personal nuisance—man with his stew of dominion and doing, his smoke, his steam, his blasphemous voice.

By man who uses such mornings for battles
and for self-improvement.

By man who strews the greensward with broken soldiers whose bellies lie open like strawberry shortcakes.

By man who picks his ears and blows his nose.

By man who sends little boys and girls through this enchantment to school.

Good morning to you.
Good morning to you.
Good morning, dear teacher,
Good morning to you.

Finnley smiled piously at Miss Busshussputts across his nasty little desk.

I pledge allegiance to my Flag and to the Republic for which it stands—one Nation indivisible, with Liberty and Justice for all.

At the word, "Flag," Finnley shot his hand outward in salute. He imagined that he could salute pretty well in case of war.

Liberty and justice.

He had learned specifically about those two American commodities in school.

Miss Busshussputts began to speak. She had a growth on her left ear that looked like a cluster of uncooked lentils. She made a whorl of her dandruff-ridden hair to cover it but the waggle of her jaw worked it through the camouflage before nine every day. She liked rock candy. She had a dog named Osiris which was one of the dozen proper names added to her vocabulary by two years in normal school. She had contrived to recall that cognomen because it had reminded her of the word "iris" when she had first heard it and irises were what she had planted on her uncle David's grave when she was ten years old. Iris and Osiris. Everyone in Finnley's town was familiar with the anecdote and many of the citizens really shared her small enjoyment of the mnemonic as a demonstrable psychological fact. When she was at school, she kept Osiris locked in the privy where his days were occasionally made momentarily lighter and then sad by the invasion of a golden bumblebee. Osiris was part spaniel, and he loved Miss Busshussputts in spite of her casual cruelty. He was like her in that when the bees stung him (or hornets, or wasps) he wailed unheard. And there would have been no bees if Les Hatcher had not upheld the sainted traditions of rustic humor by cutting hearts, clubs, spades and diamonds into the privy when he built it for the teacher. It had given him a good laugh. But it had not affected her because she had never identified the symbols of sin. It brought Osiris his mixed blessings. Miss Busshussputts' uncle had fought in the Civil War. Everyone in Finnley's town knew that, too. She wore dresses made of a stiff, gray material which looked like the paint peeled from front porches. She liked the smell of collodion. She had been in love once (they said) and the older of the townspeople could remember the suitor. Jevers Park. He had supported himself for years by milking several people's cows and he used to feed interested children from the cows direct, squirting the milk in a long, curved stream to their drooling mouths. But one day they had found him sitting on the water trough with his cheeks pushed full of pins and they had taken him away. From Sunset Rest Jevers had written bewildering letters to Miss Busshussputts until one day he had put pins in his keeper's cheeks and they had thoughtlessly beaten him to death—a fact which the teacher alone had discovered. Poetry had always reminded her of Jevers and especially of the day when his hand had inadvertently fallen and for several seconds lain unsuspectingly upon the layers of material protecting her mons veneris from public inductive logic. She was one of the best tatters in town and her nut dishes were particularly famous. Reverend and Mrs. Warren Willet had twenty-eight of them—although nuts made both of them bilious. She taught the first six grades, in one room. The house in which she lived had been built by a Swede in 1891 and he had died there, to the infinite horror of the countryside, in 1900, of leprosy, so that the rent, even eight years later, was infinitesimal. Sweet William and lemon lilies grew in profusion around the house and school boys cut her lawn for her. She also grew sassafras from which she made tea for bellyaches, sending eager volunteers home for the herbal which reposed in a brown paper bag in the middle of the shelf above the wood stove in the kitchen. She had the immemorial requisites of a teacher of the lower grades—a pointed nose and chin.

"Why was Washington a great man?"

Hands were raised.

"Clarence?"

"Because he never told a lie."

"Very good, Clarence." She looked mischievously at the class. "That was the only reason, of course?"

Hands.

"Donald?"

"Because he was the father of his country."

"And how did he become father of his country? Beryl?"

"By winning the Declaration of Independence."

Laughter.

"I mean, by winning the war for independence."

"Very good, Beryl. Yes, Solvence?"

Solvence stood and popped his mushroom eyes. "He was the bravest man ever lived. With a few hundred brave men he licked—I mean, he beat—fifteen million redcoats red soldiers."

"That is so, Solvence. Children, the father of your country was the greatest general that ever lived. Greater than Napoleon. With a few men he repeatedly defeated large armies of British soldiers and Hessians. Not millions, really. But tens of thousands. He saved America from the cruelties of the English king. From wicked taxes like the Boston tea tax which led to the Boston Tea Party we learned about yesterday. From a true slavery. Now—"

Doris Bemis began to cry. "Tears, Doris? Shame! Stand up."

Doris stood, sobbing inside her short gingham dress.

"Are you sick?"

She shook her head.

"What's the matter, then?   Did Norton pull your hair?"

She shook her head.

"Tell me, Doris."

Doris cried with renewed vigor.

"Tell me!"

"I can't."

"Why can't you?"

"Everybody—everybody'll laugh."

She took her hands away from her pink and white face. Tears had moistened her curly blond hair and the grubbiness of her hands had stained its ends.

Finnley looked on horror-stricken. He and Doris had lain together for a full hour stark naked, on the previous afternoon, in the hay barn at the far end of her father's field. It suddenly occurred to him that the results of that delirious experiment might be the cause for her present dilemma and that their secret would then become public property. His agonizing picture of the attitude of his schoolmates toward the procedure was matched by a genuine alarm for Doris. Doris was only seven and sexual exposure might have damaged her. He was not sure what damage it might have done, but he was keenly aware of mysterious pains and penalties attached to what Floyd Binger called "honey-fuggling."

He reached inside his shirt and took hold of a rabbit's foot slung around his neck. "Oh, God," he prayed, "shut up her mouth." His father would beat him. His mother would never give him another dessert in his life. Doris' father might shoot him, or cut him to pieces little by little. The kids in school would call him dirty names and laugh at him. Doris might turn purple and swell up and die and God would surely burn her and it would be his fault.

Finnley knew remorse.

Doris stalled.

Miss Busshussputts scrambled around her desk—in her haste bruising her thigh on a drawer. She shook Doris.

"Tell me what the matter is!"

Doris was now very near to hysteria. She pulled herself together, however, and pointed at Clarence, who sat across the aisle.

"It's Clarence. He smells so bad I can't stand it any longer."

Clarence blanched.

Finnley understood Divine compassion.

The teached sniffed at Clarence. "You don't smell—" then, abruptly, her nostrils were assailed. "What is it?"

The white in the boy's face gave way to crimson.

"Nothing."

She bent over his desk and peered. "Pugh!" she said. "Take it out."

Gingerly, he withdrew a large, dead, degenerating bullfrog. They laughed.

She directed them back to the channels of study, wishing that decorum did not prevent a delicate massage of her bruised limb.

Silk and olive oil, the exports of Italy.

Clarence, in the cloakroom, tried to hang himself on a book-strap, but the buckle hurt his neck.

At recess Finnley asked Doris to go to the haymow again.

"I won't, I won't, I won't," she said.

But he found her there when he reached it by the back path.

In the evening, sitting behind the Wrens' house in the lawn swing, he listened to Floyd until his mother called. Floyd whispered his deep knowledge in a hoarse, excited voice. "They wiggle underground. If you hang around at night like I do often enough, you can see the ground move. The pain's terrible. It's all that dirt. Most of them rot but some never rot. And some walk right out of the cemetery."

The soft creak of the lawn swing, the bassoons of myriad night bugs, the dark, the voice of Floyd as he told folk secrets. "You back the cow to the fence and take a long pole."

Creak and squeak.

"Finnley!"

We had highballs.

"Or," said Wren, "maybe I won't bother with the educational system."

He rubbed his face with his hand, pressing hard, as if it were grimaced by sore muscles and the strong palm brought relief.

"God," he exclaimed. His eyes traveled deliberately from person to person. "Everything's wrong — wrong — wrong. Hideously wrong. It has always been wrong. It will take thousands and thousands of years to make it right. It will take forever. And yet—it could all be set right—if it weren't for the plethora of greedy fools. Nitwits. Nincompoops. How I hate people! The young ape with his cheerful face, his willing heart, his tiny prides. What do we give to him and her at six and eight and twelve? The papier-mâché creed, code and backbone that makes the American. We teach such horrible lies. Such asinine veneration for our country. The American revolution was not a decent war at the beginning. It was the world's first racket. We grabbed our territory. We have always been a nation of blundering thieves. But education has made the promulgation of truth impossible. Ask any bank how much arithmetic is inculcated permanently by our schools. And as for geography. Jesus! How many people in this room can name the Great Lakes and how many can draw a plausible outline of them? How many can remember the capital cities of the ten greatest nations in the world? Who recalls how Tyre was governed? The great writings of the world were put upon us so unintelligently and with so synthetic an admiration that they were wrecked in every classroom. At all the millions of little Americans is hurled a gassy empire of data, uncorrelated, unexplained. They are made to memorize for a little while its dates and places but it cannot be inculcated because our educators have canonized the people involved so that they no longer smack of humanity, and dissociated the facts so that they can be remembered but not realized. A thousand thousand false facts and never a reason. The real reasons behind history and literature and the hypotheses underlying science would throw the teachers into panic. They have succeeded in sustaining a dim half-life without a word of truth or a clear track of reason in their heads and they pass on the senseless blur. They are unable even to guess at the truth and a whisper of it only makes them angry. Still—the surfeit of idiotic irrelevancies would not be so unfortunate if education were not content with it. But it is. It never proceeds. It assumes that it is more important for every little girl to know that Isabella sold her jewels for Columbus than that her navel is her point of detachment at birth and not the orifice from which babies spring. It piously indicates that God made the world and lets the world go at that. The moppets find that listing the characters in *Ivanhoe* is more significant than ten thousand fascinating and fundamental concepts for which their minds are ready and on which they secretly dwell—ten thousand—a hundred thousand. The earth swings around a ball of blazing gas a billion and more years old. Dinosaurs once stomped upon the earth. It is alive with snakes and spiders, Zulus and nuns, flowers and handsome insects. It has storms and seasons. It is made of particles of energy. Bacteria crowd it. The feet of Washington's army reddened the snow of Valley Forge while profiteers held warehouses of shoes for higher prices. Wars were lost for kissing and fornication. In such a place, the passing of too much time in an office—of a lifetime—is a dull wish even for an imbecile. But in school—in high school—in college—

such a world does not exist. It takes six years or more of learning Latin by rote to reach the blushing discovery that Terence wrote slightly salacious plays. And by that time, the plays are salacious, for it has long been impossible to think of sex as amusing in any aspect whatever. It is a wonder the brains of little girls and boys do not grow smooth as putty balls, their vaginas heal over (since they are regarded as sores) and their penises drop off (because they are made to seem like ugly tumors). Some day—some day—if all the medieval back-facing is not erased from our society—if we do not begin to contemplate facts and to admit that the truth is exciting and provocative—our fair nation will be overwhelmed and salt sown upon its moldy ruin. A healthy race will take our property. And our epitaph will be *"Here lies America, stillborn in the little red schoolhouse."* Or maybe—*"Here lies a great nation, slain by Cinderella, Santa Claus and the Stork."*

He drew a breath and expelled it in a sigh. "It's all wrong—wrong—wrong—"

Don chuckled.

Finnley paid no attention to him.

"And yet—" he continued.

Estelle leaned toward me. "I like to hear him talk," she whispered.

"He was better earlier in the evening."

She nodded and the motion impelled fragrance toward me. "He is getting tight."

Wren glanced in our direction and smiled. He had the ability to suggest to other persons thoughts which they had not yet admitted to themselves. Whether he did it by facial expression and vocal intonation or by direct telepathy, I do not know. I have seen several people who could accomplish it unconsciously, but I believe he knew what he was doing. In fact, I have ascribed to Wren in my mind a complete awareness, a lack of subconscious, an intimate self-knowledge which made him per-

ceptive of all the deep and random elements of his thought. I
have imagined him as living vividly not only with the kaleido-
scope of the mental present but with the submerged material
and concealed instincts which are elicited from most persons
only by psychoanalysis. And I have adduced, from that explanation of him, the notion that what we call genius must be
such an ability: a sort of self-omniscience and mental omni-
presence in which all possible associations are instantly com-
mandable for any use, be it the invention of electrical apparatus
or the finding of a figure of speech.

At any rate, Wren, by being aware of fragments and tenden-
cies as well as facts, could communicate the consciousness to
others. Thus, when he looked at Estelle and myself, he told
us, obscurely, that we would enjoy each other's company. The
telling embodied a knowledge of our natures and the condition
in which we found ourselves at the moment.

His glance made Estelle look at me again, and it made me
look at her. It caused both of us to hold the gaze without
embarrassment and with a minute hint of meaning.

Of course, I may be mistaken. Wren was an ordinary man.
He lived an ordinary life. At most, his associates considered
him merely gifted. And the precise light in his eyes, the particular curve of his smile may have arisen from a simpler factor:
he may well have wished that Estelle and I would become
acquainted so that she could tell me about him. She knew
Finnley well. And Finnley was, after all, talking mostly to
me on that week-end. Perhaps he merely wished that she
would amplify his spoken document.

Don refilled our highball glasses.

Finnley sat back on the chaise longue with his eyes closed.

"And yet—" Finnley repeated. "Education such as we have cannot destroy the brain. The years we waste listening to morons pass away. The inaccuracy of the facts, and the falseness of the tone of teaching—I mean to say the major falseness—the falseness of teaching people to learn things and have opinions instead of teaching them to learn processes and to be able to abandon opinions when they are outworn—" he shrugged—"neither spoils the mind. And it's all accompanied by youth."

"Childhood," Wren murmured.
"A little town."

i can smell it i can hear it i can feel it i can taste it. i can see the river moving. the stones moss-whiskered under water and summer-dried above. a damp girdle between and the sleazy unpainted houses along the river giving way degree by degree to the eight thousand dollar outlying mansions, around it all the prairies and above it church steeples.
church steeples.
there was a man in our town
named sylvester dingle a gray-bearded, antique attorney-at-law with a finger blown off at shiloh and a passion for bob ingersoll.
and a bearded catholic priest, withered and dirty
i can see them now
i rolled a hoop into their hedge and heard them talking.
—and if there is no god, dingle, how do you explain the fact that the stars stay in place and that the seasons return? surely all nature implies reason
—i didn't say there was no reason. i said there was no jesus. no virgin. no sense in formal worship.

[107]

the old priest crossing himself and peering testily at the heretic. the vast red poppies blowing around them. the hot sun. the melted tar in the wood block street stinging the nostrils and taking the print of horses' feet

—imagine, father, the dilemmas you might have been in. take just one. the cross is a picturesque instrument of torture. graceful and acceptable. but suppose they had strangled christ? then you would have had to venerate the garrote. or —at a later date—the guillotine. and if your savior had been contemporary—then the electric chair. upon your belly, dear father, would dangle a small golden electric chair and the steeple of your church would be decorated by a weather vane and a large bronze electric chair—

dingle's giggle and the priest's rage.

—i am sure, dingle continuing, the ancients would be as revolted by the crosses which bedeck and stultify our civilization as we would be to hear children sing hymns glorifying the rack or to see nuns kneeling devoutly to the gibbet.

i ran home. dingle had dazzled me. later on, dingle taught me almost all i know. he taught me how to talk and how to read and how to make copulation more than a meal. he was the finest man in our town.

i ran home. without my hoop, through the sunlight, over the wintringers' field. there was a black snake on the split rail fence. ordinarily i would have stopped. but not then.

my family was sitting down to lunch. tom and vi were cowed and when i saw them i did not need to look at father. he was on one of his rampages. i should have been cautious. but i was so exhilarated by lawyer dingle's attack of christianity that i plunged into the matter.

if christ, i said, had lived today, instead of crosses on steeples we would have electric chairs.

my mother gasped and looked in terror at father.

i felt sick and frightened.

[108]

the color came up in father's neck and spread over his face. he turned his head toward me as if it weighed a thousand pounds. he drew back his hand.

i ducked.

his hand crashed against the back of my chair, nearly upsetting it, in spite of my weight. it must have hurt him.

he stood.

doubly terrified, weak and shaking, i went belatedly to my own rescue.

mr. dingle said so, i yelled, in a hysterical soprano. i heard him—just a minute ago.

father took my arm. he had strong fingers. i felt muscle strands squirt and collapse. blue pain ran through my body.

please, i screamed.

i heard my feet moving. as we went through the kitchen he tore down the towel rack. i stumbled on the cellar stairs. the furnace room was dark and cool and mold-scented. i thought of my mother and my brother and my sister—upstairs—listening. holding their knives and forks in suspension. waiting. waiting for the first, and the second, and the fiftieth. waiting for father to exhaust himself. frozen.

blows began to fall.

the wood was hard and unyielding.

legs.

bottom.

back.

the picture of the fixed desperation upstairs departed. pain and rage rose in me. saliva dripped from my mouth. i was being tortured.

not whipped—clubbed.

an arm of the towel rack broke.

he took another.

he knocked my legs out from under me.

[109]

in his frenzy he did not realize and the next stroke hit my
neck.
i lost my sense of time and number.
like a noise heard under water, a shout came from upstairs.
my mother had fainted.
again
again
again
i saw the blood splash and spot.
with one hand he held me,
with the other, he beat.
i saw his face—fixed and hideous.
i found my voice.
you god damned son-of-a-bitch, i screamed at him.
he stopped.
he threw away the towel rack.
he hit me with his fist.
i saw the stairs moving under my face as he carried me up,
like a sack.
sobbing, gasping, i watched his inner office spin around me.
he was stripping off my clothes.   i thought he was going to
kill me.
he brought a huge bottle of iodine.
every cut.
every bruise.
i was on fire.
burning.
i could not get air enough in my lungs.
son of a bitch.
he was shaking me.
i am going to make my calls now.   when i get back, i want
to see all the blood cleaned up in this office, and this will teach
you a lesson you'll remember as long as you live.   electric chair!
never again while you call yourself my son—

i could see and hear again.

i did not answer.

mother cleaned up the mess.

she put me in bed.

vi sat with me all afternoon and wept.

i wonder what he'd do, mother kept repeating, if he was called to treat someone else's child in this condition. have the father put in prison, that's what he'd do.

she was trying to get up her nerve to tell him that.

she did—on her death-bed.

and father argued with her. argued right up to the last horrible pain.

i can still feel that beating.

but i can also still remember the strange sense of freedom given to me by mr. dingle's hypothesis.

churches were never the same to me after that.

i began to note the asininities of the minister. warren willet was abundantly asinine.

two weeks after the last bruise had vanished i had almost forgotten my fifteen minutes in the cellar with the lumps of soft coal and the rat holes, my half-hour in the office as i shrieked when the iodine burned me.

highballs

someone, becoming drunk, forgot the latter half of a sentence and, in order to hold his audience while his memory overtook his tongue, hung in the lull a giant

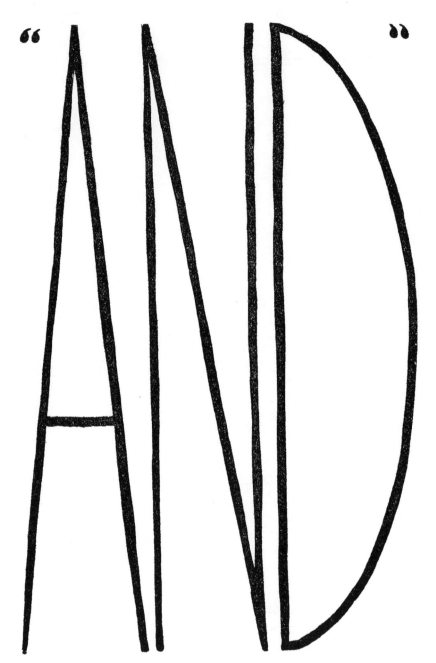

The link between sadism and sex may not be composed wholly of frustration. Observant doctors have noticed that even normal persons become lustful in the presence of wars, disasters, and plagues. Their lust may contain more than a desire for a last ecstasy before the onrush of permanent night. In *San Michele* the phenomenon is ascribed to a biological urge toward replacement. And so it well may be—an endocrine reaction like the swelling of the gonads which occurs when the hours of sunlight shorten and which brings on bird migrations. If the urge to reproduce is heightened during massacres and pestilences, then, no doubt, minor bloodlettings and the accounts thereof may be relatively slight aphrodisiacs.

In my own life I have seen evidences of it. But since the word "sadism" and its connotation of a checked and dampened sex life have made admissions upon the subject unfashionable, it would be difficult to collect data. In these days human beings detest to admit any such things about themselves.

I think Estelle was moved sexually—and sadistically if you will, by Finnley's narrative of his whipping. For my part, the story had largely sent my mind along a different channel. I had been thinking how commonplace cruelty was and how easily we accepted it—often by being unaware of it, less often by ignoring it, and rarely by forgiving it.

In the midst of that contemplation and at the end of the story I had noticed the girl.

She was leaning back on her arms with her elbows stiff. She had dark hair almost as long as a man's forearm, heavily curled at the ends. Her nose, brow and chin were aquiline but of delicate proportions and all her skin was creamy. Her eyes were black. She was smiling—a small smile to let her increased breath pass between ripe lips and white teeth. And as she sat on the floor in front of me she moved her hips minutely and with a slow, unconscious rhythm, as if in the memory of a long-sustained and completely satisfying love.

She caught herself abruptly when the telling of the incident had ended and said, "How awful!"

Then she surprised me. She turned and looked at me steadily, hotly; she admitted with her eyes that we shared the secret of what she had been thinking.

I was seized by desire for her. I tried to capitulate her gaze and no doubt my countenance sustained a monstrous leer. But she had looked away.

People were talking.

I heard Finnley say, "You don't mind if I do it right here? You are sure? You can go ahead with the party. And I'll be feeling fit in an hour. You see—" I was watching him by that time, because I did not know what he proposed to do—"I can't go to bed alone any more. And if I pass out, I want someone to sleep beside me."

Don said, "Go ahead, old man."

Jerry said, "I'll volunteer."

Finnley curled himself wearily in the chaise longue and shut his eyes.

Estelle rose then and stopped by my chair. "I think we will go out now," she said.

She took my arm. We went out on the porch and across the lawn. The wind still yeowled in the trees—a wind autumnal and yet not cold—and the sea was high.

I held her for a moment and then she drew away. "Bye and bye," she said. "Beds—pillows—clinical apparatus—girls don't give all for love any more, you know. It's grand out here. I mean, kissing is too pleasant to be wasted in this tumult. You're interested in Finnley, aren't you? Do you know him well? He whispered to me when you came in that he had brought you for me. Did he tell you that I was here for you? He has a talent for arranging other people's lives. But he's a failure when it comes to his own."

She stood on a rock overlooking the sea. Light from the house poured upon her so that I could see her dress modeled by her body and her hair standing out straight. "He told me you were married. He told me you were in love. So am I." In spite of the wind, she did not seem to be talking loudly. "I could be in love with any of innumerable men. I happen to love one. He's away. So I love the others briefly. Then I get the little rounds of conscience and concealment and quarrels and making up. He's away and I'm sure he's dancing tonight with a girl he intends to take to bed. I can be crazy about you until dawn and then weep from jealousy till breakfast time. I'm sure there's no way out of the grief that lies between true love and the hormones. No way at all—now or ever. Because they both exist there has to be conflict and wherever there is conflict, there are wounds." She glanced at me. "Why it happens to be you—tonight—I can't say. It's sheltered down there in the summerhouse."

We went to the summerhouse. It was substantial and when we stepped into it, we left the wind behind. It contained built-in chairs for looking over the water. We sat in them.

"How long have you known Finnley?" she asked.

"Since afternoon."

"Who introduced you?"

"We picked each other up in a speakeasy."

"Oh." She thought a little while. "What do you do?"

"I write books. I'm thinking of a new one now. About science and the middle classes. About people—"

She laughed. "I'll tell you about your people. No kings, no queens, no Minnesota clods—"

"We will omit those antipodal dullnesses."

"Exactly. We will write about Americans in the current year. Just the right amount about how business makes men tired and wastes their lives. A hint of the greed of big corporations. An example of the hopeless stupidity of the working classes. Socially our platform will be a resentment of government for profit, a ridicule of Bolshevism, and a blanket class inertia. A lot of sex. We'll have that in the book. We'll say the middle classes reek with it—in sublimated and transposed forms. And so they do."

"We will say," I interrupted, "that promiscuity keeps the rich from suicide and unchecked fecundity keeps the poor busy."

"Exactly. And then we will add—but the wretched middle classes, refusing either—ah, woe!"

"The book will be mostly—ah, woe!"

"Then," Estelle continued, "we'll round on the modern woman. Having said that the business man is a fool we will make mincemeat of his wife and especially of his daughter. We will say that she is selfish, uneducated, unable to think, a pursuer of petty pleasure, an—"

"—an aphid in an ant's nest."

"Giving only the high-priced honey of her organs."

"And a prim, unyielding amateur at that venture."

"We'll have all the gadgets. Automobiles. Motor boats. Radios. Elevators. Steamships. Subways. Locomotives. Motion picture machines. Musical powder boxes. Lipstick and cigarette lighter combinations, airplanes, wrist watches. What else?"

"All the gadgets," I repeated. "And all the places."

"I'd forgotten," she said. "New York. Don't make it Chicago unless you want the novel hailed as second-rate mediocre instead of first-rate mediocre."

"It must be mediocre?"

"New York. And a suburb of New York. Paris, of course. London if you will. And the out-of-the-way spot. The bullfight cities were good in their time. Switzerland was good

[116]

once. So was Rome and so was Venice. Moscow is coming in. Do you want Moscow—or Leningrad?"

"No."

"How about the new Vienna?"

"Won't do."

"Well—any place you like."

"Right. Any place where the sea is like melted wax dyed blue as if by the blood of the dead kings of forever past; any place where the cliffs come down sharp to the water's edge and end in a scowl that terrified mariners even in the days of Phœnicia; any place where the girls in native costume look upward covertly and eagerly from—"

"—their Singer sewing machines. I see you are safe in the matter of places. Now—how about philosophy? You should have a philosophy."

"I was thinking about the one that looks at stars and wonders why."

"That one is rapidly becoming astrophysics."

"So it is. How about—life is tragic?"

Estelle took my arm in one hand and gently caressed it with the other. "Do you know why Finnley is—the way he is—tonight?"

"No."

"Well—I'll tell you about him. Some. But let's go to my room first."

the man who had
said
       "and"
shouted, as we walked into the hall,

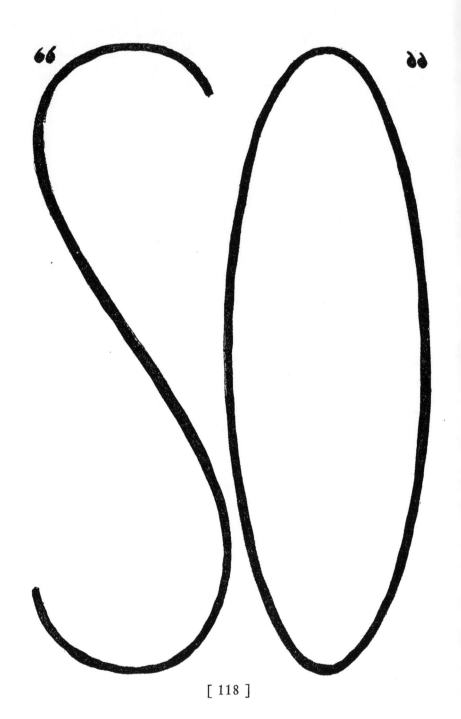

We entered the comfortable bedroom to which the Dwyers had assigned Estelle. I sprawled on a lace spread and I felt, abruptly, very silly. Futility and a mild drunkenness swam through me. The lovely brunette was removing her clothes.

"Tell me about Finnley," I said.

She stopped her intimate manipulations. She walked over to the bed. She said, "I see. Sorry."

"I don't see—and I'm sorry, too."

"I'll tell you about his second wife. I don't know much about the first. She was sweet. One of those soft, loving, mysterious little girls. Simple and good and quietly wild about him. But Helen—was different."

 You are in New York and it is the eleventh of January. Coldness and wetness fall from the sky on billions of individually visible pathways. It is not rain. It is not snow. It is a stained, frigid diarrhea. Every city except Heaven is ugly. Here is the ugliest. Its minor buildings are crystallized stupidities. Its skyscrapers, which ordinarily lift up shafts of chrome-plated hope, are now lost in a gray abyss that stinks and freezes and never moves.

Merchants whom the depression has asphyxiated still display the red and green color scheme of Christmas greed. Vehicles and crowds of people budge beneath the icy slime. Their motions resemble those of insect larvæ spilled from some crawling hibernation. Tramps and beggars thread the throng. Their hands extend and quiver. Their voices whine.

You walk through this disenchantment. Your feet are cold. Your nose is cold, and summer seems an impossibility, a maudlin mirage, as false as a religious promise. All things, you recollect, escape themselves and then turn back upon themselves. Your head aches with crackpot mysticism and snot. Your mind is like a cave, full of insensible stalagmites which mark the last resting place of dreams. Everything is forgotten except the immediate sqush.

The weather has relieved color of meaning. But it has emphasized the evil of city living and thereby somewhat confounded the machine. It has stripped life of its isolated privilege: dignified tragedy—and made it too obviously one with cold horse manure. On such a day you do not want your soul; in such a place you are made the more conscious of it.

There are people without souls.

Helen.

The grill and card room of the Hotel Mirabeau overlooks a small park by some half-story. It has humanities: many mirrors, for example, which augment the numbers of the guests, lend them the compliment of distance and diffusion, and in all ways abet their vanities; hunting prints, furthermore, which have so positive a cult to admire their feeble crimsons, their dogs and horses, that not to admire a little is (chez le Mirabeau) a very fault; spittoons of enormous (and amusing) brass.

but we do not spit in them.

A trickle of late luncheon and early dinner music pervades this civilized and elegant place, where the waiters always haughtily reply with a language different from that in which they were addressed (culture). The music also has its fans, who attend (with dramatic hand-thrusts) thematic reintroductions of feeble motifs by inferior players.

Here foregather *the crème de la crème de la crème de la crème de la crème de la crème de la crème de la crème de la crème de la crème* of Manhattan's wits, wise men, beauties, and celebrities: gentlemen from the *New Yorker* and *Vanity Fair* and publishers and persons in the advertising business and in Wall Street and ladies with fortunes and lady authors dear god and artists' models—females forsooth who have found out how to be smart by forever yawning at both ends

for bridge.

Bridge is a game played with cards of which there are fifty-two and for which arbitrary values have been set. The cards are distributed to four persons and from each they are again collected, one at a time. In a turn, then, four cards are gathered, and they become the property of that pair of players which has contributed the highest card. A score is kept, based on the arbitrary values of the cards as well as the nearness in approximation of a speculative pledge or bid made before the collection by the players.

This simple pastime, ideal for meteorologists at the north pole and travelers in lands destitute of scenery, admissible in moderation to any trivial home, has found a remarkable niche in the lives of the modern masses. It has taken the place of reading and, in a measure, of sexual activity. It has embarrassed the studios of radio broadcasting and of motion pictures. In such places as the Mirabeau it attains a near-deification. One wonders, at the bier of a bridgeplayer, whether the microscopic conduit through which his days flowed is to be considered a commentary on the state of the external world or on the state of man.

Helen was playing bridge at the Mirabeau.

A thin, red-mopped girl with eyes like green diamonds, a black hat wherein an emerald feather stood erect, a tawny dress, snakeskin shoes. Her long white fingers manipulated her cards; she hummed. She led a Jack from the dummy, finessed a King, led a trey, dropped her Queen, and then led her Ace. The King fell.

She picked up her cigarette and put it into her mouth so carefully one might have thought she had caught a stranger looking at that mouth, or imagined she was wondering what would happen to that mouth in the near future.

[121]

"Bravo," said her partner, a successful attorney who had been born on the East Side and who had not known a society in which the word "bravo" had been spoken until after he was forty.

"Mine, I think," Helen said.

That, too, was a lot of balls. Helen came from Michigan. Her first impulse had been to say, "You can gimme the rest." She never said such things—now.

They looked at Helen's cards and they looked at Helen.

The other girl at the table (dark and dowdy) said, "I deal."

Cleo Perkins entered the grill.

"Well!" said the attorney.

"Say!" said the other man.

"She has courage," said Helen.

Both men knew that she did not mean "courage."

"You mean gall," said one.

"Crust," said the other.

Helen shrugged. But the men still stared.

"I'm thinking of having a baby," Helen said.

They stared, now, at her.

"No!"

"Without marrying?"

"Exactly." Helen perceived that Cleo was sitting down somewhere.

"That's a crazy idea."

"Insane."

"Why?" she asked.

The dumpy girl held out the cards for cutting. She was unnoticed.

"Why—"

"Why—"

Both men said "why—"

Helen's strategy had accomplished her desire to revoke the minute train of subconscious attention and unrest which Cleo had lured away. Now another emotion stirred Helen—

She always thought of herself as a woman of independence and boldness, enjoying the freedom that was her due and right. Her mind ran with the mawkishness of department store advertisements: "There is a certain nonchalant liberty about us modern women. We choose our friends, our amusements, our professions—and—thank Heaven—our clothes!" I do as I please, she always thought. I think what I wish, do what I wish, *am* whatever I wish to be. If I want to be rude, I am rude. If I want to give myself to a man, I give myself. And yet,—because I have intelligence—I am able to keep all of myself for me. There is about me a clean-cut, sleek individuality. A suggestion of recklessness, but, behind that, a mental control. It is impossible for me to get so drunk, for example, that I do not know what I am doing. The world is mine.

When Helen's selfishness injured anyone, as it frequently did, she attributed the result, whether it was pique or pain, to weakness of character in the person who had been harmed.

When Helen appeared in public, the background of her thought was spark-shot with self-adulations, yet so expertly did she conceal that ceaseless good opinion (occasional revelations of it had cost dearly in ridicule) that men invariably thought her modest. Helen did not give a God-damn what women thought.

When Helen's emotions were disturbed (and, for a human being who believed so strongly in her own infallibility, they could be easily upset) she had three outlets: haughty silence, tears, and rage. Helen's rages were to be avoided as they were noisy and likely to be hard on detachable property.

Most of the latter-day female libertines are intellectual peacocks. Very few of them grasp the meaning of the biological changes which are now taking place. Such comprehension implies imagination, generosity, and lust; whereas the majority of ladies engaged in the personal evangelism of sex have only conceit, greed, and reduced hips.

Helen, with her boyish-form self-portrait to dazzle her day and night, had recently come upon a dark spot. A lecturer in a School for Social Research had pointed out to an audience of avaricious Jewesses and starry-eyed idiots from New Jersey that the birth rate of the upper castes was dwindling. "If," said the lecturer, "racial fitness is to continue together with the freedom of women, illegitimacy must be made respectable."

Helen had thought about that. It would be sweet to have a baby: sweet and startling. Sweet and startling and brave. It would set her on a pinnacle. And it was possible: she had saved from her salary (designer and buyer of dresses in a store on Fifty-seventh Street) the sum of eleven hundred and eighteen dollars. She could go away and "have it" and bring it back. However, it would be trouble—for nine long months. Helen did not like trouble unless she was its author. She had discarded the charming fancy.

But Cleo's entrance had put demands on her powers of attraction. The novelty of the meditated pregnancy had popped into her mind. It became a cause, the instant her two male companions objected.

"Why not?" Helen asked.

The lawyer smiled at her. "Quit bluffing."

Helen became a trifle pale. "If you think I'm bluffing, you're very much mistaken. I'm engaged right now in deciding who its father will be. Naturally, I'll pick him out for intelligence first and physique second."

"Naturally," said the other man, grinning. The other man was an editor. "I offer myself."

The lawyer shook his head. "Rickety," he said.

"You think it's funny." Helen's eyes began to zigzag rapidly from one to the other.

"Very."

"No."

She looked at the lawyer, because he had spoken gravely.

"Not a bit funny," he continued. "My dear child, you haven't any idea what you're saying."

Instantly she was proud and courageous. "I am not afraid of pain," she murmured in a small, convincing voice.

"I am sure you are not. But I wasn't even remotely considering the temporary suffering involved. I was thinking first, of the man—"

"I shan't even tell him."

"I wonder."

She leaned over the bridge table tensely. This was proving an even more interesting recreation than she had imagined. "When I have my baby, the father will never know. If you think that I would stoop to being wrapped in sickly sentiment for nine months—and then forever chased by a possessive male—"

The lawyer shrugged by gently constricting his shoulders. "The child, then?"

"What about the child? The hard part of life is to be born. After that—you're on your own. I'll have it cared for. I can afford a child."

"Quite so." The man from the East Side looked at her with kind, worried eyes. "And you think that it will not mind being parentless?"

"My child will revel in it."

He was on the verge of telling her what it was like to be born a bastard. But his gaze caught the reflection of the people in the Mirabeau and he thought better of it. Let well enough alone. Let sleeping dogs lie. He was kind—but shrewder still. Kindness appeared at the Mirabeau only when it did not discommode other presences.

"Let's play bridge," said the dowdy girl.

Modernistic. Compact and austerely lavish. Kept in order

by a uniformed colored maid. That was Helen's apartment. It looked as if it were trying to become a penthouse, with excellent chances of success. White leather. Natural woods. Bright metals.

Finnley eventually did get the penthouse for her.

The apartment had three rooms. Thus she was able to switch and sachet from one to another, issuing orders to her patient servant, wearing step-ins, humming only the latest music.

She had come home after the bridge game. No one had invited her to dinner. She drank a cocktail, ate half a bottle of olives and eleven cheese crackers, and had an idea.

She telephoned the lawyer. "Don't say anything about my plan to have a baby, will you? It would spoil everything. And be a dear. Call up Henry and Ruthelma and tell them. Right away? Thanks, Sam."

She ate a pretzel.

If she had a baby. She could think of twenty-eight women who would be jealous while they painstakingly ridiculed and disapproved. Still. It wouldn't do. The phone call had effectively choked the proposition before gossip made it general knowledge and people began to ask her when the big event was to occur. Oh—they would do that—if they knew. People were so lousy. They would practically force her into it.

In two weeks—or a month—dressed in something plain and dark so that she would look depressed—she could say in turn to Ruthelma and Sam and Henry—"My great desire flopped. The doctor says I can't have children."

No. That wouldn't do. If they thought she could not get pregnant, some men would thereafter dislike her. Others might take advantage of her. It wouldn't do even to say that it was dangerous for her to have a child. She would still seem imperfect.

A miscarriage.

That would suffice. I tried—and—a wry little smile—I flopped. But I'll try again.

She felt as if she had already sustained the miscarriage. She ate a few olives. The fatuity of her vision of herself, in a dark dress, telling her sad little lie did not occur to her. Instead, she was delighted: how well and how far in advance her mind made preparations for her! Even to the most trivial detail!

At eleven o'clock she whisked through a closetful of evening gowns and donned one of them. Shoes, stockings, and a dress over her head. Modern woman has conquered clothes. She started for the Newells' party.

Should she have had a mysterious dinner engagement with a man who could not accompany her to the party? No. She might be found out.

"What? Alone? My God!" Blanche said.

Helen let the others hear. "I'm kind of a lone wolf, you know."

She saw the new man—across the hall and through the living room doors.

A tall man with buff skin and eyes like an Indian's: dark, direct, luminous. A quiet man beginning his middle years with the half-confident, half-shy clutching at youth which marks the period. Some one Frank Newell had isolated from the stilted familiarity of business association.

Helen knew these facts about the other males in the room:

Gordon Bannister, the broker, liked to drink until his horn-rimmed glasses were askew and the quick motions of his head would fling half a spoonful of saliva from his parted lips. In such a state he habitually held women by one breast, which he gently massaged, while he talked to them. He was always the best dressed man at any gathering. He had a wife and a daughter and a ten room-apartment on Beekman Place. He was well-to-do. He thought of himself as a philosopher and a connoisseur of women.   A Vermont Yale boy who had made good in the big city.

Nathaniel Kitteridge designed scenery for esoteric theatrical productions.   He was a disappointed artist.   Helen could not see why he was disappointed, since he had made a small fortune. She hated him because, on an evening when he was drunk, he had told her she was a slut and a shrew, torn off her dress, and pointed out what he had called "the geography of her whoredoms."   He was a little man with pale eyes.   Every summer he went to Maine and in the autumn he reappeared, tan and determined, sober and silent.   By Christmas he was always drinking again.   His hands and arms, when he tore off her dress, had been astonishingly strong.   She knew that once he had secretly carved a huge statue, and she knew that he had abandoned it because she and two other girls, finding it in his cellar, had painted it red.   She was frightened occasionally thinking of the scene he would make if he were to discover the authors of the sabotage.

Clive Rutledge was a newspaper reporter.   He covered sporting events.   Men liked to talk to him.   He was pale and angular and shiftless.   She had spent a night in his apartment. On the following morning she had found his stove littered with pans over the neglected contents of which a green mold crept. In his bathroom was a deep pile of towels, also moldy.   The plumbing had been stopped up, evidently for days.   A short time after she had fled in nausea from his quarters she had found her pubic hair attacked at the roots by minute, itching freckles. A doctor had explained, and given her a prescription for mercury ointment.   She had been hysterical, after that, for a week.

Leonard Bellamy was homosexual.

David Tree was a radical.   He spoke Russian and—it had been discovered—Yiddish.

Jean Delacroix was an amateur golf champion. He sold life insurance. He played the guitar beautifully. He had served in the war for four years and possessed many decorations. He was the handsomest man at the party. He had a scar more than a foot long across his back. He never went anywhere without his sister—a beautiful brunette girl with lush eyes. Jimmie Barnette and Gracie Todd had climbed up the fire escape of their house on Twelfth Street one evening to surprise them. The angle of surprise had been reversed. They had found brother and sister lying naked on the floor together. They had stolen away—silent until they reached the shelter of a friendly roof and the delicious loan of friendly ears.

Billy Vanderpole was the young scion of a venerable and rich New York family. In 1929 Helen had endeavored to escape through Billy into matrimony. She had met, in a few weeks, more than a hundred competitors. And, by the exercise of diligence, she had found that Billy was impotent. Nevertheless, he desired certain repulsive activities on the part of the ladies who attended him in his drunken animal hours. Helen performed the appointed chores dutifully and with the aid of rye whiskey for more than a month. In the end, however, she surrendered her temporary hold to a girl from Yonkers who had more stamina.

Donald Gillie had told her that masturbation made hair grow on the inside of fingertips and when she had inadvertently looked at her palm, Donald and the audience he had arranged had nearly burst themselves with laughter. She had taken her revenge on his wedding night. He had married a girl from Bloomfield, New Jersey. Helen and thirty-odd people stood at peepholes bored in the wall of the nuptial chamber. Half a dozen of the people had left as soon as Donald began to fondle his bride. But Helen had stayed and she did not allow anyone to interrupt for a full hour.

Frank Newell, her host, was the editor of one of the bourgeois-intellectual monthly magazines. He was a vegetarian, a pipe-smoker, a good mixer, a gentleman who affected a great knowledge of books, the son of a banker, a theatergoer. He was fond of his wife and faithful to her. He loved New York, Camembert, and Rousseau. He had gray hair and gray eyes. His pleasant personality made it possible for him to keep a multitude of authors working on false promises. He was a known stealer of writers from other publishing firms, and a hard dealer. He had been involved in three bankruptcies and innumerable libel suits, together with suits for breach of contract and for plagiarism.

Helen had these facts documented in her mind. Her friends, on such a basis, would seem foul enough. And yet it is impossible to find a clique in New York or a group in a country town the world over that is without its amorous drunk, its frustrated esthete, its sloven, its pervert, its reluctant Jew, its war-warped young god, its dissolute rich man's son, its practical joker, and its amiable Shylock. In fact, those categories cut deep in the roster of male possibilities.

Seen briefly as individuals, or seen at any average social function, the people at this party would appear to be neither wicked nor unusual, and, indeed, they were neither. They represented run-of-the-mill human beings. Helen's compilation of their vices and peccadillos represented years of acute observation and intimate contact. If all persons were catalogued according to their major faults—a habit of index Helen had acquired—the race would look very misanthropic.

But Helen remembered only subconsciously the list of black marks. She would have flown into a rage of protest if someone had bluntly said that her friends slobbered, ripped off girls' dresses at parties, had crabs, were pansies, lied about being Jewish, slept with their sisters, taught evil copulations, played dirty tricks, and stole. The misdeeds were strewn over so long a time and the behavior of the actors during the intervals was so passive that the general perspective was one of refinement and decency.

Helen moved among the majority of those men with pleasure. Bannister was generous; Kitteridge was brilliant; Rutledge was amusing and good-looking in an austere way; Bellamy was consoling and pleasantly feminine; Tree was exciting; Delacroix was romantic; Vanderpole knew everyone interesting on earth from kings to dope peddlers; Gillie was gay and good-natured; Newell was wise and calm and entertaining.

All in all, we must conclude that humanity has a strong stomach for itself.

Estelle stopped talking and wound herself in the lace spread. She did it absent-mindedly, and her skin showing through the interstices of the fabric was like the shadow of leaves. "Be nice," she said, "and go downstairs and get each of us a drink."

I walked through the conversations:

—and the littlest kid yelled, grab your hats, boys, here we go again

laughter

—all you need to do to see the hollow mockery of christianity is to go to palestine where the religion was cradled and where the savior was born, and as you stand in bethlehem and in jerusalem and in nazareth looking at the dusty adobe and the dirt and smelling the multiple stenches, you will realize if you have any sentiment and logic that humanity is interested in itself and not its prophets for otherwise it would not permit the holy core of its beliefs to go to rack and ruin.

laughter

—go naked in the woods and worship trees and fire and have horned children

laughter

Finnley:

—memory collapses the similar days into one day and that makes childhood seem short.   you can remember the exact contour of the rocks where you habitually climbed out of the water in the quarry or the color of a fly on a dead dog's tail, but you can't remember time.   i recall a fellow named sputs who went to school with us.   older and loutish.   one summer he found a straw hat in an ash can and he wore it.   tom and i came upon it on a dull afternoon.   that is to say, we thought it was sputsie's hat.   it lay on the porch rail, yellow with age, its band sweated with a jagged profile map.   we carried it tenderly into the street and filled it to the brim with the loose material there.   we put it back.   we ambushed ourselves.   out of father's office came henry dunkley, a deacon in the church, discussing contributions. he lifted the hat to slam it down on his filbert-shaped pate, whereupon its contents trickled over his mohair suit and his white shirt.   particles clung to his never well-shaven face.   a cone of dung lifted itself up on his head.   we were terrified. father, oddly enough, thought it was funny.

laughter

—but you cannot remember the long procession of the seasons.   and when you are confronted by a place on a wall or door where, through your childhood, your height was engraved, you feel as if you were regarding the record of another person.

—the revisited scenes of youth contract and sour.   their meanness becomes apparent.   the habit of speaking well of the dead, the habit of history, in fact, is part of the phenomenon. memory contains more gilt and rose-water than truth.   its proclivities perpetually discredit all honest contemporary records. true intelligence cannot exist where there is a will to believe— or even a wish.

[132]

—day by day the size of lincoln's mole diminishes
laughter
—where have you been.   oh—I know.
another kind of laughter.

"You're sweet," Estelle said.
"About Helen—" I ventured dubiously.
Estelle set her highball spinning.   "She must be very lovely—
the lady in Bermuda.   Or you must be—"
"I do not know."
"And my husband.   Probably they have met.   Probably—"
"Probably," I said.
She drank, "Helen."

"Who is he?" Helen asked.
Blanche, without any further identification, glanced at the
stranger.   Then she looked at Helen.   She looked with nar-
rowed eyes and a smile that showed the musculature of her face.
"Terry Ames."
"Well?" Helen whispered impatiently.
"I'm not a madam, darling.   Why don't you ask somebody
else?"
"I will."
"Oh—all right.   He's the city editor of the *New York Press*.
Married.   Two children.   Aged six and eight.   Lives in Forest
Hills.   South African Dutch Colonial house.   Nine rooms,
three baths.   The eight-year-old child is named Robert and he
got 'D' in arithmetic last month."
"Not a madam but an encyclopædia," Helen said.
Blanche shrugged.   With the cigarette which she held in a
long ivory tube she wrote "nuts" in smoke, but Helen did not
contrive to read the word.   In fact, she thought it represented

on the part of Blanche an effort at arty gesture. "Very intelligent, he is. Knows everything. And he was a college athlete, dear. A very good parent—for his own children, of course. But perhaps he has a little parenthood to spare. A little passionate, intime parenthood that can be checked by chemistry."

"Fidelity is poisoning you, darling." Helen understood that her afternoon's confidences had become common property.

"I hear," she said to Terry, "that you're intelligent and physically perfect."

He had been standing alone and listening to the conversation of a group of people two or three yards away from him. He looked at the girl with red hair.

"If I were intelligent, I'd be in some other business. And no one who stays in my profession can maintain good health, quite apart from physical perfection. What's your name?"

"Helen."

Kindness, she thought, was the predominant characteristic of his face. A sentimental kindness.

"You evidently know my name?"

"I was told. I've forgotten it."

"Terry."

"Well, Terry—"

The party moved through its regular stages. It became noisy, ribald, quiet, and at last quarrelsome. Individual guests crossed their accustomed alcoholic viaducts which led variously to Hades, Lethe and Paradise.

Bannister held Joyce De Sylva by a breast; Kitteridge cursed; Melvina Rolston threw up; Rutledge hit Bellamy on the chin; Delacroix did a dance; Hortense Biltridge drove David Tree into the street and the night by a patronizing defense of Judea; Vanderpole passed out; Sheila Tomlinson sang "Frankie and Johnnie" and "The Harlot of Jerusalem" and "The Bastard King of England" and "Violate me in Violet Time."

Helen adhered to Terry—moist, aromatic, lecherous. And although God in his infinite wisdom has not yet discovered why people like to attend such parties, she enjoyed each minute, each incident.

At two o'clock she said to Terry, "Let's get out of this awful mess."

"It is awful, isn't it?" he asked in the cab.

She put her arm through his and nodded gravely. She improvised on raw Kitteridge. "This western civilization has given the world nothing of value. Its best literature is either pin-headed or ungrammatical. Its economic system has been so corrupt and greedy that it is falling to pieces faster than any other in history. Its music is the contribution of people who still speak broken English. Skyscrapers? The Egyptians did bigness better five thousand years ago."

He looked at her in the street-lamp alternations. He thought she was extraordinary. His somewhat drunken mind rushed through the fallacy of his—own—wife. His own wife would never say such a thing. (Because he would recognize the source.) And the idiocy of man—needs—inspiration.

Women hate women because so far as is possible they allow only one man at a time to see them wholly. For each woman, whether she be splendid or neutral or horrid, there is only one man to whom she gives complete permission of herself. She makes him responsible for her. He may love her or hate her or both. But for all other men she is forever part and never all of herself. Terry's wife would have understood Helen very quickly—for Terry's wife was female. She was also fine. But she could not have made Terry comprehend bitch-in-beauty. He could learn only by becoming Helen's one man either for life or temporarily.

Because Terry loved his wife in the dim and dumb shadowland where the soul's essential machinery moves, he was reluctant in Helen's lobby.

[135]

"A nightcap," she said.   Her bosom was swollen and cloying; her bowels itched.   Nevertheless she dried the libido from her eyes and became the bright, impersonal little pal.

"Well—"

Up went the elevator.

"It's nice," he said of her apartment.   "I thought it would be like this."

She made the drink and he admired her skill.   He had expected to be embarrassed.   He had intended to hurry away to the club.   He leaned back on the divan.   She was like a bird— bright-colored and swift-moving.   His feet seemed big, his clothes ugly and clumsy.   He detested himself a little for the triteness of his notions.   That detestation was pushed back in his brain, but it was never dislodged.

She very presently arranged that he should boast apologetically.   A pleasant pastime.   The Phi Beta Kappa key?   Won it on a fluke.   They gave me somebody else's grades.   (But he had unbuttoned his coat so the key would show.)   I hated college.   Rebel by nature, I guess.   Expelled once for writing an examination paper that answered the questions but contained also a criticism of the use of Latin and Greek nomenclature for modern science.   (But the paper was read before a society that was studying higher education.)   Track?   Well—if you happen to be big.   (Wrestling captain.   Weight champion in the Inter-collegiates.   Fullback for three years.)   The *Press?*   City editor is the lowest job.   (I said, "I don't agree with you at all, Mr. Coolidge," and he answered, "Maybe I'm wrong, Ames. Maybe I'm wrong."   And he was wrong.   I have a letter from him—)

"Well—the dividend.   Then I've got to go."

Terry was a man.   Terry was a good man.   It was his misfortune to be alive in this uncertain present.   He was generous and he was kind.   He hated to see people suffer.   But he was beginning to fear that his tombstone would stand over cowardly flesh. He was beginning to believe that all of us had to suffer some of the time, and not that he alone was destined to be occasionally miserable. He was commencing to identify courage with a certain moral callousness toward others—particularly toward his wife. Those incipiencies were superficial. Behind them lay an ineradicable perspective of himself. Only the doubt clouded it: is everyone becoming honest—or is everyone going haywire?

She sat very close to him. He could look down on her head and see where the white furrow of its part divided two regular turbulences of spun glass—amber and orange in the lamplight.

The crisis was quickly over. He did not touch her. He took his hat.

"You don't have to go."

He opened the door. "But I do. Work."

"I want you to stay." Tears filled her eyes.

"Sorry. I'd like to. But I love my wife. I have kids. A job. I'm a respectable old dodo. You should be—"

"A woman like myself seldom meets anyone like you. I wonder if you know what a woman like me—means?"

"Thanks. But—"

"I'd like to ask you something before you go." Helen was quite drunk, quite self-contained.

"Some other time." He was really going. In a minute he would have his thumb on the elevator button. The car would clank and rise. He would hail a cab and laugh at himself.

"No. Now. It's important." She seized the last, desperate tool.

"Good night." He smiled.

"Kiss me good night, anyway."

He kissed her. "What did you want to ask me?" He walked back into the apartment and put down his hat. He was very calm.

"To be the father of my child."

He paused. "Are you going to have one?"

"I want to have one."

"Oh."

She was earnest, intense, shining. She believed what she was saying. "I've been waiting—oh—so long. For the right father. You don't understand. I want a child for myself. I have plenty of money. I don't even want to share it with a father. You can go home—tomorrow—and forget my name. Intelligence—health—a good disposition. None of my friends can offer all three. You could do at least one biological good deed in your life. Tonight when I saw you—I knew. Years. Years. I've looked and waited. I want myself to be not a woman possessed for love. A woman possessed for a purpose. For reproduction. No man can understand that, I guess. I'll never see you again—after—it begins. I'll never tell a human being. I'll go away. And when the child is born and living and growing, I'll return to my work. I'll be different. I'll know that I've fulfilled my destiny. Fulfilled it as a woman should—by having my own child and making it my responsibility—by having it not by a man with money enough to support me, or position enough to obtain me—but by a man chosen as a worthy father and as nothing else. Can you see now why I didn't want you to go?"

"I didn't know that there were any women like you," he said, realizing that the statement was vacuum echo. "It's flattering," he continued, as his self-control began to return, "but I wouldn't want to take the responsibility."

Ire.

"That's what men think! How stupid! How unflattering to women. Your responsibility would begin and end in the simple business of making sure that spermatozoa from you could reach an ovum in me. Responsibility! It's nothing—and yet systems of civilization are founded on it. How silly! Don't you realize that freedom for women really means free-

[138]

dom to choose the fathers of their children? Nothing else. All other manifestations of the feminist movement are merely sublimations. Consider me a human being and not a female entanglement. I have decided to have a child. I have a job that is permanent—that I can leave for the necessary time. I have saved enough money—and more. I select you for the father. I request of you a simple masculine performance. You are capable of it, have the time and energy for it. But what? You are so jealous of your chromosomes, so bound by taboos, that you deny me. In the time we have talked, it could have been done."

Terry walked around the room. "All you say is true. And yet—there is something the matter with it. It can't be the whole truth. Otherwise—it would happen more often."

"It's been impossible because of the husband-bankbook code. I've abrogated that."

He stopped walking. "Suppose I do?"

She knew enough not to surrender her person instantly. "I'm not sure that you should—unless you really want to. Logic is an important attribute of the human being. Logic and honesty. I think you're a little deficient."

"Maybe you'd make up for my bewilderment."

"Maybe. Come and sit down." Then she said, "Oh, Terry!"

And that, boys and girls, is how the poor bastard was hooked.

"Now," said Estelle, "I've been pretty minute about this whole thing. Maybe you're bored. But remember that I knew Helen well, and I knew Terry. You can see them—sitting on that divan together—sliding down and down—taking off each other's clothes. Both of them half-cockeyed. Terry a little bit scared. Helen lost in the big yen. There's a Lesbian streak in me. I often imagine how love must be for men. Love is mostly running toward or crawling away. The actual moment is not one of poetry. It's generally ducked by poets as an impossibility. It wets the bed and starts perspiration. I can imagine a man going objective on himself at the wrong time —seeing buttocks like toy balloons and jiggling breasts and a triangle of curly hair and wondering what the hell. Plenty of opportunity for onomatopœia but not much for classicism. And if a woman weren't doting on her desire she might watch it with not a revolted but an amused abstraction. You almost have to put elegant garments on its approach and retreat to make up for the nakedness of coitus.

"If people love each other it can have a pleasant aftermath, and exciting recapitulations. So can it if people love love. But if the act is for any reason uncertain, its aftermath will be pins and needles. Lots of things can make it uncertain—a feeling of moral guilt—a fear of venereal disease. In fact, it is seldom certain, since most married people don't even know how to go on caring for each other, or couldn't if they knew, because a bad choice of mates is the only possible choice for most human beings."

She looked at me silently for some time. "You see," she continued, "I—understand Helen."

What might have happened next I do not know, for we were interrupted by the sad man.

"i am crying over the american male, he said. my tears fall "thick and fast because of

"golf, tennis, polo, jai alai, bowling, croquet, roulette, pool, "boule, billiards, cricket, squash, rugby, soccer, bagatelle, ping- "pong, base ball, foot ball, hand ball, push ball, volley ball, basket "ball, and all other games played with balls.

"the invention of the ball was a tragedy. it has led to cen- "turies of piddling. it is impossible to make the american male "see the gross absurdity of spending years chasing balls and "catching balls, batting balls, slinging balls and bouncing balls, "running with balls and kicking balls. even wise persons have

"rationalized ball games into noble sport and deplore only the
"most obvious abuses of this business of keeping balls in the air:
"professionalism and gambling.   the idiocy of hundreds of sets
"of arbitrary rules is overlooked.   the stupidity of coaches and
"trainers and referees and all the other acolytes of balldom is dis-
"regarded.   worse than that, oh, bitter, bitter, is the fact that a
"few men play ball while millions only watch.

   "consider the ball player
   "he does not have a good posture;
   "his right arm is big and his left arm small;
   "he cannot swim;
   "he cannot dance;
   "perchance his abdomen prevents him from touching his feet
"without squatting;
   "he cannot climb a mountain;
   "he cannot row a boat;
   "he cannot paddle a canoe;
   "he cannot keep his balance on a fence rail;
   "he cannot hoist a sail;
   "he can make nothing with his hands: not a stone wall, not a
"wooden table, not a level hedge;
   "he cannot climb a mountain;
   "he has not walked in the woods and cannot tell the name of a
"tree or a flower or a bird and he believes all snakes are poisonous,
"all insects sting;
   "he cannot even run.
   "but he is an athlete.   a paragon of sport.   a great man.
"when he walks up to a base, tens of thousands scream with
"worship.
   "for—behold what he can do:
   "he can catch a small ball in a leather glove with unusual skill
"and he can hit the same ball with a wooden club better than
"any other gentleman has bothered to learn to hit it.

"he is popularly thought to be in the class of such heroes as
"bridge-holding horatius; he is really the twin of the man who
"sat longest on a flag pole and the ineffable genius who pushed a
"peanut farthest with his nose.

"he is the home run hero.

"oh—silly, silly, silly.

"the watching millions *do not even play!*

"inconceivable!

"they cannot throw pop bottles accurately.

"are we to call ourselves men—or audiences?

"these games are not played for fun—but for the score.
"good sportsmanship is a myth since there can be neither a good
"winner nor a good loser.

"behold us living in a world full of interest with bodies capable
"of a thousand fascinating exercises—exercises to develop in-
"dividuality, and courage, and audacity, and imagination, and
"valuable skills, and balanced muscles, and health and good will.
"behold us confining ourselves to competitive sports when the
"universe cries not for rivalry but for creation, behold our backs
"turned on nature while we chase balls—or watch them chased:

"*iron* balls

"*wood* balls

"*leather* balls

"*air filled* balls

"*hydrogen filled* balls

"*rubber* balls

"there is a *gentleman's* ball game of some merit, but sub-
"stitutes have tended to submerge it.

"now do you see why i am crying?"

Estelle had ignored the sad man's excellent summation of
things. I thought to call after him that not ball games were
silly but human beings for inventing and playing them, but I

could not do so for some reason or other. Hormones were flushing through my veins like nettles. The brunette on the bed beside me had let go of the spread. Her inverse aphrodisiacs were making a havoc of my genteel notions and endocrines. Even the sad man, brilliant distracter though he was, had, in the end, profligated my composure.

"Estelle," I said, "for Christ's sake wrap yourself up. I am a married man."

"I don't see the connection," she replied.

"Go on with your saga. Finnley interests me and I am pretending that fornication does not. Downstairs and in the yard I felt different. Here on the bed, I am logic itself."

She sighed. "You'll have to spend the night with someone. It's a Whittington rule. And besides, there aren't beds enough."

"It's suburban," I answered scornfully. "I'll sleep on the divan."

"On the diva on the divan it's divine," she sang.

"I chew tobacco," I said.

"Very well. Let's see. Where were we?"

"Never mind about that. Begin somewhere else."

She ruffled her hair moodily. "I might as well. In fact, I'll eliminate sex. Hot Helen the vanity girl. And poor old nervous-smiling Terry. He was nice. You don't mind if I just mention that amorous nocturne, do you? It's necessary. You see—nothing came of it. A bar sinister was not established. Helen had to go through with the pretense because of her argument and because he stayed until time to go to the office. She lost eleven pounds between that day and the third of February. Terry was frightened. He didn't see her. She called him up to tell him of her failure. She had a lump in her throat as sweet and sticky as ambergris and as morbid. He was relieved. Elated. So he pretended to be disappointed and to pass off the whole thing as his fault.

[143]

"Helen began to torment herself again. She decided to try it over. Terry refused. She schemed to meet him. And, naturally, she reseduced him.

"She reseduced him about fifteen times.

"In the end, she became pregnant.

"She had been afraid she would reach that coveted state for so long that when it arrived it was at first less grievous than she had imagined. With the early weeks of morning sickness and the first positive diagnosis, she reverted to her original pose. A glad light came in her eye, but she told no one. She stopped seeing Terry—she informed him, in fact, that his work was done. She thanked him and bid him one of those grave, brave, Elsie Dinsmore good-byes. He departed—worried and hoping to God he would never hear of her again. She was a flashy fleshpot and he was a fumbling fellow from Forest Hills. It must be innocent and dreary in Forest Hills."

"So then what?"

"She kept her job for three months. She had a grade 'b' pregnancy, I think—a good deal of headache and vague pain, some vomit, considerable dizziness, but no melancholy. Helen became intensely herself. She went to parties and acted as if she had swallowed crown jewels to smuggle them somewhere. She stopped flirting. She had silences. She sewed minutiæ in secret.

"Bear in mind that none of us guessed what had happened. Not then. Afterward. We had forgotten entirely her discussion of motherhood in the past winter.

"She told us that she was taking a long vacation and she left for the country. Nobody noticed. Women did not like Helen and none of the men she knew had a sufficient passion for her at the moment to pursue her into the Jersey hills. . . .

"She rented a room in a farmhouse and boarded with the family. She used the name of Mrs. T. Ames. The farmhouse was run-down, tatterdemalion, ramshackle. Around it were cows and pigs and chickens. A few acres of potatoes. A hay field, a wood lot, a meadow. Schlessenger was the farmer's name. A dirty, seedy, bony man. A fat, suspicious wife. Two boys about fifteen and seventeen. Her story to Mrs. Schlessenger was that her husband traveled and that she did not want to be in the city while she was pregnant.

"Helen had a rotten time. I presume that in the first flush of impending maternity she had decided on a farm and thought that all farms were the same. She had probably seen the Schlessenger place on the midsummer day when there was no mud.

"Anyway, she went there. Mrs. Schlessenger fingered her clothes when she had them on and thought that all women ought to work and talked for hours about such matters as the relative strength of different numbers of white cotton thread and she blew her nose with her fingers. Pa Schlessenger had a habit of staring after her whenever she left a room and she used to turn back quickly in order to catch that jaw-hanging, twilight gaze. He habitually kicked his pigs to set them squealing and he serviced the cows in the front yard with a filthy, red-eyed, borrowed bull. Abe picked berries for the family's dessert and brought them to the house in an old rubber boot. Bill Schlessenger put a half dozen crayfish in her bed and his father made her watch the resultant beating.

"The worst feature of her life, however, was one that Helen had planned as the finest: from her window she could, on a clear day, see New York. She used to sit there for hours regarding the mist-hung skyscrapers and remembering how it felt to stand at their bases. None of the Schlessengers had ever been in New York. It was twenty-one miles away in an air line.

"God only knows why she did not leave the place. Maybe she felt that the reality of childbearing should be prefaced by something earthy and tough. Perhaps she was punishing herself. Masochism, again. More probably, she was preparing for what followed.

"She began to spend money. She had saved more than fifteen hundred dollars. She was accustomed to a regular income and she gave very little thought to the fact that she was now living on her capital. Spending may have been an unconscious—or semi-conscious part of the grand preparation. She went a little dotty. She bought an upright piano and a course in correspondence lessons. She bought enough material to make twenty dresses—and finished the skirt of one. She had electric lights installed in the Schlessenger house—although no doubt the family went back to kerosene after her departure. She bought thirty or forty games. She took all the neighborhood children on a picnic and gave them presents.

"It began to get cold. She bought a fur coat by mail from a New York department store. She filled the kitchen with canned goods.

"One day she found that she had less than a hundred dollars."

Helen sat with her elbows on the window sill. Her hair was not brushed and it had grown to an awkward length at the back of her neck. The child within her stirred occasionally—an activity which filled her with alarm. It was raining. She could not see New York—but only a gray place beyond which it lay. The grass in the yard was yellow and brown and water oozed through it. The trees were bare around the house and evergreens, unsuspected during the summer, were now visible—evergreens that she could imagine daubed with snow.

In the kitchen below was the perpetual sizzle and stench of Mrs. Schlessenger's frying. Today she was frying parsnips—parsnips rooted from the gummy earth by Abe only half an hour previously.

The tempo and volume of the rain increased. Chickens clucked miserably in their sloppy shed and the pigs that had escaped butchering slid and stumbled on the ground.

Helen's eyes were frightened.

The baby was not yet due. But she no longer had money enough to pay her board.

She was destitute.

She was living in a murky, muddy purgatory.

The Schlessengers and the neighbors actually believed that she had no husband.

At any minute the baby might be prematurely born with only the greasy woman downstairs to act as midwife. Mrs. Schlessenger had done it before, she said. She said it every day. Why pay a doctor?

Her friends in New York had stopped writing. They had always hated her. Now they had forgotten her.

She would die.

The father of her child had deserted her.

She had read about it in books—seen it in motion pictures. Now she was living it. The sad and sordid fate of every Hollywood star in the middle of every other movie. Maybe her child would become rich and famous when he grew up and when she still had a faded beauty.

But now—Terry had deserted her.

Never a word.

She forgot that the stirring inside her was eugenic. She ignored the fact that a few letters of explanation to her friends would bring continuous and ample funds, in spite of the depression. She thought a good deal about the depression: it made an appeal for a loan unthinkable—to her. She meditated about Terry—how weak he was, how selfish, how cruel to be willing to be a father for a night and to ignore the dreadful plight in which his casual fun had put her. That she had squandered her savings in a few months never entered her mind.

Why didn't he come?

She wondered every day.

The question obsessed her as she leaned on the window sill and regarded the external squalor.

He *had* to come.

It was his duty.

He could no more get a woman pregnant and condemn her to this hell, than he could shoot people on the street.

She needed him.

Her child needed him.

She ought, she reasoned, to humble her pride and summon him—for the sake of the child.

Their child.

Without him she might die.

They might both die.

And that afternoon, in the somber rain, she decided she had waited long enough. She decided to humilate herself for her child. She would do anything for her child.

She was a Mother.

She put on galoshes and a raincoat and went to the store a mile down the road.

She waited for an hour until the spitters had left. Then she sent the storekeeper into his loft for a ham. She put coins in the telephone.

A minute later she heard Terry's voice. "Hello!"

"Terry! It's me. Helen."

A long pause. "Oh—yes—Helen. How are you?"

"You've got to come to me, Terry. It's a matter of life and death. I'm—" She described the trains; she gave the telephone number of the man who drove occasional passengers to houses in the district.

"Tomorrow be all right?" His voice was frightened.

"Tonight. Hurry, Terry."

"Got to play bridge."

"Bridge! I'll—I'll kill myself."

The storekeeper was coming down the ladder.

"Well—all right."

"Good. Just to think that I'll see my husband in a few hours!" She ended on a jubilant note. Mr. Peezer paused on the ladder. "My husband's coming!" she said.

He sniffled.

She went out and started home. She was planning what dress she would wear.

"I'm singing in the rain, just singing in the rain, what a glorious feeling—" She shouted it at wet fences and dead goldenrod.

Terry was coming.

Terry would soon be there.

Suddenly she wanted Terry to take her in his arms and hold her and love her—as was his right. . . . .
. . . .
. . . . and his duty.

Estelle stopped and lifted her eyes. There was a sardonic expression in them. "Do I need to go on?" she said.

"Why—"

"I see that I do. But you have all the essential material in your possession. All of it. The rest of the events ran off like a string of firecrackers."

"What were they?"

"What could they be?"

"Any of a number."

"If you knew Helen and Terry—you wouldn't say that. I'll have to give you his point of view again. Remember what I said about conscience-stricken love-making. It's no good. For months he'd had two ideas in his head. One of them was that some day in the far, far distant future he would run into Helen. Helen the mother. They would smile wisely and knowingly at each other and bow and pass. Ships in the night. He unquestionably cherished the hope that Helen would keep her covenant. But the other idea was founded on surer if dimmer perceptions. You cannot associate long with Helen and fail to feel the hypocrisies and selfishness in her. She troubled him deeply from the moment they met. She looks like trouble—trouble disguised, trouble camouflaged. She looks like bait. He must have been waiting months for that telephone call—knowing it would come. Funny.

"The telephone and the telegraph have added a great deal to the shock of living. Bad news used to be brought by people who could lead up to the message and cushion its violence. Now it comes over the wire. High tolls prevent dexterous preparation of the recipient. A telegram is always curt. And a phone call is as unfortunate. Eyes and lips and shoulders don't enter into it and when you hang up you cannot remember intonations accurately, so the meaning behind the voice becomes a puzzle.

"Anyway—the call came."

"Then what?"

"You ought to be able to guess.

"First Terry journeyed to that bucolic hole. He discovered she had no money. He saw that the Schlessengers were horrible. He smelled the pigs. He learned how sick she had been. He was made conscious of her pitiful efforts to beautify herself. He sat at the window from which you could see New York. And, because he was alleged to be her husband, he found it necessary to carry on the charade by sleeping in her bed. It is difficult to sleep chastely with a woman—especially one who attributes a burning passion to loneliness and generosity in equal parts. Terry found it too difficult.

"So he gave her all the money he had—less than twenty dollars. He went back to town on the following day. Its broad light and bright, autumnal sunshine threw the situation into relief. She felt vastly better. He felt surer of himself. He told her that he could not see her again but that he would arrange an allowance, an ambulance to carry her to town in due time, and a competent, hospitalized delivery.

"Helen slipped back into the fecal routines of the Schlessengers. Terry's visit tarnished. Yearning for him increased and took many other forms than mere lust. She needed a man. The heart of her dilemma lay in that fact. It is biologically improbable that any woman can pass through nine months of gestation without having an incessant or at least a recurrent desire for masculine presence and support.

"She sent for him on the day after Thanksgiving. Business made it impossible for him to come at once. She was wild. She called his office five times in one day. She told a perplexed assistant that he had better locate Terry or she would have his salary garnisheed.

"He came again—and it was snowing. He nuzzled his caracul coat collar and swore and sweat. The ships passing in the night aspect of the affair was ended. He knew he had been scuttled. He was trying desperately to make port. Any port.

"He gave her a thousand dollars—savings. He pretended to his wife that he had hit a pedestrian with his automobile and settled out of court for that amount.

"When he saw Helen, he felt a little devotion and a great pity.

"When he was in his office, he worried.

"When he was at home, he hated himself.

"She tried to make him promise to come every week-end. He could not do that, but he managed three visits in December. He brought a silk negligee and a layette for Christmas.

"Helen started thinking in the empty intervals about Terry's wife. She was having no child. Her children were half grown. She had a fine house. She had respectable friends in scores. She had solid silver and a greenhouse and a maid and bridge dates. And yet, Helen reasoned, Mrs. Ames—Marilyn Ames—had not a tenth as much right to those comforts as she.

[151]

"Helen could see no end in sight for herself. She thought of the Schlessenger farmhouse as her doom. Her doom—and her child's doom. The unborn baby would be damned by Terry to such an existence as this. By Terry—and by his wife's smug greed.

"She began to hate Terry's wife as a thief and an interloper and especially as a hypocrite. Running around in fake swank society, she would repeat to herself, and holding her head high while all the time she is the wife of an unfaithful cad.

"She could think of Mrs. Ames as the wife of a cad without thinking of Terry as a cad.

"Terry had become dear to her—dear, sweet, and necessary. He was kind and tender and thoughtful. He sent her letters and magazines and he clipped things from the newspapers which he thought would amuse her. Terry was grand.

"She made Terry talk about Marilyn. He hated to do it. He felt as if he were betraying himself and his gods. But Helen always listened so innocently that he could not know she was storing up material for the aching, vacant hours when he was gone.

"When she was in the eighth month," Estelle said after a moment of retrospective hesitation, "she went to town. We all saw her. She told us that she was soon going to have a baby—a self-evident fact—and she refused to divulge the name of its father. She went to a party. We promised to visit her at the hospital. We outdid ourselves to be nice to her. Of course, none of us knew at the time that Terry was bleeding. We thought that probably she didn't know who the baby's father was. We hadn't expected Helen to carry through any such spectacular proposition. We were pleased by it. We believed she had nerve. When Bellamy said afterward that Helen could make a baby-carriage by putting four wheels under her navel, he was shushed. We became her champions. We promised to visit her in the country, but she gave us no address and it is doubtful that anyone would have gone out there if she had.

"Business kept Terry in the city for two weeks, in January. So Helen spilled her bile.

"She wrote a long, self-pitying letter to Marilyn Ames. She said that Terry was tired of being married, that he did not love his wife. She said that she was and would always be Terry's inspiration, and that if Marilyn had any sense she would have realized what had happened. She described the baby and the misery in which she lived. She sent a photograph of herself in her pre-pregnant prime and a snapshot of herself at seven months on the stoop of the Schlessenger house with cow tracks in the foreground.

"That night when Terry came to his home in Forest Hills he found the shades pulled and slip covers over the furniture. The children had been sent away—but Marilyn was waiting for him. When he saw the slip covers, he knew.

"He was sick.

"He shook.

"His bowels crept inside him."

Marilyn was pale. "I've known that you had a girl for quite a while, Terry. I didn't mind. But I just found out from her today how much she needs you. The children have gone—and I'll join them at mother's. I didn't think it would be—this way. I suppose infidelity leads to things like this—though—and I suppose that's why it's so generally disapproved of."

Terry said, "Don't go—don't leave me now, Marilyn," and threw himself in his favorite chair sobbing. He did need her. Christ knows he needed her. And he loved her.

She made a little speech in her mind to tell him that she would stand by, and help him. But she did not pronounce it. Maybe she should have done so. Maybe such understandings are beyond the reach of most women. The wounds inflicted by unfortunate conduct are rarely scaled down to the wretched imperfection of mankind.

She called a taxi and went away.

Terry would have hung himself if he had stayed at home.

When a good man harms those he loves he can go mad from believing he is already mad.

He returned to the city and sat all night in front of a mirror in a speakeasy.

He hated Helen then. He realized that he had always hated her.

In the morning he shaved and went to work. Marilyn acted quickly because she was in pain. A lawyer telephoned and refilled Terry's viscera with anguish by saying "divorce." He wanted his wife. Nothing else. Then he was called by the company from which he had recently made a loan.

Helen was frightened after she had sent the letter. Two days passed. Fright became panic. Then Terry appeared. He was extraordinarily kind to her. He brought a hundred dollars. He said that his wife had somehow found out about them and that she was suing for divorce. Helen thought that Marilyn had not disclosed the source of her information and Helen thought that she would act in the same way if the situation were reversed. There was a bond between women, she thought.

Terry went back to New York and stayed drunk for a week. It almost cost him his job.

"The day he came back to his desk," Estelle said, "Helen phoned wildly that the ambulance was needed. He got one in Montclair, New Jersey. Helen will tell all comers what it is like to ride in labor across the Jersey marshes. She thought—and she made the driver think—that she was going to have the baby in the car. But she reached the hospital in town by a margin of about sixteen hours. She doesn't tell that. She says she just made it."

Suddenly Estelle laughed.

"Why laugh?"

"Because at the end of sixteen hours a funny thing happened. Helen had twins. Illegitimate twins. Can you imagine!" She shrugged. "That's all. That's the end of the story. Except—she made a perfectly hideous fuss about it. They gave her every known anæsthetic. The twins were sound enough—two girls. They took them in for her to feed."

Helen was conscious. She felt, as yet, no pain. She ran her hand across her bandaged abdomen—and it was flat. She shouted with delight. The awful weight was gone. She had not died. She was alive. Her job at the store would be waiting. Her friends would welcome her. She would be a heroine. She could go to parties again and make love again.

"I want those babies on bottles," Helen told the nurse. "I can't feed them. I'm weak. Take them away. They're simply too grotesque."

They took away the babies.

Terry came in. "My dear, my dear," he said.

He was resigned, now. He would make the best of the wreck. He would give his life to his two new offspring. A pair of girls. Not bad, Terry thought. He had already seen them in the nursery. They had dark hair—like his.

"I'm sorry you had to suffer so," he whispered, taking her hand. "Get well soon. What are you going to name them?"

"Terra Ames," she answered, "and Thalia Ames."

"Swell! And don't fret. As soon as the divorce—that is—as soon as we can—we'll be married."

[155]

"Married!" Helen's green eyes widened incredulously. "Married!"

Terry was flushed by noble feelings: self-sacrifice, courage, and the pleasure of giving a splendid surprise to an unfortunate fellow human being. Doubtless Helen had expected that they would be compelled to move stealthily through a half-life. But now—he was going to tell her that they would be married—to insist upon it until at last she believed.

"I'm divorcing Marilyn." He lied that much because he wanted to feel masculine, powerful and generous. "And I'm going to marry you."

Helen thought of the babies with their toothless mouths—funnels for a ceaseless, nerve-eroding sound—and their opaque eyes forever staring at nothing. She thought of Terry—stupid, insensitive, unchivalrous, unromantic Terry—stomping in the muddy Jersey snow, blowing his nose, floundering sweatily in bed, breathing hard.

She was disgusted.

She shut her eyes for a moment. She drifted—safe and sound and whole and stunning—into her past and into her future. The sales floor prim with the smell of new fabric and gaudy with color. Her own svelte apartment where she could lie in a slip on a white leather divan and hum songs. The babble of party voices, the first soft fingers of alcohol in the brain, kisses and taxicabs, bright bathrooms and glittering gowns.

No man had ever seemed as stupid or as unsympathetic as Terry now seemed to her.

"Married!" She laughed. A small, mewing laugh—not loud, but sharp and cruel enough to disembowel a stone idol.

Terry chuckled contentedly——and stopped.

He muttered to himself that she was out of her head.

"Married!" she repeated.

"Soon." He looked at her carefully.

"Do you think—"

[156]

"Be quiet now, Helen. I'll discuss it later."

"—that I'd marry you after all you've done to me?"

"I thought you'd be glad."

"Glad? Glad. Oh, my God, glad."

"Somehow—I thought that."

"That I'd be glad? Well, I'll be God damned."

"Please—honey—"

"Thought that I'd fail in this, did you? Thought I wouldn't have the nerve to stick to my original agreement? Thought I couldn't pull through by myself. Thought—"

"It's different—now."

"Oh Lord! I should never have told you that you were the father of my children. I knew that I'd have to face scenes like this if I told the father."

"You're out of your head. You're sick."

"Not that sick. Look here, Terry. Get yourself together, will you?"

He dropped her hand and silently stood.

"You're a weakling, Terry."

He said nothing.

"My life lies before me. I've been through hell and I've come out with all sails set, all colors flying. You've been through not one little part of it, Terry. And you're mawkish and sentimental anyway."

He stood there, twisting up the coverlet.

"If you've got a spark of manhood left in you—you'll leave. You'll never trouble me again."

"What are you going to do with the children?" he asked, after a little while.

"Find them a good home."

"I don't seem to understand."

"Have them adopted. They're mine, aren't they? Mine to do with as I see fit."

"Oh." He dropped the cover. "I—I don't suppose you'd let me adopt them?"

"And have their lives influenced by a middle-class shrew like Marilyn? I'd rather give them to a washerwoman. Much rather. It would develop them through hardship."

"I—see."

"And another thing—since I've been silly enough to share my knowledge with you. Don't make any recourse to law. If you do—I'll let the whole world know how you treated me."

He looked at her then until she looked away. She said something about regretting that her principles made such sternness necessary. She moaned and said she was very tired.

Terry left the room.

He walked down the corridor of the hospital. Gloom. Stillness. Pain. The faintly pleasant aromas of hell. Step. Step. Step.

His finger slid off the elevator button, so he pressed it again.

He descended to the lobby. In a white box with a glass front was a fire axe. He stopped in front of the box and he seemed to peer at the axe without seeing it. He unbuttoned his coat. He glanced patiently at the elevator doors. He shuffled and pondered.

He shook his head.

He went to the revolving doors. They bumped and shooshed. He began to walk.

After a long time he put on his hat.

A bit of paper blew along the slippery sidewalk. He thought to himself that it was a gum wrapper.

"You can see Terry," said Estelle, "any time you like. There's a speakeasy on Forty-third Street where newspaper men gather. Terry comes regularly—every night—at ten. I daresay you'd recognize him if you went in. He's not exactly on the bum.

A circulation man keeps him in a job of some sort. And the reporters and editors who know Helen buy most of his drinks. If you buy him more alcohol than you'd think any man could drink—he'll tell you what I've just recited. I did it once. He calls it a story about a lady."

"Mmmm."

"And how is your libido?"

"Meager."

"Well?"

"Well what?"

"It is my assumption that when I've satisfied all your curiosities—extraverted your repressions, so to speak—you'll be amenable, tractable, ductile. "

"Did Finnley teach you to talk, by any chance?"

"Finny taught me a great many things."

"Such as—"

"More alcohol than you'd think any woman could drink. I call it a story of a nice young man. Too nice a young man. That's mean. And it's not true. Finnley was good to me. Only—"

"Only?"

"He loved me—in a way. And I—"

"You?"

"I love my husband and I love Finnley and I love you, but most of all I love myself, I guess. Or I love to be loved. Or I love love. That's how I get by. When life grows difficult I invent a confusion and dive into it. The confusion magically becomes somebody's arms, as a rule. When it stops doing that —well—maybe it never will stop. And maybe I'll lick left-alone with a mustache and a menopause. Finnley comes to see me. He was coming tonight, perhaps. And he made me a present to you because he likes you. Or because he wanted me to be soothed instead of saddened."

"How does it happen," I asked, "that Finnley married Helen?"

"Finnley's life is a joke—a trifle more flagrant than other lives in that respect. Then—Helen was wild about him. Desperate, delirious, delicious, dramatic, diabolic, debauched—anything that begins with 'd.' She was anything that begins with 'd' about him. You've heard of rebound? Well—he was on the rebound. He was bounding back from one of the neatly wrapped flatirons God drops on us. She met him. She put him over various hurdles. She made him think that she was sane and free and tragic and courageous. And she was hot. Even I feel curiously passionate when I watch that thin red girl breathe and move.

"Oh Jesus that girl was pitiful and brave when she returned to our crowd! Her babies were in a Home. When she met Finnley—she didn't muff. He was very happy with her. Puzzled—but dizzy with ecstasy. He had been thinking he could never love again. Then he found her. The realist. The woman of iron nerve. The woman who could not be frightened by the facts of life. The one woman of whom he could be sure, about whom he would never worry. Ha!"

"Ha?"

"Ha! How she woopsed on him!"

"Woopsed?"

"That's his trouble now. Poor Finnley!"

"What's his trouble?"

Estelle ignored the question. "You know," she said, "he never had a chance to see that girl in strong white light. He believed her story about Terry. And he's not the sort of person you can warn. In fact—you can do nothing about Finnley's fates. If you intervened—you might be included in his destiny —but you would not prevent it."

"Well," I said, "why don't you tell him the truth?"

"It isn't necessary—any more." Abruptly her eyes brightened. "But I think I will. He would understand it now. And he'd enjoy it."

She was no longer languorous. Her eyes sparkled. She looked at the door as if by looking at it she could make it pass over her like a quoit. "You are a great man," she said.

I understood that she was going to leave me, that I had become a bubble in her highball or an ear for her loquacity or something equally trivial and frustrating.

"Before you go," I said, "you might at least tell me why in hell Finnley lost Hope—and has lost Helen, too. It's a small price for my condition."

She stopped at the door. She stared at me oddly. She opened her mouth. She shook her head.

"He'd better," she said.

I picked up the lace spread and ran to the head of the stairs. "Here!" I called.

Estelle said, "Thanks," and caught it.

I have not seen her from that day to this.

I went out on the lawn again. En route, I poured myself a drink. I heard Finnley in the middle of some further exposition of his childhood. It had to do with *ants*.

It made me impatient. He lived a myopic life, I said to myself. Ants, frogs, snakes, horse manure—he had his nose on footpaths.

The wind had subsided but the sea was not mute. It arrived at the shore and folded and fell in a running collapse somewhere down in the dark.

I drank.

Nuts, was my precise comment to myself.

I though that I had entertained *strictures* of *good sense* to neglect the overtures of so *languid* and *healthy* a lass as Estelle.

I thought I was a *college boy* at heart.

I thought I was *middle class*.

I thought I was a *fine fellow*.

I thought I was a *tragic figure.*

The stars were invisible and rationality was impossible and the absurd was pitiful. I looked at the trees in the light from the house and I estimated that some of them were *saplings* before my great-great-grandfather was a *sap.* My eyes had been tear-flooded on account of the *darkness* and *disease* of it all, but now I giggled.

I went back to my comment of a previous instant on Finnley's minutiæ-gazing. I thought about crawling along on the street and I said to myself that *cities,* for example, look *clean* to human beings but would appear *filthy* beyond description if we were suddenly reduced to the stature of *one inch.*

I said that life was like that and briefly I desired to cut my throat for saying it.

Puns and *banalities,* I murmured.

Platitudes and *bromides.*

I thought what a *fine imagination* I had.

I thought I was *cockeyed.*

I sat down at the foot of a tree. I sat resignedly, lugubriously, as a *tramp* sits. I put my half-empty glass in my lap to take the place of a bulging bandanna on a stick. If atoms were solar systems, I thought, then suns and planets would have to obey the laws of protons and electrons which turns that fancy into rubbish.

I contrived a doleful little song on the spot, for I am an inventive fellow, handy at rhyme, and full of whim. I sang it:

"The elevator boys are rude
The porters scream and yell
The swill is better than the food—
God damn the Mills Hotel!"

I was in fine voice. I sang it over.

"Sing it again," somebody said.

"With pleasure."

On the third effort, the interloper, a lady, joined me. She lent to the ensuing rendition a tenor harmonization which was exceedingly pleasing.

"Where did you hear that song?" she asked.

"I made it up."

"Not really."

"Really. It was a nugget of self-expression."

"I'm sure," said she, "that I have no idea what you mean."

Perceiving that she was correct, I made no response. She sat down beside the bole of the tree. "Everyone here talks about things I don't understand. I'm not very intellectual, but my sister is. My sister brought me here. She is a doctor and a college professor."

"I see."

"I'm an actress. This year I was in the front row of *Hot Mama* and it's too bad it is dark out here because I am very pretty. I was in the bathroom when you came so you didn't meet me. My name is Flora. I'm a perfect thirty. And I'm a natural blonde. I saw you walk out. You looked very sad. Are you sad?"

"No. I am drunk."

"Oh. That's too bad. I'm drunk myself. That's why I was in the bathroom. When I drink I seem to have to go to the bathroom all the time. It's too bad you're drunk, though."

"Why?"

"Because I brought you another drink."

"That was thoughtful of you."

"One for you and one for me. I put them down on the lawn back there but you'd better let me get them because you might kick them over. I think Finnley's nice, don't you?"

"Yes, indeed I do."

"Nifty," she added.

"Tell me," I said in sudden consternation, "are you an old friend of his?"

"How silly! I never saw him before in my life. I just either like or don't like people on sight. My sister—the professor—says that judging people quickly is pin-headed. But it doesn't seem pin-headed to me. Does it to you?"

"Well," I answered, "what do you think of me?"

"I think you're ridiculous."

"Then the system's pin-headed. Why do you hold me in such low esteem?"

"Shall I really tell the truth?"

"Why not?"

"You might be embarrassed."

"Not I."

"All right. I will. The reason I think you're silly is that—is because—" she miscorrected herself—"I was looking and listening to you and that dark girl all the time you were talking, up in the bedroom. My sister thought I was taking a nap."

No apt comment blazed in the bewilderment of my mind, so I held my peace. However, she did not object to silences. She filled them with apparent ease.

"Why did you keep her talking when she was trying to make you?"

"I'm sure I don't know."

"Well—I said to myself that it was for one of three reasons. Either you were in love with someone or you didn't like her or you were silly. And I decided that even if you were in love you'd be silly not to let yourself have experiences and I decided that if you didn't like her enough for at least a little experience you were very, very silly. So I figured that any way you looked at it you must be silly."

"Rather neat, I think."

"What? Oh—yes. Wasn't that Helen a stupid person?"

"You thought so?"

"Oh—of course. She probably didn't know that you don't have to have babies these days if you don't want to. How not to have babies was the first thing my sister taught me when I went into the chorus. She makes me come to see her every month. She takes a little glass full of blood out of me and does a lot of other things and then she says I'm all right. I don't know what would have happened to me if it hadn't been for my sister. I was there for my regular visit only the day before yesterday and after she found out I was all right for another month she invited me up here. Otherwise I'd have missed the whole week-end."

"What's your sister a professor of, Flora?"

"Didn't I tell you? She teaches ob—oh, dear."

"Obstetrics?"

"That's right! You're just like all the other people here. Words don't seem to bother you."

"Only in special arrangements, anyway," I said.

"Still," continued Flora, "I'd have had a week-end if I hadn't been disappointed and it was my sister who made up for my disappointment. I had intended—that is, till Thursday—to go to Florida for the week-end."

"You'd spend most of it on the train, wouldn't you?"

"You're foolish. We were going to fly."

"We?"

"Ralph and I. He's a man I know. He has a—I forget the name of it. But it flies very fast. I've flown for quite a few week-ends with Floyd—I mean—Ralph. Floyd is another man. Laugh and forget—that's what I say. Men are like trolley cars. There's always another—"

"I know. Don't quote it, Flora. People are always talking about the weather, too, but nobody ever seems to do anything about it."

"That's cute."

"Well," I said, rising.

"You're not going?"

"I think so."

"But I came out here to have an experience. It wasn't very snappy in there. I thought," her voice was unhappy, "that at least you'd want to neck me. Maybe if you'd seen me in the light—"

"You're sure you're a real person, Flora?"

"What a question! Pinch me and see." She held up her ankle.

"I think it would be better if I pinched myself. Do you ever wonder what will happen if all the people get to be like you?"

"They would have a pretty good time."

"But who'd run the power houses? Who'd make the laws? Who'd milk the nation's cows?"

"I can milk. I milked once. I was at Saratoga with Jerry. We went to a farmhouse to spend the night. It was just like the jokes, I said. And—"

"There must be twenty-five millions of you," I continued, talking to myself in a furious, lurching sotto voce. "Soon there will be fifty millions. Then a hundred millions. My God! Who is going to work out astrophysical equations when mothers haven't a sufficient intelligence quotient to sew on buttons? Help! I am mired in pulp magazines. I am smothered by the five and ten cent store. I am trampled by motion picture audiences. I am terrified. Birth control! Eureka!"

"Just what I was talking about," quoth Flora, "only I was being polite in the way I mentioned it."

"Too late," I murmured.

"Too late for what?"

"I am going, Flora."

"You're making a big mistake."

Someone opened the front door. Flora had her wish fulfilled. Yellow hair in ringlets and a variety of less complex curves. A really lovely neck and an impudent profile. Puckered, cherubic lips. She might have been twenty-five. Or more. The light was cut off.

I floundered into a lilac bush. I flung my glass against a tree. I heard it smash and tinkle. I heard Flora say, "Where are you? I'm coming after you."

"Hell!" I shouted. "Damnation! In all phylogeny there is no precedent for the ontogeny of a moron. Not even the pea-brained dinosaurs."

My foot slipped. I toppled into a bed of acrid-smelling leaves which were damp under their crackling surface. I heard Flora calling.

And then the alcohol suspended me.

I embarked upon a long dream. I dreamed that Flora the moron caught up with me. I dreamed I said to her that her charms had quite overthrown the essential snobbishness of my soul. I dreamed that I rose to my feet and told Flora that there were upon them the wings of Mercury. And in my dream I encircled her palatable waist with my arm and led her to the house of the Dwyers. There I quaffed nepenthe and traded witticisms with those guests not yet abed. Finnley was absent. I dreamed I found him taking a shower in the downstairs bathroom—naked and singing.

I dreamed furthermore that Flora and I finally ascended the wide, mahogany-railed staircase together and devoted ourselves to a lavish and mutually agreeable love-making which lasted until dawn. We occupied the interval, it appeared, by painting upon the oval mirror with mascara and lipstick and a paste we compounded of face powder and certain other materials which we melted in various ways, a lewd pastoral.

It was a fine dream—full of long dissertations on my part— a dream vibrant and realistic.

PART III

SATURDAY MORNING

WOKE.

It was morning and I lay in a bed.

My first thought was for my condition. Did I dare move my eyes? They had dropped by chance on the curly maple of the bedstead and located a gargoyle or two. I budged them and there was no pain—only a sense of billowy contentment. They fell next upon the screen of an open window and penetrated it. The outdoors was maudlin with pacific beauty. I could see the Sound, calm as glass, and the haze-draped sky shading from white on the horizon to blue at the zenith. A day of Indian summer was beginning.

My next object of attention was the room wherein I lay. I looked. And what I saw was an oval mirror whereupon were painted in a primitive style and outrageous colors a shepherd and a shepherdess piquantly and personally interested in each other.

I appreciated my rationalization of reality into dreaming.

Oddly enough, I was not horrified. My opinion of Flora had subtly changed. Stupid she unquestionably was in the superficial coin of social usage, but in another currency, Flora had genius—at least—if my memory (now flooding the interstices of my cerebrum) was correct.

Only then did my senses announce a running record of touch: there were tender filaments in my fingers.

As I turned, I gave a thought to headache. But there seemed to be none. My hangover was of that rare sort composed only of opalescences and warmths and tentative melancholies.

Flora was awake.

She was looking lazily at me and smiling. Half her face was aureoled by her curls.

"Good morning," said she.

I felt a recurrence of desire and so, I soon perceived, did Flora.

By and by we were sitting on the edge of the bed together and laughing.

"You are a nice girl, Flora," I said. "I like you." I felt expansive.

Flora rubbed a bare shoulder with baby-like vagueness. "You are nice, too," she answered. " 'In all phylogeny there is no precedent for the ontogeny of a moron. Not even the pea-brained dinosaur—' I'll remember that. It was rather neat —to use another phrase of your own."

I said nothing at the moment.

"If you pull that bell cord—a miracle will take place."

I pulled.

I went to the window and feigned an interest in the sea. Flora put on a negligee and gave me a bathrobe which she took from a closet. It was striped in yellow and chocolate brown. I still said nothing. There was evidently a radio in the room for it was presently invaded by liturgical music played on an organ.

Someone knocked on the door. "Come in," said Flora in a most cultured and casual tone.

A negress deposited a large tray on the bedside table. The tray was set for two. There was coffee in a glass decanter. There were eggs. There were two tall, stemmed glasses which contained an amber fluid.

Flora handed one of the glasses to me. I tasted its contents and gazed at her over its rim. The flavor was bitter.

"A recipe I gave to Don," she murmured, "or perhaps it might be called more accurately a prescription."

I decided to say something. I said, "You are your sister and your sister has no sister."

"In that giddy envelope," she replied, "I have occasionally found pleasant access to some human relations that are made artificial by an M.D., a Ph.D. and an M.S. Men go clinical on me. They are really much nicer to chippies than to ladies who lie beneath an involved predicate and a pince-nez."

"You are a superlative chippy."

"I am. And I like philanderers better than gigolos."

I peered at the warm morning. Whatever I had drunk floated through me like ambrosia. "It's too bad to break the enchantment."

"It is. But wouldn't you rather break it here than in public? Suppose we had descended the stairs and that insufferable chemist had asked me something about tissue immunity from water extracts of placenta?"

"You are gracious."

"I wonder," Flora murmured speculatively, "if we aren't justified in having a second pick-me-up? Yes—I'm gracious. But this morning I seem to remain stubbornly female."

I had dressed in a brown shirt and reddish brown knickerbockers. I had a green woolen tie and golf hose of the same shade and I put them on.

I walked slowly down the front stairs. The Dwyers' front door was divided into halves and the upper portion was open. Through it I could see Finnley's back. He was leaning into a pale yellow coupé. I heard Estelle's voice.

"Good-bye, darling."

"You appear in my life," Finnley said gently, "at precisely the right hour with the exactly proper solace. I wish you wouldn't go."

"I'll always go."

"And always reappear?"

"I hope you won't need me again."

She drove away.

Finnley put his hands in his pockets. His back was towards me. He watched her car until it was lost from view. His shoulders relaxed a little. He seemed tall, then, and a specific frailty was articulated by his figure. He walked under a lattice arch and into a rose garden. A single crimson flower hung its lost luxury on one of the bushes. Finnley started to pick the flower and then let it slip back to its stalk, reluctantly opening his fingers. Petals fell from it to the bare earth.

In my melodic mood I wanted to weep. He was still suffering and I did not know why.

But Finnley's evanescent Gethsemanes served mostly to vary and clarify his imagination. For I saw his shoulders shaking and I heard him chuckle.

"Ho, ho!" said Finnley.

I stepped into the weak, warm treacle sunshine.

He turned and spoke as if we had been engaged in a conversation momentarily interrupted. "You've heard of Circe?"

"Her work," I answered, "is virtually complete."

"And all men are beasts? Nonsense. I was thinking of a red-headed Circe who made one temporary transformation and I was thinking of the anodyne I had found for it. Only last night. You had a hand in its composition, by the way."

"I was unaware of it at the time—and unwilling to share it."

"And the accident that befell you has made you conscience-stricken?"

"Apophysis."

"In reference to your comment about Circe? Ah, me! There isn't any cure for acute lechery. What a pity the word has so bad a connotation. Let's talk about you for a moment. You've made a good impression. My friends like you. Tell me—would you bring your wife here?"

"Certainly."

He shook his head. "I wouldn't have brought Hope. I was jealous of her.

"Not to be jealous and still to be fond—"

"That's an achievement or a gift or the dawn of a new era," he said. "The Church wouldn't admit the possibility of it. Most women wouldn't want it. Too much risk involved. But logic prohibits any other form of affection in this plastic century. The brain finds it out but the heart and navel are inept pupils of the brain. The Dwyers are subsidized."

"Subsidized?"

"By an eccentric Yale alumnus. He left his fortune to them. It was his opinion that problems of government and economics and the machine are susceptible of a sane solution which will be arrived at by humanity in the extended future. But he had no formula for the interrelations of adults. He wanted one. He left the Dwyers his money for hunting out facts." Finnley looked at the gables and wings of the big white house. "You can do as you please here."

"And what have they found out?"

"Nothing," said Finnley. "Nothing much."

"The new school of week-end polygamy."

"Maybe."

"An extravasation of suburban fluids."

"You are enjoying yourself?"

"Yes."

"You weren't sore about Estelle?"

"I was drunk."

"They don't often drink. Just—sometimes."

"Oh."

He regarded me in a thoughtful and friendly manner. Less than twenty-four hours before this moment we had been total strangers. I guessed from the expression in his eyes that he was as surprised as I at our intimacy. However, in a moment he stopped thinking about me and returned to his subject. "Why

[175]

shouldn't statistical experiments with your friends, and guests be endowed? Every imaginable sort of investigation these days has wealthy sponsors. The Dwyers fervently believe that in a generation or two casual promiscuity will accompany marriage and the family life, as well as adolescence. They want first-hand material for their book. What is jealousy? Why is it caused? What is modesty? Is it innate or is it an environmental product? Does married love tend permanently toward monogamy? Must it be essentially disturbed by extramarital sex relationships? Would the opportunity for numerous sexual interests which did not involve the obligation of marriage or the danger of undesired conception or the risk of disease tend to increase an individual's happiness and efficiency? And so on. Those questions will be chapter headings in their book, I suppose. Maybe it will be a valuable study."

I said, "I believe their procedure is wrong. No human beings act normally when they know they are guinea pigs for analytical study."

"Well—you weren't forewarned. You probably consider yourself normal and intelligent. A little healthier than most people, I'll bet, and brighter. And you're right in both matters. You were taken blindly to a party—"

"Is this what my report will say?"

"Of course. You'll be listed as a newcomer, uninformed of the experiment. And right away—"

"I see. Right away I made goo-goo eyes at a svelte brunette and was nearly seduced and then I picked up a blonde who was pretending to be a moron chorus girl and slept with her—"

Finnley grinned. "Did Flora do that? Anyway—there you are. You're married. You're fond of your wife. I'll tell you how I know that. In the first place, you're worried about the fact that she is barging off to Bermuda alone. I noticed it last night. In the second place, Estelle said you had fidelity inhibitions of a high order. In the third, when I asked you if you were having a good time you said, 'yes'—a most perfunctory remark under the circumstances and one that showed you were in trouble with your conscience. In the fourth place, although I've reassured you in respect to the possible consequences of your deeds, you are still exceedingly sober-faced. You have certainly had more than one love affair in your life. Therefore I conclude that your attachment to your wife is partly what the Dwyers—right or wrong—would call medieval—and all your fine intelligence is not powerful enough—the Dwyers again—to enable you to emancipate yourself without the aid of darkness, exile, exacerbation, alcohol, and I daresay a drunken but obliquely searching preliminary examination of the ladies you approached."

I laughed. "I would like to make a suggestion to the Dwyers. A suggestion based upon my own limited experience here. On the basis of my interest in you I came here, tired, not at all interested in love, preparing to spend this day planting tulips at my house farther up the coast. First Estelle and then Flora attacked me. I claim original innocence of desire and of approach. I would like to suggest to the Dwyers that this prophetic household of theirs is revealing the fact that in the future casual world women will instigate all such matters."

Finnley laughed. "The Dwyers will tell you that women always did—and they will regret that the observation is trite. They'd like to be the first to make it."

"I'm embarrassed," I said.

"You shouldn't be. These parties aren't as laboratorial as that. There are just house rules. The tools of contraception are as accessible as faucets, no marriage is sacrosanct, and people who get mad aren't asked to return. Husbands and wives are discouraged by laughter from pursuing each other around the house and grounds. If the Dwyers invited you to bring your wife, would you come? Don't you think your children's chil-

dren will accompany their husbands and wives to such week-
ends and only such?"

"I don't know," I said.

"About what?"

"I don't know what my children's children will do, and I
don't know whether or not I'd bring my wife."

"You'll be asked."

"I'll give my wife the details, in that case, and refer the invitation to her."

"You think it's mawkishly modern, don't you? Affected?
Self-conscious?"

"I'm not sure. It's a nudist colony that doesn't wear loin
cloths, at any rate."

"Ha!" Finnley replied.

"And what do you think?"

"Me? I think it's all right. I wouldn't have brought Hope
here, though, because she would have been saddened and disturbed. It would have been the same if she had come alone.
The removal of individualism in a heretofore delicate matter is
appalling to the immature. I wouldn't have brought Helen
because secretly I would have been afraid that she would turn
an experiment in human relations into a nautch dance." He
shrugged. "Funny. I'd not have given words to that fear yesterday. Nautch dance. Do you meet any people who talk
about anything else but sex these days?"

"They find room for the depression."

"A little room. There's always a little. Still—I understand
that preoccupation with the subject is dated. Listed as post-
war. Odd. Nation's been ruined by it. Depression was
caused by it. I've been beached by it. You're confused by it.
But I hear in town that it's out of fashion. As for me—in one
way or another—I think about it a good deal. And if I lapse
into an hour of pure science—which is the only non-sexual subject on earth—the spell is soon broken. Not a newspaper, not

an advertisement, not a story, not a human being clothed or naked, not a look on the street, not an office or a library or a railroad station—not a haunt of human beings except for a few nerve terminals in the head—that isn't eternally conscious of male and female. We've discontinued at least for the nonce religion and patriotism, and only morality remains. If there isn't a great discovery made soon to sop up this preoccupation—and I mean a great sociological-psychical-sexual discovery—the current deluge of its decayed backwash is going to suffocate us. I should have said—rediscovery. Because the original surcease is lost, together with other ancient arts—pyramid building and glass staining and such items."

"What was it?"

"Copulation."

I said nothing. He scowled at me. "Well? You're surfeited now. How about tonight? How about tomorrow—or the day after? You and I belong to this wretched age of transition, this day of mass sublimation, this hour of hypocrites. The conquest of three unicellular organisms—spirochætes, gonococci, spermatozoa—will put a period after the word society. It will lead to changes greater than the transition from empire to soviet. It will slay bigger organizations than the Catholic Church. It is of the magnitude of the first word of articulate speech or the first use of fire. And how are you today?"

"I'm very well, thank you."

"And how is old Mrs. Bevins?"

"So nice of you to ask. Her other eye fell out this morning."

"How too, too bad!"

"Still—the dear soul couldn't see with it and it was a terrible expense to Henry as long as it was in."

"Too true, too true. Lovely day."

"Humid."

"Humid. The very word. Humid me—"

"what I am today—"
"I hope—"
"you're sat—"
"is—"
"fied."
"fied."
"You dragged—"
"me down"
"and down"
"until"
"the soul"
"within"
"me died."
"died."

We walked to the boathouse. The ocean was glassy to the eye, but the ear detected gurgles like laughter under the piles of the wharf and among the rocks. A door of the boathouse hung open. We entered without spoken suggestion. We saw a canoe on beams overhead and we found paddles in a corner.

In a few minutes we were out on the Sound, looking back at the Dwyers' point and their many-faced white house. Finnley paddled in the stern.

"You know," he said, after a while, "I feel totally unreal this morning."

"So do I."

"When the air becomes hazy and the sun warm at an abnormal period in the solstices, it is difficult to maintain a certain realism about yourself and your life. Such a day recalls others. I remember an afternoon long ago in New York. It was January. But by some necromancy the thermometer rose abruptly to seventy-two. Hope and I got on a bus without coats and hats. We rode to a place where neither of us had ever been and we had tea at a restaurant we had never seen. It was two stories high inside and filled with curios. I'm reasonably sure that it existed in space and time only that one day. The proprietor looked Irish but he spent most of the time we were there reading a book printed in Japanese. The upper region of the place contained innumerable canaries which sang incessantly—although we never saw any of them. We tried to find it again on a blustery winter day after we'd had a number of cocktails somewhere, but neither of us remembered the street and we couldn't locate a place in the metropolitan scenery even remotely reminiscent of its vicinity."

He paddled with energy so that the shore melted into a blurred pastel and we rode specklike on the calm water.

"I like a canoe," he continued. "I like to swim and dive and paddle canoes and carry packs. I like to portage and put up tents and build fires. I like to fish and hunt. But I don't care much for formal sports."

A gull made a planetary revolution around us and squeaked and flew away.

"Have you ever spent much time in the woods?" he asked. "No."

"Funny. Your life seems to you like destiny and to anyone else like the result of multiple jostlings. I've had lots of side-tours from those shoves. Last night I was thinking of my childhood and of what a savage, stupid bastard my father is, and of the monotonies by which I learned the petty perquisites of education from how to swim to how to parse an irregular verb. The whole period was unpalatable. This morning's mist has reflavored it.

"It doesn't disturb me any more. Not to hate. Not to laughter. Not to a churning of miserable memories, anyway.

"It seems romantic and glamorous. The doctor's boy in a little mid-western town. Gardens to tend, lawns to mow, quarries to swim in, little girls to play with, school to while away the years.

"God's good Indian summer and one or two other things have blown the bugs from the potatoes and rooted the dandelions from the lawn, and removed the turtles from the quarry—"

The promontories of the coast had lost their capacity to approach nearer than the bays. In the far distance on our right was a white line of beach, close to the water.

"Beyond that beach," I said, "I live in the summer."

Finnley turned the bow of the canoe eastward gently. I realized only afterward that he was making for the place I had indicated.

"When my father came east," he began presently, "he operated on a wealthy citizen of Orange Park named Briggs. Briggs had been abandoned to mother death by the medical profession but the old man snared a tumor from him that was not malignant after all, and Briggs got well.

"Briggs paid pop five thousand dollars in gold and as an additional reward took me to Canada with him. At that time I was in high school. I had another year to go. Briggs was a middle-aged, curly-headed, lean Christer who owned a hardware store in New York. It was generally and correctly believed that he had made his fortune by selling lethal weapons to South and Central American governments, but he was like most of the contemporary churchmen: his trade and his religion were never brought into juxtaposition.

"He went to Canada to prospect for gold—not that he needed a gold mine while political bitterness existed in the banana republics—but he was an amateur geologist and fond of the woods and he liked a picturesque explanation of his fun."

Finnley was silent for a moment.

"Sitting here in this canoe makes me think of those days. Briggs was a tough man and he knew a lot about the woods. There's a lot to know. I'm often accused of being a Boy Scout when I talk about what is called the 'outdoors'—and I can only think that if the Boy Scouts did what their handbooks suggest, the reference would carry no lampoon.

"Briggs and two French-Canadian Indians and I left a huddle of log cabins called Rangadam in June and we did not view them again until the end of October. During the interim we saw no human beings, we paddled and portaged eight hundred miles, and that was in nineteen-seventeen. We lived on moose and deer which we illegally shot and on ducks and partridge and fish, and on johnnycake and rice and raisins and tea and beans and brown sugar and oatmeal and onions and raspberries and chocolate. We slept for four and a half months in a tent.

"There aren't as many places in North America today where you can do such a thing—but there are still many. It was great—"

The cool mornings, the shining water of an unnamed lake, the smell of a campfire, the song of birds, the richly blackened pots hanging over the fire, the carpet of pine needles, the slow awakening into a primeval Oz

the dip of a cup into the bark-flavored water and the sharp passage of that water along naked loins

a tin plate of oatmeal and brown sugar and another and tea

the organized industry of striking the tents and packing sweaters and dish-towels and glittering equipment in duffel bags

the push-off into the lake and a backward glance at the virgin camp site where the memory of man would remain for a week in a keel-rut and for a year or two in sooted stones and a ring of ashes, where silence and falling needles and leaves and the wind and the rain would at last efface that blemish

water beneath the tireless blades of the paddles

swift water, where the heart expanded, the nerves perceived more than was their wont and the leaping muscles boasted of latent reserves ready to be tapped for a vivid peril of rock or foam portages—makeshift pathways through burned slash among scrub birches and tangled evergreens always defying passage, always conquered by sweat: by sweat that leaked out on a thousand stinging deerflies and soaked leather harness and dripped with each cautious footfall—gothic corridors through the dim prodigious realm of timeless trees which held the sun far away on upflung boles—and swamps where the feet slid in fecal ooze, where obscene fish lived among the hummocks and reeds, where herons rose clumsily, where the lily tubers floated like dumped garbage

small rivers that bent into question marks answered by the inquiring eyes of shoulder-deep moose, and the querying eyes of deer, by the slap of a beaver's tail and the swift angle of water at a muskrat's nose, by the shimmer and splash of an otter or the quick retreat of a mink

lunch on a ledge from the cold pot of rice and the pan of corn bread—lunch of chocolate squares and tea boiled over a fire so small that a handful of whitened sticks sufficed for its fuel

afternoons that ended with the crack of a rifle as a man would drop a buck kicking into the water or less fortunately send it flinching into the forest whither he would pursue it by rubies on the huckleberry leaves, red stains on the stones

in the evening the sky would turn chrome yellow and parallel shafts of blue-black clouds would float upon it; a coldness would fill the air; the wolves would practice for the coming of the long crystalline hell; owls would hoot; and a wildcat might incarnate a female fiend;

then in the ruddy dome of the campfire with the racially sad smell of smoke—peace

peace while the chrome faded and the stars came out so well that the nebula in andromache was like a far-off, faded moon and the dipper seemed large enough to hold all the water on earth, near enough to be lowered into some wet, ecstatic sea

where polar bears played

[184]

and slick seals swam

and the aurora borealis made mummeries over the waves, the seals, the bears, and shrimps with ogling eyes and penguins and icebergs and silence

sleep.

sleep.

sleep.

"In Africa," said Finnley Wren, *"the jungle drums may beat, rhinoceri with trident snouts may gallop through the heat; maybe the birds are brighter there—the night may be more horrid—and you may find a witchman with a diamond in his forehead but in the north your flesh will creep, your hair become as gray and its advantage is that it is not so far away.*

"A thing happened to me there," he continued, "which influenced my life or at least my philosophy. It's a thing not connected with the local magic—because I imagine that particular magic is the product of emptiness. No doubt if the first men to reach Mars find absolutely nothing alive there they will nevertheless have many and many a bad moment just because of their own nerves. I had plenty in Canada. I don't mean unpleasantnesses—such as getting caught in a whirlpool that had no place to be where it was, or being bayed by wolves; I mean—the psychic kind. If you knock around the unpopulated regions long, you'll soon see why Mr. Kipling's invention of the Red Gods was plausible, and why people believe in white things under the sea, and why Mr. Poe's Mr. Pym embarked southward on a highly credible junket.

"The thing that happened to me was in the category of my other adventures in this business of living. And the philosophy I derived from it? I suppose it was—that more things happen to you than you make happen—and the corollary that nothing ever turns out to be what you expected. Look at you. Yesterday evening you were probably going to do a little work. You planned to go to your summer house and plant tulips today.

Very well. You didn't work, because you met me. I took you on a week-end party at the home of some valuable nuts I know —which eliminated the tulips. We found a canoe—and lo! in another half hour we'll be digging in your lawn. Look at me. Any point in my life. I met Hope because I happened to be on the same boat. I got a terrible beating because I happened to overhear a conversation and was excited by it and because my father happened to be sore that day. I won an impressive medal because I had volunteered with a lot of boys in war time to stoke commuters' locomotives and because a nitwit named Meekel drank so much that he balled up some switches. Why did Meekel drink? Because he had a foot that ached him terrible, he said in court. Why did his foot ache? Because someone had vomited on the steps of a trolley car and Meekel had slipped and strained a ligament. The investigation didn't probe into the nausea—but I won a medal at least partly because of it. And in Canada I went through another phase of the involved network we call a plan.

"When Briggs and I with our Indians returned to Rangadam we stepped into a forest fire. It came over the hills from the west at a distance of several miles that same afternoon. A nasty-looking thing with a red edge and a fog of smoke. The local boys back-fired. Rangadam was on a lake—so—if the worst came to the worst—there was always refuge.

"In the middle of the night, the fire jumped across the protective burn and spread like hell. They woke us up."

Unconsciously, Finnley began to paddle with violence. "It was a spectacular thing to see. Anybody who has been waked in a burning house in the middle of night can understand at least part of it: the unusual color and fitfulness of the illumination as you open your eyes; the sense of having been coughing or strangling from smoke while you were asleep, and shouts both nearby and distant.

"I hopped to the window. Some of the cabins at Rangadam were deep in the woods. When I looked, many of them were burning. The tops of a cluster of giant pines were blazing in the center of a wall of fire about a mile away. Indians and French Canucks were running out of the forest to the clearing. Their kids were following them. They carried, down to the smallest youngster, bundles on their heads and packs on their backs and things in their hands.

"Porcadeau, the trader, was on the wharf trying to get his gasoline launch started. To my amazement Briggs was standing beside him, apparently doing nothing. His face was turned toward the roaring woods and although I could not see his expression, I sensed from his attitude that he was insane with fear. I thought then and I subsequently learned that he had a latent phobia about fire. That outpost was no place for such a phobia, because I've never seen or dreamed of so much fire either before or since.

"It shook the earth. It roared and boomed. It made a sort of super-crackle that vibrated the skull. Even at a mile, it was baking hot. Tremendous flames bounded into the air and other flames came into being high above the treetops consuming an invisible and almost explosive fuel there. It was like a close approach to a miniature sun.

"I stood at the window for some little time. The wharf, the shore, the buildings and the people were stagy in that light. The water began to reflect the horns of a crescent of incandescence which had encircled the village. Sparks fell—bushels of them at a time. I saw a man beat himself as his clothing caught. Apparently he failed to put himself out, because he jumped into the lake. He couldn't swim, either. I could hear a dim little note from him as he came up and I saw them throw a rope from the boat to him.

"Presently firebrands began to drop. Not pleasant, symmetrically spaced drops of fire like the arrangements in a Doré hell, but heavy things, ablaze.

"Canoes pushed into the water, loaded to the gunwales. One canoe turned over. Another caught fire.

"It occurred to me finally that it would be a good idea to get out of what was called a hotel, even if I didn't take an active part in saving the property and lives of the stricken people.

"You must bear in mind that I haven't any abnormal fear of fire whatever. If I get too warm, I move, and if something burns me, I move quickly. Otherwise, I'm not impressed. I take that word back. I was impressed by that fire.

"Anyway, I pulled my head in the window. My room was smoky. The night had originally been cold, so I was wearing for a nocturnal garment a suit of woolen underwear. I put on some heavy breeches and wool stockings and moccasins and a couple of shirts and a round, white sailor's hat which I had affected on the trip. The hat had a bunch of grouse feathers pinned in it.

"I had twenty-eight dollars in Canadian money and I stuffed it into a pocket. Also I took a knife and a revolver and some shells and perhaps I was more excited than I remember, because I pocketed a box of waterproof matches.

"I started down the narrow stairs, but as I did so, fire burst through the door at the bottom, a blast of smoke and heat started sweat on me, and I returned to my room, closing the door. That was the first notion I'd had that the big log structure we had stayed in was ablaze.

"I went to the open window and crawled out. I hung by the sill and dropped on the grass. It wasn't far, but I turned my ankle. So, for a minute or two, I sat in the grass rubbing myself and looking around. The fire was pretty close. Rangadam was hemmed in on all sides but the lake front. Still—there were plenty of canoes on the beach and the lake was nine miles wide and thirty-two miles long, so I felt unalarmed and only indignant at hurting myself.

"By and by I stood. My ankle didn't pain much. The night was bright as day, and furnace hot. It consisted mostly of roar. People's voices were no longer audible. I walked toward the wharf and the beach. I saw Briggs paddling furiously out onto the lake. The moosehead we had brought out was still resting in the bow of our canoe like an oversized figurehead. He stopped long enough to throw it overboard.

"The superstructure of the wharf was burning, now. I could see the men still trying to get the engine of the launch started. They were not more than fifty feet from where I stood. But I couldn't hear them, although they were yelling—yelling and sweating and cursing and socking their women and pushing one another away from the flywheel of the motor in a hysterical egotism of effort.

"I had an impression that children kept falling in the water and men kept hauling them out on boathooks—although it may have happened only once or twice. The launch was jammed. It had a normal capacity of about fifty. I presume there were a hundred in and on it.

"It passed through my mind that the men were making such a desperate effort not because it was impossible to save their families in canoes, but because the launch had been brought there piece by piece—on their backs—and it represented the major factor of their civilization.

"It also occurred to me that the fire on the wharf was under and around a four hundred gallon gasoline tank. I looked over the situation and decided that it was not hot enough to explode yet, so I ambled up on the place and yelled to as many people as I could that they ought to abandon the boat and the pier and get the hell out on the lake in canoes.

"Nobody paid any attention.

"A falling branch hit my shoulder and I got mad because it hurt me. I kicked it into the water and it steamed out.

"I went over to the gas tank and found a bucket and poured some water on it by lying on my belly and scooping it up in the pail. It wasn't any use. The heat was unendurable. I finally made some of the people in the boat look at me by throwing half a keg of nails among them and I pointed to the gasoline drum and the boats—but everybody merely yelled at me to get away from the tank. I thought then that they had probably never seen a gasoline explosion and fire—which they hadn't—and that they had planned to get away after it caught—which they evidently had. At least, those who planned anything, had planned that.

"My ankle hurt, my shoulder hurt, my clothes were singed, I was coughing, and I was indignant. I stalked off the pier and I yelled back, 'I hope the boat doesn't start, you God-damn fools.'

"I hurried about two hundred yards down the shore and I picked out a good canoe with paddles in it.

"Then something heavy hit me on the head and I fell in the water. The water brought me to in a hurry. I sat up in it. A fair-sized log, still burning, was floating near me. The burning trees and the burning cabins made my face hot. I looked at a picture of the people on the wharf and in the boat and realizing that I had been hurt again—this time on the head—I merely sat in the water and swore stupidly and steadily. It did not occur to me that anything serious could happen to me.

"While I was sitting there a man came out of the very flames with two bundles over his shoulders. He was running in a wild, tottering way. He reached the water a few feet from me and rushed into it with his bundles. He ducked himself. His bundles floated away and he did not come up. One of the bundles moved. All of a sudden I saw that it was a kid wrapped in a blanket.

[190]

"I jumped up then and waded to the bundles. Two kids. I picked up both of them and put them in my good canoe and pushed it into the water and paddled like the devil into the lake. I remember feeling at that time that I had stalled around so long because I had an inner motion that there was something for me to do. I remember attributing my anger to the fact that my necessary delay was being made needlessly uncomfortable.

"The kids were sitting in my canoe, choking and vomiting and splashing water on their faces.

"I remembered the man who had brought them. I gave the canoe a yank that spun it around. I went back to the beach. Now, however, I was scared—terrified. I kept my eyes on the wharf. It was blazing brightly.

"I looked over the whole surface of the water along the beach. Finally I saw the man. He was floating face down. I went to him and rolled him over. I didn't even try to get him aboard. It was an Indian—and he had been burned so badly in the face that I couldn't see how it had been possible for him to locate the water.

"I turned the canoe again. One of the kids—they were about half-grown—grabbed a paddle and hopped up on the bow seat and fell into stroke with me. He was still coughing and throwing up, but he didn't stop paddling. Whenever he had a spasm he just let it go. The other kid, on shouted orders from the paddler, began to splash water on all three of us."

Finnley abruptly tossed his paddle on the thwarts and let our canoe coast. "I'm reasonably strong," he said, "and at the end of that summer in the woods I was in extraordinarily good shape. It wasn't long before we were half a mile offshore. There was a moderate smoke on the water—about twice as much, I guess, as there is haze today.

"I looked back—Lot's wife wanting to see the last curtain on Sodom and Gomorrah. I saw it all right. The tank blew. Everything went up into the air—piles, people, planks, parts of the boat. The assorted entities in the explosion sailed up in dolly-silhouettes against a large light and dropped into the water. The lake surface supported a spreading fire.

"We turned away and paddled and paddled. We passed a few islands, but we gave them a wide berth, because we were afraid the fire might be carried through the inflammable night to their trees.

"We didn't see anyone else.

"It might have been an hour—or it might have been three when we stopped. . . ."

Finnley leaned on his paddle and looked at the furnace-fringe of the water. It was far away. Rangadam was already beginning to glow and smolder. It gave little light now.

"You kids talk English?" he asked.

"Certainly," one of them replied.

"Who are you?"

"Clarence and David Montgomery."

"Good Lord! Americans. How old?"

"I'm ten. David is eight and a half."

"What were you doing here?"

"We were hunting with dad."

"Where's your dad?"

"A tree fell on him."

"That," David explained, "was when we were all running. The wind blew it down. There was lots of wind. It whooooed all the time. Pierre picked us up after that. He went in somebody's house and got blankets and put us in them."

"Who was Pierre?"

"The guide, of course. He was Indian, mister. A real Indian."

"He wet the blankets," Clarence said. "And told us not to let our heads out."

"We were camping on Petit Lac," David said. "It was the first time we'd been in camp."

"It was father's vacation."

"Mother didn't want us to go."

"The tree killed father, I guess. He was all mushy."

"It didn't hurt, though, because he didn't holler."

"I guess mother will cry a lot. But I won't." Clarence promptly began to cry.

Finnley paddled aimlessly in the smoke, in the dark—aimlessly but always away from the red shore.

"Where do you live?" he asked.

"Chicago."

"Lake Shore Drive," said Clarence, sobbing.

"Do you think you kids could lie down in the canoe and sleep a while?"

"It's too smoky."

"Try it, anyway."

They huddled together in the boat on the ribs. Clarence continued to cry, and presently David cried also. Finnley paddled on and on through the penumbral gloom. A steady breeze now drove toward the fire and the canoe tossed on swells of gradually increasing magnitude. The wind was fresh, however, and after a long time the smoke was dissipated, the stars thinned, the east became pallid over the burned region. Then the wind veered and Finnley allowed it to carry him north and west.

He felt well—and tireless. There was a bump on his head, but it did not ache. His ankle did not hurt unless he pressed hard on his foot. His shoulder had recovered from the blow it had sustained. He was damp from his immersion, but exercise and woolen clothes prevented the dampness from chilling him.

Dawn came. Visibility was low. Within range of his eyes he could see nothing but the running waves.

The sun rose.

The two boys woke; they shivered and beat their hands together.

Their clothes were blackened by smoke. Their faces were grimy and sooted.

Finnley looked at his own garments. Half of the outermost of his two shirts was gone—burned and torn away. His neck and face and his hands were covered with red spots where sparks had fallen.

He was hungry.

The boys were frightened. The day was gemmy, crisp, autumnal. It would have been freezing cold during the night had not the world been on fire.

"You men grab a paddle and take turns," Finnley said. "We'll find an island and camp. I've got matches and a revolver so we can make ourselves warm and probably if we keep our eyes peeled we can find a duck to eat." He was not at all sure that he could shoot a duck with a revolver.

After a while he stopped and filled his hat with water. The grouse feathers had been burned away and only their charred ends remained pinned in the brim.

He began to think.

Half of the population of Rangadam or more than half had escaped by canoe. What would they do? Some would return to the site of the settlement. Others would make the carry over Table Mountain and down to the Poitières River. If they hurried and if they had luck, they could take the news of the fire to Williams Point before nightfall. That would result in the arrival of aid on the next evening—or afternoon. Of course, if there were a flying boat available in the district—help might arrive in the early morning.

What could he do?

It was dangerous to stay in the middle of the lake. A high wind might blow at any hour from the northwest and upset their bark.

If they landed on one of the hundreds of islands in the lake it might be days before they were found. Meanwhile there would be the problem of food and shelter.

The position of Rangadam was marked by a slow fan of smoke ascending into the blue sky. Finnley at last turned toward it.

"Listen, kids," he said. "This is the kind of thing that used to happen when your great-grandfathers were pioneers. The Indians used to burn their villages. The kids in those days were very brave. They never cried. They didn't mind going for a whole day without food. They grew up—those kids—and they were so courageous and so strong and so tough that they were able to drive the whole English Army out of America. Now— the boys alive today aren't supposed to have as much nerve as that. But I've been looking over you two and I think you're just like your grandparents—"

"My father's uncle Ned," said Clarence proudly, "captured three guns from the Johnny Rebs when his arm was shot off."

"That's what I thought. Now here's another thing. We can go on an island and hide and take it easy and have fun till we're found, if you say so. But before you agree to do that, I'd like to have you think this over. Back in Rangadam a whole lot of people have been hurt. Burned. There's nobody to take care of them. They'll be screaming with pain and they'll be helpless. It will be pretty bad. But maybe—see what you think—maybe three fellows like ourselves who haven't been hurt at all ought to go back and do all we can to take care of them. What do you think, Clarence?"

"Sure."

"How about you, Davy?"

Davy considered. "Would we have much fun?"

"Not very much. But it wouldn't be cold. And they need us back there. Only—the people will be pretty badly off—so you'll have to have a lot more nerve to go back than you would to stay here on an island."

"I got nerve."

Finnley paddled toward the smoke. Waves lifted the canoe's stern in long, regular glides. The boys said very little. They sat in the bottom of the boat and looked ahead. An hour passed. Two hours.

The shore was becoming visible. Finnley's heart sank. Not a cabin was standing. Not a sign of life could be observed. From a thousand separate spots smoke rose—so that the black and white terrain looked like a place of volcanic activity. A few hundred yards to the left of the cremated town there was a patch of green woods—an oasis in the charcoal and ash desert—a freak, a familiar freak of such conflagrations.

As they drew closer to the land a wind came to them. It was a hot wind. And it carried a subdued murmur. Finnley could not understand the sound and, as it was reiterated, he listened with bemused concentration. He felt as if in his brain there was a clue to that eerie whisper, but he could not analyze and uncover it. It came only on the burning offshore wind and it made his spine tingle.

David explained. "Well—I can hear people moanin'."

He turned out from the town and approached the green semi-circle near the water.

There were people among the trees, yet no one came to meet him. The shore was rocky. Waves broke upon it. He could see the blurred bottom now. His eyes scanned the edge of the land. Finally he perceived a tiny cove under some bushes. He made two quick strokes. The bow of the canoe slid under the greenery. There was a yeowl. Overhead, on a limb, a lynx glared at them and vanished.

The boys had seen it and crouched in the boat, quivering.

[196]

Finnley gulped. "Nothing but an old lynx," he said. "Why —we used to kill those things with clubs!"

"Honest?"

"Honest."

The canoe had grounded. He stepped into the water and pulled it up, his head touching the limb on which the cat had crouched. He helped the boys out. They walked stiffly into the woods, parting the bushes.

The fire had spared less than twenty acres of trees. It was warm even on the fringe of the green region. As they walked forward, they were conscious of things moving around them, of animals hiding where there was scant cover. They saw presently a moose that looked at them and went away. Then a bear. The bear walked toward them and coughed. Finnley took out his revolver and loaded it with slippery fingers and aimed it. But the bear also went on.

They penetrated deeper into the place. Innumerable little animals scurried around them. It was as if all the beasts of a vast tract of forest had congregated in a small spot—and, indeed, all those that had been trapped by the fire and had escaped being burned alive were in this tiny sanctuary. They saw beavers walking in the daylight and more moose, stately and aloof, and deer, and another bear. Wolves trotted past them—wolves making a perpetual, fretful round of the edge of the prison—looking for escape and confronted always by hot coals or rough water.

Then they found seven people.

The seven people were lying in the middle of a clump of white pine trees.

Two of them did not move at all.

Two moved and moaned. Of them one, a woman, occasionally raised a face that did not look human but that looked like an ill-butchered ham cooked too long, and in that red and gummy gobbet she opened a hole from which she emitted a long, agonized shriek.

There was a terrible odor around those people.

One was a child. The child walked about. It was blind. It kept bumping into things.

The other two had few clothes on. A woman with crimson breasts and a scarlet face. A man who looked up at them and then looked down at his hands. From his hands he pulled with his teeth a strip of flesh and skin as big as a carrot. He spit it out.

"They've come back," the woman said to the man. "They're here."

The man held up his hands. "Voyez," he said. "Voyez."

"Medicine," cried the woman with crimson breasts. "Have you brought some?"

"We went out on the lake in a boat, and we saw no one, and we had nothing," Finnley answered. "Now—we've come back."

The woman with no face screamed. The child bumped into a tree and began to whimper. A man sat up. His skin hung around his face like tissue paper and his naked back was split open as if it had once sizzled and snapped. Through the slits in his back his lungs bubbled redly.

"They're burned," said Davy. "It smells terrible."

Clarence stared. His eyes were unblinking and sickened, but he held himself steadily on his feet.

"It was the gasoline," the half-naked woman continued dully. "It blew up. Everyone in Rangadam that hadn't left was on the pier. It come out all over us. Them as could swim afterward found themselves a-swimming in a lake of fire. My husband was in it jumping and hollering when I came up. It threw me high and I got out of the worst of it. I was blazing and I doused myself and the steam done this." She looked at her breasts. "It hurts cruel." She paused. "I was a-feared

[198]

to breathe fire because it dries out the lights, so I held my wind till I got cool air. My husband was dead or quiet anyhow by then. He's a Canadian. He got me up here nine years ago from a matrimonial magazine called *Hearts Desire*. Maybe you've heard tell of it. That's our boy runnin' here blind. He's a-dyin' too. Burnt right to the innards an' don't seem to know it. Kinda out of his head—and can't see. I was thinkin' of puttin' him outen his misery before you come, but I hadn't the stomach for it, though I'd picked up a goodish sized rock for to do it with. It's terrible, all this burnin'. Him peelin' his hands there is the best trapper in the province." The man heard and looked. "Worth ten thousand dollars in Quebec, they say. Won't set no more traps, though. I went down near as I could to town a while back. There's a few crawlin' around in the ashes and a few still standin' in the water. I couldn't do nothin'. Every time I grab somethin' my skin slips off onto it."

"Do you think you could mind these two children for a little while?" Finnley asked.

"Leave 'em here."

He turned to the boys. "Listen, fellows, I got to go down to—town—for a little while. Stay with this lady."

He turned and walked through the trees. A hundred feet from the opening in the pines he stopped. On the ground, still trying to crawl, was a man. The wolves had been eating him.

He went back for David and Clarence. "I'll take you along after all," he said. He held them by the hands and walked slowly. He avoided the place where the man was crawling, but he could see the fronds of ferns moving as he passed.

They walked near the water. In a little while they reached a ledge on the other side of which was the beach. They crossed the ledge, holding their arms up to protect their faces from the heat. The ledge was about a hundred feet wide. At its summit was a mêlée of hot ashes. At its base the water. He told the quiet children to wait for him at a point from which he could see them. He started. He turned back. "Can you swim?"

"Sure."

"Real well."

"If any animals come out on this big stone—yell like the— yell as loud as you can—and jump in the water and swim right out in the lake. I'll come for you."

"Right straight out?"

"Right straight out."

Finnley went toward the sand. He could tell where the hotel had been and the store. He could see the blackened stumps of some of the piles that had supported the wharf. There were heads in the water—in the shallow water.

He pulled out three human beings.

"I'll take you around to a green place in a canoe," he said.

Farther along, sitting on a stone, was a man. When he saw Finnley he began to roar with laughter. A moment later he rose and dashed up into the glowing coals of what had been Rangadam. There were other persons on the beach.

He returned to the stone ledge and the boys. "How would you feel about getting the canoe and taking these people to a place where they won't burn or drown?"

"All of us?"

"Sure. We three."

"They'll get the boat nasty," David said.

"I know. But they've been hurt and if we're as good as the boys who lived long ago—"

They made eight trips. They helped the moaning, shudder- ing, tormented forms of eight people to the dubious security of the green oasis.

Then Davy had hysterics. He wept and kicked and shook. Finnley took both boys offshore in the canoe away from the heat and away from the voices; away from the smell of the people and away from the silent, puzzled beasts.   Finnley gave Davy a drink of water.

He had nothing else to give.

Even if there had been food in the ruins of the store, he could not have reached it without being cooked.

He sat in his canoe, not speaking.   He kept it headed into the wind.   He moved neither forward nor backward.

By and by Clarence saw another canoe approaching.   It contained an Indian and his squaw, and two children and a dog. It veered to approach Finnley.   The Indian smiled at him.

"Fire she is varee bad, n'est-ce pas?"

"There are about fifteen people in the woods yonder," Finnley answered.   "Maybe you can do something for them."

The Indian shrugged.

"Il y a quinze personnes là-bas dans le bois.   Ne pouvez-vous pas les aider?"

"Non."

"Ils se sont brûlés."

"Oui.   Naturellement."   The Indian regarded the village that had been his home.   "Fini!" he said.

"Have you anything to eat?"   The canoes were gunwale to gunwale.   "Avez-vous quelque chose à manger?"

The Indian smiled and rummaged in his boat   He passed to Finnley a pail.   Finnley lifted the lid.   Inside was a noxious mess of meat stewed with potatoes.   Finnley's eyes widened as he looked at it.   Abruptly he turned away from the Indian and puked a thin slime onto the water.

"C'est bon!" said the Indian.

Finnley handed back the pail.   "N'ai pas faim," he said. "Merci."

"Où sont les autres?" Finnley asked, after a while.

"Un bateau—she is—" the Indian made a whirling motion with his hands.   "Les autres—la—" he pointed to a dim island —"et les autres she go to le Williams Point."

"We went into a bay eventually," Finnley said, as he resumed paddling our canoe. "The heat from three shores made us comfortable—although it was smoky. The wind died. The kids dried out. So did I. There was nothing on earth I could do for the people in that unburned place—unless I had shot a couple. I did shoot one man on the beach.

"Funny." The tone in his voice was odd. I turned. He was gazing at me. "I've told this story a number of times. And I've always said that I wasn't able to shoot that man. That's a lie. You might as well know the truth. There wasn't an unburned place on his body—but he was alive and he could think. He saw my gun. He asked me to do it. I gave him the gun. He couldn't hold it in his hands. So I shot him. He sat still and I shot him through the forehead. I could have done anything that day. Anybody could—under the circumstances. His head jerked back and he toppled over and lay still. That's all there was to it. The blob the bullet made was almost indistinguishable from the rest of the marks on him. I don't think I saved him from more than another hour or two. But maybe I saved him from days of it. Some of those people—lived a long time.

"That's the way you meet death—occasionally. You're in a subway shooting along under the street—when suddenly—crash —and everything's blood and horror. An elevated train jumps the track. Three automobiles collide. A gas tank blows up and destroys a city. A hurricane comes. A tornado. A fire. A steamship hits an iceberg. It's not as common as a slow diminution of consciousness in a hospital bed—but it does happen. Still—people do not want to think about it; they almost don't believe it. And such things in our civilization are swamped by relief organizations, whisked away in ambulances, quieted by opiates. It's seldom that you come upon them although you read about them every week. I wonder why people don't think more about death? It's inevitable. And you've only two possibilities—really: you can go peacefully and in a dream at a hospital—or you can go as those people did in Rangadam. I'd like a different death—sudden and unexpected. I'd like to die when the world looked rosy for me and when I was feeling fine—to die without foreknowledge of death. To die so suddenly that there would be an imprint of interest and fun and aliveness on my brain until the worms made off with it. Most people would like that, I think. And it's so rare. You hear of it occasionally—but usually there is first the hideous arm-pain of angina or the struggle to get to the surface of the water or the agony before the doctor decides to give a hypodermic or the dreadful war between fear and creeping oblivion. I'd rather not have those moments. I wouldn't mind dying young. I've got nothing in myself to give the world that others lack. Nothing but the common property of my chromosomes. I've got no panacea, no revolution, no philosophy of distinction. And if I died young abruptly—no—instantaneously—I'd never lie in regret for what my years might have produced. Because they would not. I'd give the world children with curiosity and reason and I hope with courage—nothing more. But whenever I've felt the pressure of the grave on me, I've vowed that if I live I'll make my name an illustration of virtue and when I've healed I've forgotten. Forgotten. That's it—isn't it?"

I noticed that we were approaching the shore. The observation made me uncomfortable. I imagined that genteel Connecticut seascape surrounded in fire. I envisaged it a bed of embers with stinging, screaming figures trotting at the water's edge.

"That's why"—I said—"you spoke of the effect of a burned sleeve on you—yesterday—at the speakeasy—"

[203]

"Oh—" said Finnley. "No. Not that. Why did I start that episode? Oh. I know. To tell you about my philosophy of the unexpected.

"Help came to Rangadam on the following morning. We—the boys and I—were damn near crazy. We went back to the oasis late that afternoon and I shot a deer that was just standing still—as if it had given up. We cooked it—Davy screamed when I lighted a fire—and everyone who could—ate. We could even eat among those people. Anyway—we got out of it. I accompanied the kids to Montreal. Somebody had given me clothes. Briggs had run all the way to New York. He telegraphed me five hundred dollars and five thousand words begging me to keep his flight a secret—which I have done till now. He hid in town till I got back—and I've supported a joint story with him ever since. But this was the thing. The Montgomery kids' mother was at Montreal. They'd been bricks. I still love those kids. And when anyone tells you that kids are realists—you agree—because they are. Their mama was an ex-actress who had married a millionaire.

"I thought she would be grateful. But she was just hysterical. And angry. Nothing makes any sense in relation to anything else. That's my point. Here. Imagine me. Seventeen. Delivering the kids to their nurse at the hotel and accepting an invitation to dinner with Mrs. Montgomery. Pretty proud. I'd walked through graves in which the dead were still turning—and I could still boast of an appetite and smoke the cork-tipped cigarettes I elected to use in those days. I thought of myself as the rescuer of the kids and I'd saved what was left of several other people. I'd also dispatched a man under rather difficult circumstances. Of course, I'd been rather icily dazed while I floated and walked in that charnel house. It had seemed like being marooned in a river that turgidly drained a battlefield. Still—if there was a hero of the Rangadam disaster—I was the guy.

"What happened? Reporters didn't come to see me. My name wasn't in the papers. Briggs' telegram had prevented me from telling the facts. When the rescue boats had arrived, I'd taken the kids and scrammed.

"I went into a dining room where three hundred smart Canadians and Americans were having dinner. An orchestra was playing war music. There were dozens of birds in uniforms. And girls. Mrs. Montgomery was big and blond and handsome. She looked like a cross between a Gibson girl grown older and a madam. The boys weren't there.

"She shook my hand—but she didn't thank me. Instead, she balled me out furiously for letting her boys see so much of such horror. I tried to explain that it was more important to try to help those poor shriveled devils at Rangadam than it was to keep youthful memories clear of evil sights. She couldn't see that. The boys had talked some. And they'd taken a nap after their baths that afternoon. A nap that included several voluble nightmares, I guessed. No wonder. I had a few.

"I had a feeling, however, that her point wasn't yet made. And it wasn't. It appears to have been common knowledge in the society of Chicago that Mr. Montgomery had ceased caring for his wife. She'd married him, beyond peradventure, for his money. And when news of his death had reached the city a newspaper not ungifted at innuendo had hinted that Montgomery hadn't died but had taken advantage of the fire—after sending his sons to safety—to escape to a foreign clime, a foreign savings account, and, no doubt, a foreign enchantress. Mrs. Montgomery was wild. She was afraid it would block her inheritance.

"We had reached the demi-tasses, however, before she leaned forward and offered me a thousand dollars if I would go back to Rangadam and recover the body of her husband."

I wanted to laugh. It seemed so silly. So out of place. So unpredictable. And, of course, I was bitterly disappointed. I told Mrs. Montgomery that you could shake her husband's remains through a tea-sieve in five minutes—if you could pick them out of fifty square miles of other ashes. She didn't like that. And the thousand dollars seemed a shade meager for such conspiracy.

" 'A thousand dollars, then,' she said, 'if you will testify that you saw his body before it was burned and were sure he was dead. Or—say—a hundred dollars for a written statement to that effect.'

"I said, 'Make it a hundred and fifty.'

" 'Very well.'

"She sent for stationery then and there. I wrote out a piece—it said, 'I don't know what kind of a man your husband was, but, judging him from your two boys, I'm pretty sure that tree fell on the wrong parent.' "

"I excused myself for a moment, rose, flipped the missive to her, and said, 'That's the only guarantee of your husband's death I can make.'

"I went out into the lobby and sat down and laughed. It passed through my mind that she might come belting out of the dining room. I departed for the street. I went to a café and had some beer. End of story."

We beached the canoe and walked inland from the shore, standing for a long time at the Post Road to discover an interval in traffic through which we could pass. An inspection of the cars reminded us that it was Saturday and that there was a football game at New Haven. Finnley spoke about it.

"I'm not a loyal graduate. Or I'd be in that parade. I don't believe in college loyalty. I don't believe in many loyalties. They're stultifying—like faith. Whenever human beings get together in numbers, however, the first fine flower of their association seems to be a loyalty. College spirit—club spirit—

church devotion—teamwork—patriotism—the loyalties in acquaintanceship that prevent what is called gossip even where it would do the most good. I can't subscribe. It's a nasty word —loyalty. It doesn't mean helping the weak. It means sticking up for yourself, your crowd, your country, and your prejudices. It engenders precedent and tradition. It checks criticism and perspective and change. Reason doesn't indicate the adoption of blanket principles. Cases alter from hour to hour. Loyalty—somebody ought to think it over."

It was noon and warm. We walked on a country road. There were yellow leaves over our heads and red leaves on the hillsides and brown leaves under our feet. The sumac was gaudy. The air was as fragrant as a sweet-grass basket and there was no one on the road, no one in the houses we passed, so that when we descended to the valley where my wife and I have lived for many years we walked down into a deep silence. It is true that the stream at the mill dam dripped from moss beards and birds occasionally thrummed through the air but the lack of human response to those timeless murmurings made them organs of quietude. The fields surrounding my dooryard were stiff with tarnished goldenrod and dock and mullen and over my vegetable garden—where tardy bees still hummed— was a sweet anæsthesia, a warning that summer was gone, summer was spent, spring was unthinkable, winter was near, winter the bleak, the bitter, the barren, the blowing, the white, the cold, winter the casket, winter the tomb, winter the dismal, winter the further stillness. The grass in the orchard was littered with apples and apples offered themselves on the branches. There were leaves on the porch. A nest had dropped on the roof. The woodpile grew brackets of fungus. The bed of the brook was nude. The corpses of hollyhocks, cosmos, daisies and asters had toppled upon their faces. The frogs were gone, the insects stilled, the pig had been sold and butchered, the hens were dead. Squirrels remained and rabbits; pheasants and rats and

[207]

grouse. Moles had rutted the aisle of grass under the arbor where grape-blood fermented and ants had built themselves a skyscraper upside down in the driveway. It was a swan-song day, quietly sweet, exhausted, distilling its ultimate perfume into the sunshine, lost, unregenerate, hopeless.

"I meant to tell you," Wren said, leaning into the well-house and deeply inhaling, "why I spoke of that charred sleeve."

I could not even be curious then. "The tulips are in the pothouse," I answered. "Wrapped in burlap. The colors are marked on separate smaller bags. I marked them myself. Let's get them."

We walked through a perfume of rotten apples. "It's because," he said, "it has a reason. You'd think with all that experience in the matter of ashes, I'd be spared. One catholicity of conflagration—you'd say. But I wasn't.

"Hope burned to death. Do you see?"

"Oh."

"In the yard. On Sunday. For no reason at all. We'd come back from tea and I'd fallen to fondling her in the car so I went directly upstairs. It was a day like this. I wasn't in any hurry. We never were. I sat there—waiting. I think—she walked around the back of the automobile—and lighted a cigarette.

"I loved her more than my life—remember. Maybe that flame also burned me—backwards—taking away the centers of feeling—leaving only the sensitive ends of my nerves.

"I loved her so that I could cry from thinking of her—and often I did.

"There was a flicker of light. A soft explosion. A trick of the eye, I thought. A noise in the machinery of a distant vehicle.

"I heard her call—so strangely and so passionately that I brimmed with love for her.

"She called once and twice and again. And only then did I hear an undertone from which I'd give my soul to emancipate myself. 'Finnley' she called.

"I jumped all the stairs at once. It was no use. She was like a torch, a mouthless spew of fire. I brought a blanket. It was no use. I caught Hope in it and I covered her with it. I took it off. Dark, delicious Hope was already gone. In her place—one of those monsters from Rangadam. She sat on the grass beside me. I'll call a doctor, I said. Don't leave me. But I must. It doesn't hurt at all, she said. I telephoned—somehow. Somehow. A motto. We sat there—waiting for her to die. It doesn't hurt, she repeated. I can't see you, you know. Her eyes were opaque and they swam in a small carnage of flesh that I had seen burn like fat in a fire. The doctor, I said. He'll fix everything. Naturally you can't see. The light—must have been awful. Is the car still burning, she asked. No, I replied, and I wondered she could not hear it and feel it when she could catch my quiet voice, when her hand—reached for mine. It's useless—isn't it, she said. I'm sorry I can't see you just once more. But you'd be frightened now. You'd look sad. And when you went upstairs you were smiling —oh—so nicely. We sat still for a long time then. Maybe, I said, a pill. Don't go. Don't go any more. Oh—Finnley— I'm so, so terrified. I loved you with all my heart and please, please don't drink too much for too long and don't—don't put all that sugar on your cereal because you'll get fat. And tear up all the pictures of me because maybe—oh—I'm sure—you'll forget this picture a little—and the rest are so stupid. Won't you, dear. Of course. Isn't there anything—anything—? Could you kiss me?"

Finnley suddenly yelled at the top of his mighty voice and threw himself at my feet and began to kick and bite the earth and to beat it with his fists.

I was ready to speak to him when he scrambled to his feet. He put his arm around my shoulder. "I had to get that done," he said. "Every so often. Every so often. My God, it's a wonder people can live at all when you think what happens to them in the light of what they are taught to believe. I'm sorry."

I didn't say anything.

He had restored himself, however. We went to the pothouse and carried the bulbs and some tools out on the lawn. We took turns spading up the bed. I set strings and we planted the tulips.

When we had finished, Hope had washed back into Finnley's terrible mind and its surface was again serene. I went to the house and fitted a key in a rusty lock. He followed me. I descended to the cellar, unlocked a cupboard in the wall, and thrust in my arm. I brought out a bottle of brandy. I had smuggled it from France, years before, by suspending it from my loins with adhesive plaster. It was waiting in our closet for the proper hour.

Finnley took the bottle from me and stared at it with concentration. "The back yard, I think. Straight. But I imagine we might have glasses. And other glasses for some of that well water? It must be very cold now. Cold and clear. I'll remember this beneficence. The distillate of an autumn afternoon in Cognac transferred to a similar time in Connecticut. A personal miracle, eh? A mile-post you laid down long ago for my destiny. You must have known it would be me—a beater-on-the-earth, somewhat exhausted, and at the lower edge of a hangover. An artistic cadaver with a thirst—but no hunger, my friend. No hunger.

"So—underneath this orderly cloak of existence—underneath this pleasant pretense—lie the suffering ribs of human beings. And all our grandeur is a false smile. Fire for me. A beating. A scared girl swelling with child.

[210]

"How pretty your house is! How fine these gardens must be in June. Yet—in the two hundred years this house has stood and that elm yonder has stood—what pain!

"The poor live close to those things—and because of an aching littleness of expression, the middle classes hate them—the poor:

" *'I had to go to the doctor every week for the needle.'*

" *'His leaders tightened up till his neck broke.'*

" *'Stir-daffy.'*

" *'I set all night fightin' rats off'n the baby.'*

"Such things frighten the middle classes—

" *'My God-damned Wassermann was plus.'*

" *'He was under morphine to the end.'*

" *'Suppose he did do a little drunken driving and kill an old slow-poke? Is that any reason why society should lock him up until he stops caring about anything any more?'*

" *'I had to fire my maid. You have no idea what uncleanly surroundings she lives in.'*

"And the rich assume there are no such things—

" *'My dear, Graham is worth millions and I don't see what his complexion has to do with that.'*

" *'Three dozen of the big lilies. Doctors are so stupid!'*

" *'Not one cent. Our prisons are too comfortable as it is!"*

" *'You must ignore those obscene, fictitious newspaper stories, Rutledge'.'*

Finnley chuckled and dropped the bucket into the well. Its rope raced over the rusty wheel and from the stone tube came a splash. He poured. He threw the remainder of the water on the roots of the rambler. I took the cork from the cognac.

We clinked two small glasses of topaz liquid.

We drank.

The bouquet of the brandy blended with the aroma of autumn. An immediate peace, the forerunner of delight, entered our beings. We sat down on a bench together and refilled our glasses for slower imbibition.

Smoke from the far-away bonfire of leaves came to our nostrils; the whole world smelled seasoned, and spiced, sun-cured, benevolent, and poignant through the intellect but not the soul.

"I wrote an Epistle," said Finnley, "about a man who could make lightning by rubbing two sticks together. And I wrote the middle scene of the middle act of a play. The back drop was represented as the riveted side of an ocean liner and halfway down, canted at an angle, was a lifeboat full of people. As the scene progressed some fell overboard and others jumped in. The blocks were jammed. And all the while the side of the ship leaned out and out and out so that the boat on the ropes swung steadily farther away from the sinking vessel. Then, I wrote a fine melodrama. It had to do with a room in a church where the light entered as if through the skins of purple grapes. A man and a woman were in the room and the woman was naked and the man was strangling her and all the while the organist was playing Te Deums and on the farthermost pew a cat sat, watching and listening. I wrote another Epistle, to the Galatians, which had partly to do with an acromegaloid who became a peeping Tom because he could look through transoms without standing on his tiptoes. And I have various things here."

He reached into his coat pocket and withdrew a sheaf of papers. These he set out on the bench one by one and what Finnley Wren had in his pocket I have indexed here as follows:

1. A hotel bill for seventy-three dollars.

2. A postcard from a girl in Hyères.

3. A scrap of paper on which was written: "Fleas, flies, lice, mites, ants, worms, slugs, beetles, caterpillars, toads (to step on), grasshoppers, locusts, gnats, mosquitoes, rots, smuts, molds, other fungi, droughts, wet spells, acid soils, manures, weeds, weeds, weeds, sunburn, stones, lack of drainage, price hazards, poisons, tree roots, tetanus, lumbago, frost, overeasy abundance

of meager vegetables viz. Swiss chard, radishes, and the like, exhaustion, arguments with quarantine officers; bad grammar in government bulletins, unjust competition with the farmer, bites of extraneous insects caused by exposure, poison ivy, increased thunderbolt hazard, increased danger from meteors and bolides, tool-risks, etc.

4. A wedding invitation.

5. A page from a magazine containing part of a story called "He Asked Her to Say No," on one side and on the other an advertisement for Monobilt Automobile Bodies.

6. A cocktail recipe.

7. A counterfeit twenty dollar bill.

8. An envelope in which was a lock of dark, curly hair.

9. A newspaper clipping about the discovery of a woman's body, a boa constrictor and a paraquet in the subway.

10. A card on which were the photograph, fingerprints and typed record of Barney Mistraro.

11. A jingle written on the inside of the cover of a toilet-paper roll:

Beware the dawn, the noon, the night!
(The earth is full of dead)
Beware the stair, the electric light!
Beware, in fact, the bed!
Beware the corner of a rug!
Beware the zephyr's breath!
Pins may kill you!   Bathtubs lug
Their thousands down to death.
The tack-wound victim oft is rued—
Trust no stool or chair—
And as for eating any food—
Beware! Beware! Beware!
A splinter is a thing of doom!
Beware the sun, the shade!

The bread-crumb beckons to the tomb
And so does orangeade.

12. A gardenia petal.
13. An article torn from a magazine.

"You live here," said Finnley, after he had scrutinized each object, "and you write. You cultivate all this"—he waved his hand—"vegetation. You talk to the people whom you invite here. Me, for example. You mail your stories to an agent and he mails back checks. The checks you turn into tools, and paint, and lumber, into food and clothes and wages for the people you hire. You pay a tax on your land and a tax on your income. You vote. You travel. You buy gadgets. I read your stories and I say they are terrible. You read my advertisements and you do not even hypothecate—you know—the extent of their vainglory. Your stories bring my advertisers customers, my advertisers' customers bring you checks for your stories.

"The matters I have collected in my pocket were mostly suggestions for further Epistles, which I have been carrying about. All that has the very pleasant quality of being neither here nor there—and I will have another brandy.

"You go into New York. You peer at the buildings and you walk into the theaters and the motion picture houses and you dally in someone's apartment. Perhaps you go to Hollywood for a while and write a few motion pictures. You amble along in a big car under the sunshine and watch the snow melt on the distant mountains when spring comes and you argue with people about wholly trivial alternatives in arranging a scene for photographing. You stop in El Paso on the way home—and Chicago—and Cleveland. There, too, you look at the buildings and the lakes, if they are to be seen conveniently, and the parks.

"You get on a boat and you go to Paris. You gaze at the buildings and shop and you take the Blue Train and sit on Mediterranean sand for a while.

"You make love to your wife and you gossip with your intimate friends. Occasionally you let yourself wheedle yourself into the compilation of a long prose junket you call a novel. A publisher brings it out. I buy the damned thing and I enjoy it. A readers' club mails it. You order a copy of the first edition bound in leather and after it has sat for a few years on a shelf you pick it up and wonder what in God's name could have been the matter with you when you wrote that one.

"In your observations you will find out several million such facts as that people all over the world turn on lamps when the sun goes down and that the duck-billed platypus is an egg-laying monotreme, that a nasty noise can be made on a B-flat clarinet and that nuclear physics is an extraordinarily recondite branch of science.

"But you won't find out much, even so. You'll look blank or, worse, you'll begin to talk, when I ask you what in hell is the matter with people these days. You'll have a number of fine recitations at your tongue's tip but you can't tell me why people are such fools. You'll find it still harder to explain how fools manage to give their aberrations such an orderly aspect. And you'll go into a dither when I ask you why more people don't get mad at the way things are and do something.

"Why do they sit like the goggle-eyed inmates of a sanitarium unmoved by such a spectacle as the near-starvation of ten million people in a land of copious resources? Why do they who call themselves intellectuals imagine that a vestiture of power in the proletariat, the rabble, the riffraff would be an improvement? Why do they allow a form of constitution which insists on the equality of all men and which provides for the election of amateurs by morons? Why do they go through life unable to mention certain parts and functions of the human body in each other's society? God damn it all, my fine friend, a moment's thought would convince a sane foreign creature that nothing superior could exist under such stupid rules. Why, my boy? Why? I'll tell you. We're still in the Middle Ages. The Industrial Revolution was a mere shift in wages. It wasn't a human, social thing. The Renaissance wasn't rebirth. It was merely a lifting of censorship that has in the subsequent decades permitted a very limited dispersion of facts. Can this be anything but an extension of medieval times when the masses still believe in God, sin, immortality, horseshoes, husband's rights, penology, purity, and whatnot? It cannot. Moreover —we are befouled. America! Land of the dimwit and jackass! They crowd the theaters, flood the boardwalks, surfeit the streets and reproduce like microbes. Withered fruit of the unfertilized ova of New England witches. Tinpot leaders from the Continent. Cheap desperadoes. A few pioneers. Myriad misfit nincompoops. Greedy-eyed and beady-eyed. The covered wagons were filled with harlots and hypocrites, those who had nothing to lose, nothing to give. For generations the ships brought in the garbage of the world. Seldom did the illustrious migrate. Good blood, good brains, and good intentions were accidents in that sniveling motley of something-for-nothing seekers. And from the rock-bound coast of Maine to the sunkissed shores of California their progeny has multiplied, still hunting something, still with nothing to contribute even if the urge were there. They do not want sense. They do not want system. They do not want universal and coöperative construction. They concern themselves never with helping. Only with getting. Aid. Aid. Help the farmers. Rescue the bankers. Destroy our insect pests. Support our unemployed. Make our municipal bonds good. Help us to get a profit from the crude oil we are pumping. Pay our bonus.

"Could you tell them about robbing Peter to reimburse Paul?

Or about the structure of society? You could not. They would elect a Congressman with a bigger mouth and a louder voice and a shrewder species of weasel-wit.

"They could all be killed and it would not matter. 'In the year nineteen-thirty-four,' history would say, 'more than ninety millions of people were legally executed in North America after careful tests of their mental capacities and a chemical analysis of their hormones, hereditary factors and so forth. The remaining twenty-five per cent of the population speedily rebuilt the nation, repeopled it to the present stationary population level, developed the existing upcurve of mental and physical standards, and obliterated every trace of the now impossible-seeming follies and stupidities which existed before the passage of the Ass-reduction Act.'

"Our people!" Finnley exclaimed, upsetting his glass. "The melting pot has turned out to be a cesspool. Not a crucible for the amalgamation of a fine alloy but a gigantic receptacle for anthropological waste already reduced by the bacteria of publicity and precedent and custom and fashion and education to a vomit-green, gelatinous mess in which only the toughest kernels still remain undigested. Putrid America! Rotten to the core. Corrupt to the guts. Stinking, flatulent, bubbling! The odor goes over the radio. The color inks the rollers of the press. And the sound of its beshitted fermentation is the voice of Congress.

"I used to love this country," he said, moodily throwing an apple at a hole in one of the trees. "But the earth of it has been defiled and the people in it haven't a purpose. There's nothing fine left here but individuals. I could do without the individuals if most of the citizens were moving together toward"—he shrugged—"almost anything. Still—a leader couldn't lead it. A prophet couldn't evangelize it. Its sensitive minority differs from one man to the next in adherence to dozens of false gods and they cannot convene to plan a street without quarreling over worship. I despair to see light grow dim in the West. Or to think of sunrise in the East. The Russians are such emotional eggs and the Chinese are so silly. Maybe panics will purge us. Maybe science will render out the fat-headedness. But today's props are not foundations. At the moment, we're licked. If an individual exhibited the symptoms of our society, he'd be sent to a hospital for the criminally insane—and he'd die there quickly. America! A close race between science and the archæologists of the future. Thousands of people know what to do. Most of the procedure has been made self-evident by patient research. But nobody knows how. Nobody. And I try to love this country."

PART IV

SATURDAY AFTERNOON

"IN the great city of New York," said Finnley as we sat beside my well, "I have become a lesser big shot. My vocation is that of advertising. I adopted it because of Hope and I waxed exceedingly successful under the leadership of the petulant, cigar-throwing Ricardo Jones. Advertising is a fine trade because it gives its guild members a cross-section of the florescence and morbidity of big business.

"Sitting here in the mellow sunshine a spell is cast over my present and makes my past seem impossible. I have been wondering about it.

"You wouldn't think that an adult male could concentrate so much of his time and emotion and thought to business. You'd say it was silly. . . ."

Monstrously silly. Finnley picked up the article and began to read:

THE OFFICE

Suspended halfway between the street and the sky. With a view; architectural misalliances and clutter, two dirty rivers full of integrated débris, smoke and steam.

Machined, immaculate. A stained-glass window in a Gothic chamber. Next door, hand-hewn beams and wooden floors with butterfly joints. Next door, Chippendale and glazed chintz. Next door, the moderne.

THE DESK

Gargantuan rosewood. Bare. A panel of discreet buzzers on its flank and a chair behind for the behind of the Mind.

A period item, worm-holed by larvæ that understand dynamic symmetry.

THE SECRETARY
Bronx Parisian

THE MIND

	%
Intelligence	9.19
Taste	.00000000000004
Greed	17.67
Treachery	21.905
Imitativeness	18.141617
Memory	.00000000368
Imagination	.00000000000001
Sympathy	.00000000000005
Coöperativeness	.000000006
Vanity	32.434445
Miscellaneous	.6589379903199
Total	100.0% *

THE BUSINESS

There are ten times too many gasoline filling stations in populous centers, but we have more stations than most firms in all places.

By inventing activities and incidents which may be made to appear as legitimate news we supply you with inexpensive publicity.

We manufacture and distribute the patent Cosy Home. A false fireplace on casters electrically run which may be about-faced in summer to become a wall fountain with an electrically-driven pump feed. F.O.B. $198.50. Easy payments.

* Table based on maximum possibilities of individual possession of characteristics listed.

"Business . . ." Wren repeated.

Once upon a time power and wealth were the accompanying features of noble birth. Rich dynasties rose rarely from the common herd and then so slowly that their successive generations had ample time for the accumulation of culture. Moreover, since their ascendancy demonstrated a possession of intelligence, that very quality, together with an equally self-evident acquisitiveness, made possible a ready emulation of the virtues instilled by tradition in the nobility.

In those days the reign of a moron emperor was not impossible, but it was unlikely. In those days it did not behoove a king's banker to be a vulgarian. And in those days a wheelwright could not become a duke overnight, so that the spectacle of a landed gentry with kitchen manners was contemplated neither as an ambition nor as a fact.

The earth sustained vegetation. The vegetation fed cities and made ships. The earth also contained gold and iron. If a man owned the land or ruled it, he was safe from competition. The evils and abuses of such a system became finally evident to the penny-headed hordes and they overthrew it.

Out of them came the new governors, but, as soon as they found that political power in a democracy was not profitable unless an attitude of recklessness toward the penitentiary was adopted, the leaders of revolutions and their slightly superior offspring abandoned the offices to still lesser men.

They had accomplished one major task: they had removed wealth from a basis of birthright and opened it to private acquisition by each and any individual.

A puff of steam in England, meanwhile, had ushered in the gadget era and the gadget era was destined to become the little father of an infinity of fortunes.

It greatly extended the arms and legs and eyes and ears of mankind. His fragile body was speedily provided with steam shovels for hands, telescopes and microscopes for eyes, and a variety of vehicles to abet his running, so that no single person can have a faint idea of his possible resources. Enough people did hear of a sufficient number of extensions, however, to run up the world's riches in a geometric progression, and inventors and adapters presently found ways of bringing their fabrications to the public attention and creating a want for them where none previously existed.

A few men and women, furthermore, appreciated the fact that gadgets could open the road to knowledge and applied them accordingly. But the majority merely made them for each other and sold them to each other so that they might have more funds to buy from each other. The uses of the items were for pleasure and to lighten needful work. A woman wanted her muscles extended so that by pressing a button she could wash her dishes. A man desired to make a few motions with his hands and feet and thereby to reach his office without the need of a half-hour's ambulatory effort. Neither wished especially to investigate with gadgets or to be taught by them.

Not only were idle hours thus multiplied, but the bulk of the trivial interests of the masses was elevated in scale so that the earth is now agog with them.

To extend the facilities for saving the labor of numskulls and to magnify their tepid enthusiasms and poor tastes until they are as numerously available as the light of stars was not to change the race.

The changes that might have come, did not.

Housing conditions remained almost the same. A few diseases were put down but the public was apathetic toward the conquest of all but the most dramatic and disfiguring. Morals were maintained as tribal customs in spite of the revelations of the new arms and eyes. Heaven and Hell yielded here and there to astrophysics but a god without a country was still essential for crumb-witted millions. Law, the inexorable epitome of human stupidity, did not budge from its centuries of paralysis. Only the physical presence of the principles of thermodynamics differentiated today from our wretched yesterdays.

When a minority gathered a glimmering of the records of the gadgets it did not set out at once to remake the world in accordance with facts and needs. On the contrary, it bewailed the loss of the credulities and prejudices and synthetic arrangements of notions which had hitherto sustained it. It felt lost. It scanned the horizon for a new center. A god. A religion. A pap to suck imaginary liquids from. The gadgets revealed a nakedness and even the wise men ran to hunt for clothes without waiting to discover what amount of nakedness could be tolerated.

The gadgets have made us naked indeed. One by one they have removed the foetid garments of our collective ideas.

Goodness and virtue depend more upon circumstances than principle.

Justice is a rare accident.

Loyalty is often the mark of an ignoramus and perseverance of a fool.

Sin can be more accurately defined by sociologists than by the Pope.

Lust is as noble as compassion.

The innocence and sweetness of children is a myth.

Freedom is the concept of a dolt.

Hope is limited.

Purity is a vice.

Law is extraneous to fact.

Honesty is the slowest road to riches.

Most history is counterfeit.

No war is noble.

Morality is the product of exigency.

All men are unequal.

There is no free will.

There is no god.

A good pituitary is more important than a saintly mother.

Naked indeed. The theologians yelled folly. The reformers exhibited their own frustrations. The believers were not thinkers. The thinkers were misinformed. Nothing is what it was once thought to have been and the church and the schoolhouse remain the sounding boards of ignorance.

Naked indeed. Perhaps it is no marvel that the gadgets have driven mankind into a retreat from himself—for it is himself he will have ultimately to face—not judgment, not god, not torment or milk and honey—just himself. Bare man, an animal under the sun, born to live and die, born to dream and feel, his functions to evolve expandingly in his environment and to help his fellows—functions shared with the beasts—and to study the enigma of his surroundings—which is, perhaps, his occupation alone. All his inventions to conceal the limits of those offices and to make their exercise simpler have proven absurd. His recent compromises and subterfuges are even more comical. And yet—how difficult it is to drop the vanities! How hard to stand before a mirror nude and say—This—am I—and—that's all there is to it.

Hard? Impossible!

Perfidy and pretense will go through the ages. What the intelligent few cannot relinquish must continue to sustain ten trillion tomnoddies yet to come. Under the surfeit of their slough a thousand civilizations may well smother. And in its meaningless meander ten billion miserable martyrs will struggle and choke.

Until tomorrow or never when the gadgets check the geometric progression of human sewage.

For we are committed to the gadgets. Whatever is left of us belongs to them, depends upon them. And if they were taken away from us, we would be compelled painfully to reconstruct them. We are committed, even though they have yet made little change in most of us and though their authors are held up to ridicule. Men who cannot think toss science aside in a pooh and demonstrate that no scientist is fit to govern because such and such a one cannot live with his mother-in-law without recourse to the obvious malpractice of letting a hatchet into her head.

No rhetoric can destroy the gadgets. No pin-brain can confute their discoveries. They are our hope. They are also—

Let us study the lens. To one man it was a corrector of strabismus, a sleuth of bacteria, a ponderer of stars. To another it became a photograph projector and while the lens peered into the unknown world it was simultaneously multiplied a thousandfold to portray the wet dreams of the mugs. Fifty cents a week will buy a microscope wherewith to inspect reality. Fifty cents a week will rent a seat in a dreamy peep-show.

It did not take long for the self-deputized leaders of the multitudes to solve the ratios of applications of the lens to possible customers. Paramecium caudatum vs. Patricia Candy. Cilia vs. legs. A vacuole vs. a mons veneris. Give the public what it wants. At best, make the public want what you have to give and if your gift has a sufficiently low common denominator you will be showered with nickels from every purse in North America.

Then came the parade of the gadgets all calculated to bring profit to the manufacturer.

A radio for your automobile.
Your coffee in a vacuum.
A tooth paste for your breath.
A telephone you can use in one hand.
A polish for your automobile.
A refrigerator with a fancy ice pan.
An automobile with airplane parts.
Synthetic heels for your shoes.
An automobile that can roll over and over.
A paint that will not blister.
An antiseptic that kills countless germs.
A linoleum in cubistic patterns.
A tire that scarcely skids.
A shaving cream that softens your whiskers.
A cigarette that tastes cool.
Shoes that support your arches.
An oil that comes from Pennsylvania.
A coffin that will not rot.
An oil with a tough film.
Trucks that wear.
A floor enamel that smooths itself.
Pipes that will not rust.
Prunes that contain sunshine.
A lipstick that will not make lips seem painted.
A pencil that spawns its own lead.

Maple syrup that is all maple syrup.
A walled bottle to keep fluids cold or hot.
A white sauce to make your shoes white.
A refrigerator that runs on a small current.
A waterproof varnish.
A detachable boat motor.
An automobile that tells time.
A chocolate with vitamins.
A razor that changes its own blades.
An electric plant that runs on gasoline.
A pipe with demountable viscera.
A motorized garden cultivator.
Electrical clocks.
A tooth paste for your gums.
A light to wear when bicycling at night.
An animal-shaped balloon for bathing.
An alarm clock that does not tick.
A bath for birds.

The gadgets and their brood. Raise any list however long to the twentieth power and you will nonetheless discover that invention keeps abreast of your arithmetic. Consider that these things are fabricated for a profit. Note that they duplicate each other until rivalry between their manufacturers is over minutiæ or irrelevancies. The automobile that rolls downhill competes with the automobile that runs headlong into a sand heap. The tooth paste that sweetens the breath and removes stains wars with the paste that checks receding gums and cools the mouth. The refrigerator with loose ice cubes is the rival of the refrigerator with a quiet motor.

In every dominion of the gadgets it might seem that mankind would choose to perfect a strain and produce it for himself as cheaply as mass creation would permit. Standardization of gadgets once terrified him but since variations in each species occur so often there is little danger of monotony. However, kings and queens rule no longer, the land is not the all-in-all of living, and engineers vie with each other for money when they should control for economy. The mugs dictate to themselves through the more self-aggrandizing of their numbers.

Each gadget has given rise to a colossal factory (Our Plant), a chain of sales outlets (Our Agencies) and, since there is no sensible government arranged for any of them, a business hierarchy (Our Executives).

Credit was expanded to abet the golden flow implicit in the gadgets. The

[227]

master minds of credit finally swallowed the plants, agencies, and executives—but that was a later jest.

Let us first consider the Hercules of the machine.

Whether he originated in Iowa or in Queens, whether he invented his gadget or stole it or developed it from another, whether he had never matriculated in a grammar school or graduated from a university makes no generic difference. He laid his hands upon the better mousetrap. That is all. Now if, after this triumph of invention or this lucky break he had relegated the better mousetrap to the means of an excellent livelihood, all might have been well. He could have used his days for many pleasant purposes.

But the good life is invisible to the boobs or its attainment is difficult, for the mousetrap maker voluntarily hoists himself by his own petard, and is caught in his own trap. Leisure and a private life cease to interest him. The decent profit to be obtained from persons troubled by mice is not enough. If all people had mousetraps, he reasons, then I would become very rich. I would be the mousetrap mogul. So, until the problems of springs and wood supply and western sales resistance pop him into the clod limbo of the ground, he spends his every hour upon the proposition.

In his own words—in the words he speaks to his children—he eats mousetraps, sleeps mousetraps, drinks and dreams mousetraps. He goes mousetrap goofy. He spends a million dollars to tell the world about the depredations of mice. He hires bacteriologists to prove that mice carry disease. He causes to be published photographs of mice ten inches high yawning at men one inch high and upon them he puts labels: Destruction; The Farmer; and underneath them captions: If His Size Were Proportionate to His Menace.

A few statesful of persons are terrified into buying mousetraps.

Then sales lag. Almost everyone who needs a trap possesses a dozen. The mogul's profits dwindle and his tables show that he is selling traps only to replace those that have worn out or have been lost or broken, and to outfit the homes of newly married persons. It is conceivable to a casual observer of this dilemma that he might conclude that the mousetrap market had found its level, that his invention had earned its just reward, that he could at last accept his dividends and interests and cease to annoy himself night and day with the trifle of traps. But to him the thought smacks of defeat, resignation, failure. He burns the midnight oil. He thinks. He grows testy. He abandons his annual two weeks of salmon fishing. J. Morton Gleet licked? Never!

Then out of the toils of his piddling mind and the darkness of the night come

[228]

Mousetraps in colors!

The mousetrap is always with us. Who wants the dirty, red-painted horror that for too long has made the kitchens of the world a revolting spectacle? The modern mousetrap—the mousetrap of the hour—will be exclusively set in the houses of the élite. Effective, painless, quick, self-sterilizing, self-deodorizing, and *cute!*

The mogul has banished the lean years and once again he and his associates and employees can dine and slumber on mousetraps.

Now, our dear Gleet may suffer when he is compared to other tycoons. A motor-car maker has chosen a finer object for his thought. But to the gods, the difference between chrome-super-mesh and enamotraps is nil. Piddle for profit. A way—a wasteful way—of making a living. But certainly not a fitting career for a man.

Finnley stopped reading. He tore the article slowly into strips and the strips into squares. He threw them on the ground and they blew against the barberry hedge. I found a scrap of the essay long afterward when I was cleaning leaves from the bush stems—sentence middles—indecipherable and yet full of meaning.

"Nonsense!" he said. "Sheer nonsense. I thought it would be good. Someone tore it from a magazine and gave it to me. 'You'll agree with this,' they said. I don't. Give any writer in North America what is called an 'angle' and he will produce just such ringing half-truths. The gadgets do change civilization. And Mr. Gleet does boost his sales by high-pressure blither. I invent it for him. But you can say only two impressive things about business: it's a cinch, and it's a human activity."

Because he was silent and poured more cognac into his glass, I repeated, "Cinch?"

"Certainly it's a cinch. Buying. Selling. That's all there is to it. Everything else is superadded technique. There isn't a branch of any business on earth that couldn't be learned by an intelligent man in two weeks. In fact—there isn't much that couldn't be learned in two weeks. I don't mean that you could capture every detail of any gross enterprise in that time—but—I'll bet you could run a country bank after an intensive course of that length—or even perform a creditable appendectomy—if you had the nerve. Matter of nerve entirely.

"The human side is discounted—but that's the other important aspect. Business isn't economics, or sociology, or even psychology until it's history. Then you can name it. Until then it's human nature. I had a secretary—"

Miss Clerrindger always arrived at the office at ten minutes of nine. The leeway in time was for subway accidents, fire lines, and brimstone rains, probably. Her entrance was greeted by the nods of eleven other secretaries who occupied a large room from which they could be individually summoned by push-buttons. Electrical contact established by one of those buttons created no efficiency—destroying noise, however. Ricardo Jones had been at pains to eliminate noise ever since the invention of the word "decible." Instead, a green light was made to burn, and it turned to red with the second touch of the concealed stud on the desk of whatever executive wished to dictate, or to ponder to a public, or to view a member of the opposite sex.

On a day in March in 1932 she proffered her usual salutation and then hung up in a steel locker her raincoat, rubbers, and umbrella. It was a sunny day—but the papers had prophesied rain. She sniffed as she closed the locker, without knowing that the derogatory exhalation was due to man's sloth. In his unwillingness to improve his estate, man has permitted to exist for himself all manner of anti-rain habiliments which, when moistened, exude odors so foul and nauseous as to make their wearers faintly sick—odors so rank and vomitous that thousands of persons refrain from collective human society whilever the clouds are ominous.

Afterward she went to her desk. Finnley's mail was neatly

heaped upon it. She opened the letters one by one with a long fingernail file. There were reminders from clients, and solicitations from advertisers whose profession was to advertise for advertisers, and requests for data; there was a note from a man in Idaho suggesting a slogan for a brand of soups; there was a cheering missive of praise which concerned a campaign in progress; there was what Miss Clerrindger called a "complaint," and a note about the possibility of the sale of goat meat in America which Miss Clerrindger filed under "Misc." although she knew that Finnley would have enjoyed the letter.

"I want to read all nut letters," he had said.

But Miss Clerrindger disapproved. Once he had answered a nut and the man had come to the office. He had invented what he called a trapless fly trap and in order to demonstrate it he had let loose one thousand flies in the room. The invention had been about eighteen per cent successful. Swatters, diligently wielded by Miss Clerrindger and her secretarial associates had eventually accounted for the rest of the flies—but not until a long reach for a bluebottle had started Miss Clerrindger's most severe attack of lumbago.

When Miss Clerrindger had read all of Finnley's mail she found herself with time on her hands. A few typewriters were ticking semi-noiselessly and one girl sat with the stethoscope of a dictating machine in her ears, her face quite immobile, her hands rapidly typing, as she listened to an impassioned love appeal from the assistant head of the art department. The clock made up its mind to jump a minute and did so. The hour hand then pointed to a phrase of Ricardo Jones stenciled under the temporal engine: "Every minute leaves one less."

It was a slogan to which many employees often added, "Thank God."

Miss Clerrindger found an occupation—cleaning her typewriter—which did not require much thought, and she was thus enabled to sink into her favorite pursuit—daydreaming.

Now it is true, but it is odd, that people have become unself-conscious about their nocturnal or formal dreams. People are rather proud of them, in fact. "Last night," they will say with charming candor, "I dreamed I was walking through a hall in the shape of a woman's body. When I had reached the middle of the first vestibule I saw my mother. She was reading a novel and poking at a dog's belly with her foot. The sight enraged me so that I picked up a baseball bat and brained her with it. Whereupon her brains tumbled out and I saw that they were all little red mouths like kisses and I woke up feeling both depressed and extraordinarily excited."

At any moment any person may be expected to produce such a rigmarole.

But daydreaming is different. It is daydreaming that should interest the fortune-telling amateurs of what is alleged to be the science of psychology. People are not just reluctant to discuss daydreams: they refuse to discuss them. They will give any lenience to their sleeping minds, but they will disavow all the exotic flowers of their semi-conscious reveries. Snap your fingers at a subway-riding moron or a belimousined theatrical producer when you catch him in that opaque-eyed, dandle-chinned state and ask, "What were you thinking?" "Why," the answer will be, "I was thinking about the World's Series"—or "About the plight of the coal miners." The answer will never be, "I was wondering if any woman had ever had sexual congress with three men simultaneously."

Miss Clerrindger's daydream was a wow.

It concerned, naturally, Finnley. March, 1932, represented a high point in the lush flux of popular fiction and motion pictures having to do with skyscraper love, lust and libido. There was scarcely a secretary in the edifice which housed the Jones Agency who had not looked for several weeks with new eyes at her boss—wondering if his wife was discontented, his sex life unsatisfactory, his Buffalo appointments bona fide, and so on. There are fashions in such things.

Miss Clerrindger began with Finnley's new suit. He had bought it on the previous Wednesday and he had displayed it—although God knew she had seen it the instant he entered his sanctum. He had stood up, in fact, for her. She had observed the lithe curve of his left hip.

Her fantasy removed that suit in a trice. There stood Finnley in his underwear, looking like the men in the garter advertisements.

He smiled at her.

She frowned. "Rather proud of your figure, aren't you, Mr. Wren?"

He was embarrassed. "Really—my dear—"

"What are you doing in my apartment almost nude?"

"I couldn't stay away. I stole in here. You were absent—"

"Don't you think you better go?"

He stared at her—a man utterly under the spell of the fierce and stirring passions which she held locked within her rather commonplace exterior. "I can't!" He spoke hoarsely—the way he had spoken to his second wife on the telephone one day. His second wife was going to lose him now. They had been alone together too long to go on as they had been—alone in their modernistic aerie above the cruel, voluptuous city.

She toyed with the handle of the samovar that stood beside her bed. "Well—Finnley—"

She undressed him completely, and tried to visualize. There was a mist here and there—

The green light became red.

As she trotted through the corridor toward his office, not in the slightest perturbed by her recent intimacy, she found herself sniffing again. Into her nostrils seeped a sweet and fœtid odor. Sinus. She remembered half-sensing it on the subway. She was coming down with another cold. In thirteen seconds she had garnered a dozen symptoms from her slightly passé carcass: chilly feet, scratchy throat, burning nasal passages, sweaty armpits, vague pains in the back, eleventh magnitude headache, heavy stomach, quivers, a bright flash, incipient canker sore, coated teeth—and the characteristic smell.

She reached Wren's door.

She opened it.

He sat at a broad desk upon the top of which was nothing at all: an ant egg would have been conspicuous there. Finnley had copied the caprice from Ricardo Jones, who, in turn, emulated a fashion: most of the routine of life is due to the age of the individual performer or to a reigning fad. The fad of empty desks for big executives may be considered, as an illustration, a lulu.

"Yes?" said Miss Clerrindger, and, although she would have given her soul to avoid it, she felt compelled to clear her throat—which she did in a manner that made Finnley conscious of three-quarters of his nerve-paths.

He said, "You have a cold!"

"Oh, no. Really, Mr. Wren—"

"But you're getting one. Why not take the day off?"

She shook her head. "It's impossible. I have a mountain of work that must be done."

Neither of them had a damned thing to do—and Finnley had summoned her in the hope that her presence would necessitate the invention of an activity more engrossing than sticking back with library paste a corner of the Chinese silver tea box paper with which Genevieve Jones had caused his walls to be decorated.

However, the sight of Miss Clerrindger with a cold was always repugnant to him. He could recall days of hours during which he had sat dictating while his mind blazed with the thought: if she would only blow her nose and get it over with! No cold was bad enough to force her to take a holiday. Sometimes, at the apogee of her infections, Finnley himself stayed at home to avoid the spectacle of martyred diligence a-drip.

Miss Clerrindger would have preferred falling liquidescent on the floor to allowing another secretary to do her work—a younger secretary, or a prettier. There was none more efficient, she was sure.

She sat down and opened her book.

Wren walked behind her and thumbed his nose at her. Then, with a start, he wondered if she had been able to see his gesture reflected in her glasses. He grimaced at her from one side. She wore no glasses. That, he reflected, was strange, because he had always imagined her as wearing glasses. He was about to remark upon the fact when he realized that it might hurt her feelings.

"A letter to Blake and Robbins," he said. "On that matter of shoe copy. Dear Ed."

Miss Clerrindger began to write. She could feel cold browsing about her intestines. She could feel it gnawing at every pore. Dew appeared on the chromo make-up of her plain face. Her brown, overshiny and thinning hair began to separate into strands as her arm-motion jiggled it. Finnley dictated on and on—using his most effusive and hence time-taking system: paragraphs of numbered points.

7. *Mr. Jones and I both feel that you will reach a larger audience by - - - - -*

8. *An examination of the campaigns of seventeen shoe manufacturers shows - - - - -*

9. *Class presentation of your product, while it might build a certain prestige, would nevertheless - - - - -*

Tripe, Miss Clerrindger thought.

And Finnley thought that the back of her head looked like a water-logged cabbage.

Presently Miss Clerrindger sighed heavily and sneezed.

[235]

Finnley walked lightly and quickly away. Particles of sputum twinkled on a sunbeam.

Inside the garments of Miss Clerrindger there was, concomitant with the biphase explosion, a genteel pop.

Now the nature of that really inaudible popping sound was obscure, delicate, and disastrous. Miss Clerrindger was a virgin spinster of well-tailored outer aspect. She wore suits, as a rule; she purchased them at Macy's, had them dry-cleaned regularly, and kept from four to sixteen months behind the trend of fashion in order not to be embarrassed by the possession of a garment that would become obsolete before it became shiny. However, the long habit of subsurface privacy had made her less careful in the matter of undergarments.

Miss Clerrindger's undergarments were made, I regret to say, of rayon. They were of the sort one sees on counters—not in neat piles. And the rayon, with a little washing, took on a cartography of assorted hues. Because the price of laundering is excessive in New York, and because no human eyes had seen her in her scanties since her fifteenth year, Miss Clerrindger had grown remiss or perhaps economical in the matter of change.

One of her intimate vestments was a pair of bloomers: pink rayon. They were upheld by an elastic around her waist, and her maidenhood was further protected by two more elastic circles which clinched each leg of the garment firmly below her knees. Her bloomers were of such an inferior quality that the rubber tape within them usually lost its vigor in a short while and had to be replaced. When that condition occurred in bloomers already donned, a temporary repair could be made by pulling a section of the elastic into a loop which, after it was knotted, took up the slack. On the morning of this day she had resorted to the measure.

But now, under the strain of orange juice, milk, and butter cakes—which she had eaten at Childs—together with a sigh and a sneeze—the master cord had ruptured.

In other words, if Miss Clerrindger stood up, it was likely that her breeches would slump around her ankles.

Of course, there was a chance that she might clutch them. There was a chance that they might be stuffed into the upper ridge of her corset and thus be made to remain in suspension, so that by leaning forward and pushing her stomach out, she might contrive to escape eventually from Finnley's office with no greater embarrassment than that caused by being observed in a mildly idiotic posture.

However, as she reached the nineteenth point in Finnley's letter and as she made a furtive and tentative manual inspection of the situation, she confirmed the worst of her expectations. Already, her midriff was badly askew. The broken bloomer elastic had dropped below her waist line. She could not distinguish between the fabric of her slip and the fabric of the bloomers through the material of her suit. Relief by corset suspension was out of the question. Moreover, she found, with a new prick of alarm, that one of the straps of her singlet had parted with the same sneeze, and now it hung down in the area of confusion, contributing two inches of loose elastic to the mêlée.

Miss Clerrindger decided that she would have to sit in her chair until Mr. Wren left his office. She did not have the courage to risk a quick grab as she rose.

Finnley, meanwhile, had not been unconscious of her fidgety dilemma. At first he thought with sympathy that her cold might have been unexpectedly complicated by woman's blight. But his memory was so accurate, and her powers of dissimulation so feeble, that he recollected the precise past date. By the subcutaneous torture on her face and the sly snatchings she made, he eventually realized not what undergarment would fall if she stood, but that some undergarment had slipped its moorings.

He continued to dictate. But now he was amused. His

morning had improved. He felt that fate had given him an instrument for revenging himself on Miss Clerrindger's colds. He knew perfectly why she would never surrender to her afflictions. He even knew about the wave of office-lechery—and its source. He understood that his secretary did not love him, that she could care or think emotionally of no one but herself and of herself only in the feeblest terms, and he deduced that she was jealous of him because she was vain about herself. Usually her tangle of small mental vice and prodigious inhibition made no difference to him. Occasionally he was annoyed by it. Today he was pleased.

He finished his letter.

"That will be all," he said.

Miss Clerrindger did not budge. "You should answer Mr. Newt, of Tumult Hot Showers."

"So I should." He dictated a brief note to Newt.

"And Mr. Lusk, the man who wanted information about silk."

"Dear Lusk—" he began. And afterward he said, "If you'll just transcribe those letters now, Miss Clerrindger—"

She blushed.

She recovered.

Danger threatened.

"I believe," she said calmly, "that Mr. Jones wanted you to step into his office when you were through answering your mail this morning. He mentioned it to me last night as I was leaving after six."

The fact that she had stayed an hour overtime did not interest Finnley. Many people stayed overtime—generally because they had nothing more interesting to do. It was certain that Miss Clerrindger spent her pleasantest hours in the office—a certainty born of comparative sterilities. But Finnley was delighted that even at a crucial time she could not omit entering a bid for trivial kudos. Six o'clock indeed! The hell with six o'clock!

He would have liked her better for leaving at three o'clock without excuse or apology.

Finnley sat down on the top of his desk. "You know," he said, in a casual tone, "people are always getting into trouble because of their personal habits. A little carelessness, a little slackness about the most unimportant thing may lead to all sorts of embarrassment."

Miss Clerrindger paled. She said, "Really?"

"Take Ricardo," Finnley continued innocently. "That habit of his of throwing cigars whenever he gets indignant. Hazardous performance. Most hazardous. Genevieve has covered the floor of his office with fireproof stuff that feels like art gum under your feet. That helps—yes—indeed it helps. But it's not enough. Day before yesterday—I was in with him for an important conference. Leslie Borden Beasley, as a matter of fact. The automobile manufacturer. We were trying to get a piece of his account. Destiny is a peculiar thing, Miss Clerrindger. You don't mind? A little interlude rests the anterior lobes. I sound like my father. Well, we were talking about destiny. Mr. Beasley had arranged to meet Mrs. Beasley in Ricardo's office before lunch. She arrived with one of those lap dogs—you might as well have a rubber one—because all they do is squeak. And a rubber one wouldn't have to be housebroken. I beg your pardon. However, this atrobilious canine nuisance did have one trick—it proved. Mrs. Beasley was on the heavy side of fifty and asthmatic. Snorted. I sponged off the best chair and dangled her over it till she fell. She was wearing purple orchids—the worst kind, I think. Hate purple orchids. The green ones are interesting. But the purple—or orchid orchids—nix. Anyway, we fell into a discussion—Beasley, Ricardo and I—while his wife and her dog wheezed in the big chair. Presently, Ricardo began to fume. Beasley had told him the design of their new line of cars. They're going to have cars that are quasi-streamlined, with enormous front fenders. Ricardo forgot himself and forgot Mrs. Beasley enough to shout, "God scalp me! Why don't you hang elephant ears on them!" Then he threw his cigar. The Pekinese let out a yelp of delight—the first time I ever heard the breed emit any sound of pleasure—and leaped from his mistress' lap. His eyes followed the arc of the cigar. It hit the ceiling, showered sparks, and dropped. The dog, with commendable skill, caught it in his mouth."

"Very funny," said Miss Clerrindger.

"It cost us a hundred thousand dollars the first year," said Finnley.

"Perhaps that is what Mr. Jones would like to speak to you about."

"Oh, no. No. He'd rather I didn't speak about it. The dog recovered, too. Mrs. Beasley sent us the veterinary's bill. Sixty-three dollars and a half. It was worth sixty-three fifty. But not worth a hundred thousand."

"Anyway—he wanted to speak to you about something."

"I'm not in the mood. I think I'll spend the day here. Very congenial. Have my lunch sent up."

Miss Clerrindger perspired.

Finnley made a tour of his chamber. "Reminds me of another odd thing that happened here yesterday. A man came to sell me a bleached grizzly bear skin. Helen wanted it for a rug in our new apartment. She'd read of it in a swopper's ad in a western magazine that she'd noticed frozen in the ice at Lake Placid. Man's name was Taylor. John Taylor. He'd been on a whaler once. Harpooner. Offered to throw a hatrack through a partition. Said it was only wall board. Said he could throw a crowbar through a brick wall. He's trying to get a job as a fireman. He writes a little, too. Anyway, he told me a story that would curl your hair, about climbing a mountain in Alaska. It was winter. They were after gold. The Yukon. Cold. Eighty below, he said. By the way—you can throw hatracks through walls the same way you can shoot candles through two inches of pine with a shotgun. Matter of inertia. Anyway, they got to the peak of the mountain on their last strip of pemmican and what do you think they found on top of a rock cairn there?"

"I'm sure I don't know."

"You'd never be able to guess." Finnley shook his head in solemn amazement. "He gave me what they found as a souvenir. It's in my desk drawer—the middle one." Finnley looked at his watch and walked to the door. "Better see Jones after all." He opened the door—to the infinite relief of Miss Clerrindger. "A souvenir of a strange exploit—a strange object in a strange place. Take a look at it, Miss Clerrindger. A safety-pin."

He departed.

Miss Clerrindger pulled open the middle drawer. There was nothing inside it at all.

She resigned that same day.

"Business," Wren repeated. "Maybe we'd better start back. It's a long paddle. And I'm a shade squiffy."

"We could leave the canoe—and I could have someone take it down."

"Paddle it? I'm afraid you might not find another day as calm as this for weeks."

"I mean—truck it down. We could put the canoe on a truck and ride with it."

"That sounds promising."

We walked from my garden to the road. Finnley carried the cognac. At the nearest house we telephoned Jimmie, the local expressman. He met us between my place and the Post Road. We drove to the beach, loaded the canoe, and started for the Dwyers'. In a state of pleasant exhilaration we clambered into the back of the truck, righted the canoe, knelt inside it, and very slightly assisted our forward progress by paddling the air. We were met by the returning stream of Yale graduates and their friends. Traffic was slow; Yale had won; we obtained from passing enthusiasts several chrysanthemums, a banner, and two ornamental badges.

We had planned something in the nature of an arrival. But as Jimmie drove us toward the Dwyer residence (with what thoughts no man can tell) there drifted to our ears on the cider-smelling air of that Indian summer afternoon music from a piano. Finnley put down his paddle and turned his coat right side out. I did the same. He beckoned Jimmie to the boathouse. Quietly we lifted the canoe onto its rack. We paid our truckman. We walked toward the house, listening.

"It's Vi," Finnley said.

Vi meant nothing to me.

"Vi. My sister. What the devil is she doing here?"

We went inside.

A half dozen of the people who had been introduced to me as Whittingtons were sitting in the Dwyers' living room. At the piano was Violet Wren. I had heard her play once at Carnegie Hall and I would have recognized her, I think. On the previous night I had vaguely connected Violet Wren and her chamber music society with Finnley's sister—but I had given no thought to the connection. Her orchestra, in any case, had been hushed by the depression; her success had been minor.

Violet Wren was about thirty. She still had the dull golden hair that Finnley had described, the pale oval face—and white arms and hands. She did not look like Finnley—although if he had been blond and pensive, she would have had a spiritual resemblance to him.

She saw him come into the room, but she continued to play. He sat down beside her on the bench.

"What?" he asked.

"Been looking for you." The music did not falter.

I deliberately eavesdropped.

"Trouble?"

"Not exactly."

"Well?"

"Tom's entered a monastery."

PART V

SATURDAY NIGHT

INNLEY walked toward the window. Tom was his brother. A younger imitation of himself, he had once said. Nothing more to complete the portrait. But assuredly cowls and cloisters were foreign to Finnley Wren and hence to imitations of him. The music reached a whirlwind passage. I walked toward Finnley.

He was grinning.

Grinning sardonically.

"My brother," he said, "entered a monastery."

"I heard."

He spoke underneath the music. "You play football. You break track records. You go to the head of your class. You turn communist and make speeches in Union Square. You dwell in a house run by a woman who has elephantiasis. You live with the daughter of a speakeasy proprietor. You go to South America for a copper company, next. You come back with malaria. You then decide to be an astronomer. Through it all, you lead a second life in your own home, enjoying parental patronage and pretending that you are taking postgraduate work at Columbia—with a field course in Peru. Astronomy excites you, but you haven't the stamina to study the requisite amount of mathematics. One day you find yourself selling neckties from door to door. Disgusted by the discovery, you hire yourself to a road construction gang. You have your ankle broken, lie in a hospital for a month, fall in love with the patient in the next room, and become increasingly confused when she moves from town with her family, making no explanation of her actions at all. You then come to your older brother

Finnley and ask him what the hell." Wren looked ferociously at me. "What would you have told him, Phil?"

"I can't say."

"What could I tell him? Think of that for a life. He was bright. He was filled with energy—not much perseverance—but plenty of energy. At every street corner in the maze of his soul he stood and begged the world to take him and use him. Sometimes he was foolish, sometimes he failed, sometimes he had bad luck. He had plenty of courage, though, and a good education. He never wandered with the bums on the road today because he could always find something to do, somebody to interest himself in, some cause to espouse. I put him to work in my office. He stayed five months. He wrote the best copy we've ever had. Then he got himself drunk one night and fell down an iron fire escape. It didn't hurt him, but when he reached the bottom he sat up and decided that the advertising business was not worthy of his aspirations. I tried to explain that not what you did mattered so much as how you did it, and he argued so furiously about money and property and human life that we very nearly had a fist fight. That was last August. The next time I saw him, he was operating a cigarette-making machine in a white uniform in the window of a store on Broadway. Then father wrote me—he always writes such things because, I think, he likes to dictate them to his stenographer-nurse, that he was treating Tom for syphilis. He said that Tom had caught it from a toilet in the Metropolitan Museum of Art where he had been seized with diarrhea caused by eating cherries while he was making sketches for an art course he had enrolled in. I telephoned Tom and got him a good doctor. He decided to write a book on the vitality that his enforced celibacy would give him. I rented a room for him and gave him an allowance. He wrote one sentence, 'We gathered round the devil's table for a tasty dish of roast stuffed

Long Island cherubim.' Then he quit and went to Canada with some college pals for a week-end. I had a letter from him saying that he had decided to stay there for a while. Now—"

Vi came to the end of her concerto. The final beatitude ceased to hum in the copper-wound strings. Several of her listeners rose and praised her.

Finnley crossed the room. "How did you find out where I was?"

"The doorman at your house suggested I go to a particular speakeasy. The man there said that you'd told him on Thursday night that if you were alive at all you'd be in Connecticut. I knew you came here sometimes—so I telephoned."

"I see. And about Tom—"

"A monastery. He's taken a billion vows. We won't be able to see him for a number of years."

"How many?"

"I forget. Five. Maybe it was ten."

"Well—that's the end of Tom."

"His letter sounded very somber and yet very happy."

"Those letters always do." Finnley grunted furiously. "He ought to have his ass kicked."

Vi flushed. I felt sorry for her. It was evident that Finnley felt that an affront had been put upon him by his brother. He was closer to bad temper in that instant than I ever saw him. He would not apologize, however—unless his next words, grumbled in a reduced voice, could be taken for a sort of retraction: "It's like committing suicide. It's the same thing, as a matter of fact. Come on, Vi. Let's run off a measure."

She walked back to the piano with him—obediently and yet with reserve. They sat down together—brother and sister. He began a simple exercise and presently they were engrossed in an impromptu elaboration of it.

I was listening, spellbound and bewildered, when someone

[249]

touched my arm. It was Flora. Her hair was still curly and her body was as insinuatingly rounded, but Flora seemed aloof and mature. She looked like a youngish widow about to retire from excessive philandering and settle down to one or two lovers and social service.

"Where have you been?" she asked. The words might have carried criticism, under the circumstances. As Flora pronounced them, they did not.

"At my house up the shore planting tulips and getting tight with Finnley."

"What do you think of his sister?"

"I've just met her."

"Well?"

I made a thrust at opinion. "She seems nice. Cold. A bit frightened. Too virtuous. Why?"

Flora shrugged. "Folliculin, Theelin. Sex hormones. She hadn't enough. I gave them to her. So now she's come to Dwyers for the rest of the cure."

"I thought she'd come because of her brother."

"Fuff!" said Flora, giving the remarkable word considerable emphasis. "Think of the things her brother has done without even getting her out of bed on a warm summer evening! She had an endocrine insufficiency. I've been fixing it up. The poor kid has been a sexual zombie for fifteen years. Good pianist, though. Finnley's more fun to listen to. She plays better. Tonight will be her big night. Nobody to chaperon her—"

"Finnley—"

"Finnley's going away. This morning at dawn while you were checking up on your sheep count I walked out in a perfect lather of sunrise and Finnley was ordering a car for tonight. Talking to the gardener. Going to leave before supper and get back before morning on Sunday."

At the piano I heard Finnley say, "Play your new opus, Vi. What's the name of it now?"

She replied in a low voice. "The bolero? It's called 'Locomotive.' "

"Shoot." He leaned back on his arms. She began to play.

"What's he going away for?" I asked. "And where?"

"God knows. Or maybe he doesn't."

We had steamed clams at dinner.

They followed a procession of cocktails.

Finnley was gone.

i was satisfied to devour clams and then a lobster and innumerable soufflé potatoes. enough people were talking merrily to make conversation unnecessary on my part. they talked about the result of the elections in new york and the new deal and the blue eagles president roosevelt had plastered upon the fatherland. they talked about the fact that technological unemployment among farmers was a general but little recognized condition. they talked very learnedly about yields per acre and efficiencies of soils and fertilizers and about irrigation. it bumbled through my mind that finnley had said people discussed nothing but sex—and i realized even then that he had used a sort of hyperbole to make his point. he would have held to the assertion on the grounds that sex brought these people together. but it was different conversation from the chitchat of my early era, my student days, and my later youth. when i was young we learned words and subjects and we imagined that the world would never change much. airplanes might go faster —but the major differences would be of that kind and magnitude. in college in the once highly romanticized and now already vanishing post-war years we talked about god and women and gins and beauty and art. we seldom thought of business; politics meant nothing to us. even through the depression we had clung to the substance of that youth; we had believed in the western intellectual desert and in rococo speakeasies and in an eventual upturn; we had never thought of attempting to uproot tammany hall and we wanted to keep down the income tax because, if our incomes were small then, we expected that some day they would be large.   a lovely girl at my right was engaged, even as i meandered through those reminiscences, in saying that she could run a tractor if it became necessary, and the man at her right described an experiment in farming for his own consumption which he had concluded with great success that summer.   i had a presentiment then of america changing into a nation much different, much more honest, much more difficult for the existence of parasites—and i thought of myself as one, for a while—although i can run a tractor and i have lived on farms.   my presentiment was evanescent, but it was very strong.   the people around me were twenty-five and thirty and thirty-five.   they were taking hold of this new world —taking hold wherever their fingers touched substance.   they were not especially frightened—although they were well born and accustomed to many luxuries.   perhaps, they said, we would still have luxuries.   certainly we would, they agreed a moment later.   only—

only what? they didn't know.   this reaction from the wrongs of our economic system appeared to me to be far stronger than the rejection of biblism and ancient morals by that nearly forgotten generation once called young.   and when i contemplated the broad effect of the latter revolt, the future implied by this calm insurgence was startling.

then i thought of tom wren in his monastery and i thought of a few other young men whom i knew.   very young men. they had matured in the arms of defeat.   they spawned into consternation.   those who immediately preceded them had obtained stances in the nation before its revealing debacle.   those who were to follow might have greater opportunities than had ever existed on earth: they might grow up in a world consciously adopting civilization and its social and economic consequences. but there was a group now young that had no especial hope of reward for virtue, that had fear of punishment for only the less attractive self-indulgences. they were surely at a loss: a by-product of evolution. the history of their tens of thousands would never be written and their failures would belong to the unimpressive and unimportant tragedies of individuals.

then they began to talk of france and germany and russia, and i who had come conscious thinking of those nations only in regard to their reputations for bravery in trench warfare, sank back to my alcoholic remembering. another stream of melancholic truth poured over my brain. the war had ended a race, a philosophy, a social form. and the succeeding race, philosophy, and form was now also about to vanish. we had all precipitated it—first by insisting on being sensible and rational, and finally by doing something about things. voting, maybe. or writing. or merely talking.

the singing, frittering, white-shirted college boys marched into oblivion with flappers and partly remembered songs, and in the procession now nearing the great blank gate went rugged individualism and prohibition, while overhead our now recognized perplexities loomed appalling and grim. so wound the windmill of my thoughts while they talked.

rome was not burning. but rome was purging itself, and any single person might be caught and killed by the cleansing tide.

"You can see what to do," one of the men said. "And that's a lot. How to do it will be the next step—and a bloody one."

"Not bloody," a girl replied. "But painful."

They were watching the same shades pass into history as myself. They had no regrets.

Why should I be sobered by anything akin to regret?

[253]

The fire in the grate was burning. Vi came and sat beside me. I could detect a change in her face that had occurred since afternoon. She was excited and vivacious.

"Talk to me about Finnley," I said.

"What shall I tell you?"

"What you think of him."

"Oh." She considered. "My opinion of him has changed. I used to think, when I was little, that he was wonderful. Of course, he never paid much attention to me. And he was stand-offish even with most of the kids at school. He had a million hobbies—I couldn't possibly list them. He collected everything from stamps—to mushrooms and toadstools—which rotted. And he learned to do all those handbook things—carpentry and masonry and making musical instruments from tin cans and resined strings. Then—when I was about seventeen—" she paused and seemed to make a decision before she went on—"I tried to hate him. He managed to disgrace us all a little. After he became successful in advertising—I seldom saw him. So he grew to be enigmatic and fairly unreal. Recently—how-ever—we've been together a good deal. He took me to Flora—did you know she is a doctor? And a good one? Off and on we go places together—have been for months. So that now I feel that I know him well."

"And now you think—?"

"I don't believe he's mastered himself yet. He ought to be quite a useful person in the world. He wants to be."

"Useful!"

Vi nodded complacently. "A great many people think he's a genius. He's not. He's talented. So—was everyone in the family. That's all people ever are—talented. Day in and out he's a quite unphenomenal person—although he's shrewd and controlled and he has a lot of fun—two kinds—private and public. I don't believe, for instance, that with the exception of Ricardo Jones, any of the people who work for Finnley think there's very much unusual about him. And why should they?"

"Miss Clerrindger must have thought so."

Violet laughed. "Wasn't she funny?"

"She must have been." I thought a moment. Violet was no more communicative than most sisters. After all, it undoubtedly seemed to her that there was little to tell. "How is your father these days?"

Her expression changed. The original aspect of her face gave place to an unwilling concentration as she considered her father. By and by she said, "Some day I would like to see him die the way my mother died."

It was a curse.

She stood up and walked away from me to the piano.

A couple relinquished the bench.

She played the "Second Hungarian Rhapsody."

Finnley Wren drove toward New York on a mission which it was not his business to undertake. He was passionately eager to succeed in it and he was at the same time almost sure he would fail. He was going to enter into and to meddle with the lives of other human beings. He was going to call on a woman he had never seen. He was not even certain that she would be at her home.

He sat at the wheel of a gray roadster, wrapped in an old, borrowed coonskin coat. His flat-brimmed hat was pulled over his eyes and he drove faster than the rate permitted by the square roadside signs, but so smoothly that his speed seemed normal. At Bridgeport he encountered a succession of traffic lights, but he moved unruffled from each to the next as the bright ruby eyes winked down to green.

He drove past hundreds of houses and factories and stores,

past myriad fly-specked collections of stuff in windows that blazed and windows that exhibited their stale chocolates and cut-out lithographs in the glimmer of a single bulb. Fairfield, Westport, Stamfort, Norwalk, Greenwich. At Greenwich he turned right and wound through wooded, night-chilled hills where golf flags leaned in their pools of grass and polo ponies whinnied steam into the fecund air of stables. The Saturday night main thoroughfare of White Plains took his attention from the infinity of his almost thoughtless mind and bestowed it upon hundreds of horribly ugly people who stood in the markets gazing at vegetables and who crossed the street with that snotty carelessness of stupid pedestrians which through God's good justice gets many of them killed.

Then he turned into the Bronx River Parkway and bowled along its shadows toward the city. In the daytime the land-scaping along the banks of the river is visible, pretty, and sometimes even beautiful; but at night the narrow strip of half-hearted return-to-nature gives place to the real estate developments it has pushed back and becomes only a decent road through the revolting flats that represent centralization. His eyes caught window-squares from thousands of cubic apart-ments, yellow rectangles where we sad fools make our patently tentative abodes.

For a while thereafter the city roared around him. He drove through it wishing that he did not know it so well in order that he might make a stranger's assay of its personality. Then he wished he could come to it from another age and experience the shock of a century's changes in one night like this.

A bridge over the East River. Traveling upon it was very much like flying—its slow curve imparted the same sense of lift and its height above the black water was detached and disquieting.

At a single-windowed restaurant with a name upon its vitrine in enameled block letters Finnley ate two hamburger sandwiches and drank a cup of coffee.

Then he drove out on Long Island.

Once he stopped beside a policeman who stood in the center of a cross-street, stamping his feet on the blue rails of a trolley line. He asked directions and moved away with the three moaning crescendos of changing gears.

At last he found his goal: a brick apartment house with grilled iron doors and two coach lamps. There were maple trees in front of it and their leaves had fallen.

He parked his car and went into a vestibule. The brightness there and the warmth gave him a delirious feeling which did not depart when he rang a bell marked "Sloan." His fingers were so cold that the button had roused no tactile response in them.

It passed through his brain that perhaps he was a ghost.

The buzzer on the lock startled him. He turned a brass knob and started up a flight of carpeted steps. A woman's voice dropped anxiously down the stair well. "Yes? Who is it?"

Wren went up. He took a deep breath.

On the third floor, half inside a door, was a woman of thirty-five. She wore a white satin blouse and a long satin skirt. Her eyes were dark and nervous. She smiled—a curious concession to a dishonest convention. "You must have rung the wrong bell."

"You're Mrs. Ames?"

"Yes—but—"

"My name is Finnley Wren. I want to see you very much. I want to talk to you—about Terry."

He could see her grow pale. Her ears were silhouetted against the light of a silk-shaded lamp and the color went out of them. "Has—anything—?"

Finnley shook his head and spoke very quietly. "No. Nothing like that. I'm not even presuming on an old friendship. I've never seen your husband."

"He's no longer my husband. I'm sorry—but—it's late—and I have no interest in Terry—in him."

Finnley was some distance away from her—far enough so that, if she wished, she could easily retreat into the house before he could reach her side. He did not move. "I drove all the way from New Haven—farther, as a matter of fact—to see you. A girl named Estelle gave me your address. Estelle—" Finnley could not think of her last name. He halted for a crippled instant and then went on. "You see—Helen—is my wife. She left me two days ago. I assure you I mean no harm. But I have something to say to you. If you'd just allow me to talk for a little while—"

At the word "Helen" Marilyn Ames had recoiled. "Oh," she said bitterly. "I'm sorry you troubled yourself to drive here. But I can't see you."

She started to close the door. "You must," Finnley said then. His voice was low, but it was imperative. He had not budged.

"Please go." Suddenly she shut the door.

Finnley did not know what to do. This state of glacial suffering that masochistically rejected all solace was familiar to him. But he had known of few people who could maintain it for so long. Most old wounds in human beings are healed, and only a sense of duty makes them attempt to keep the scar raw-appearing. Marilyn Ames' hurt was more grievous than that. It was eating away her charm, devouring her composure, destroying her very consciousness.

Then—he was a stranger. A stranger in her hall at night. While he turned those alien sorrows in his mind and while he considered making a gentle knock on the door, she screamed, yanked the knob and reappeared.

"There's a man on my fire escape!" she said shudderingly.

Finnley rushed through the door.

"The living room!" she called.

In the living rom, which an overabundance of steam heat had

made stifling, a curtain blew. Finnley looked out the window. A series of iron steps leading to the ground and to the roof hung in the night, untenanted, and bizarrely patterned against the pink of the metropolitan sky.

"Gone now," he said.

She sighed tremulously. "He was kneeling there—just about to come in."

Finnley nodded gratefully. He knew that there had been no man on the fire escape. "I'll go now. I'd speak to the janitor, if I were you. Perhaps you have a watchman—"

"Oh—I can't let you go after what you did."

"Nothing," he replied truthfully.

"It was a great deal. I was frightened. You have plenty of nerve. Please take off your coat and sit down for a moment."

He took off his coat. She went into a kitchenette and connected a coffee percolator. "My children are asleep," she said. "I live here with my mother, but she is visiting in Bayonne."

The illumination of the room revealed her careworn face. Finnley was usually ribaldly vexed when he studied the disintegrating features of an aging woman and saw what they had been. This woman's countenance was not beyond hope of restoration. She was very thin. Love would have turned that characteristic to slenderness.

He caught sight of an evening paper—a sporting final with a double column of football scores. "I missed the game today," he said. "New Haven—my university. But I heard it was good. A long run and a tied score in the last quarter. A march down the field and a fumble. An intercepted pass and a drive back and a touchdown."

She had returned from the kitchen. She was listening to him without any specific knowledge of his words. She said abruptly, "So you were married to her?"

"If you'd rather not talk about it—"

Marilyn Ames shrugged. "I don't mind—now. You looked terrifying in that mothy coat."

Finnley scanned the pieces of the puzzle that was his life and they did not fit together, they did not even belong to the same picture. There was no integration, no reason, no clue to a symmetry. On the tortured fragments were the brush strokes of several artists and the daubs of many more amateurs and vandals. But he might make one bright segment.

"If you do want me to talk," he said, "I shall." He heard the coffee percolator spurt once. "I married Helen a long time ago. It seems a long time. I knew she'd had twins. I thought that they were a brave adventure. What I learned last night I will tell you—if you wish.

"I don't know, Mrs. Ames, how well I could interpret the special allure of that girl for you. Maybe it would be better if I did not try.

"We lived downtown in New York in a rather handsome modern apartment which she and I had furnished. I've been married once before. My first wife—burned to death."

"Oh—" said the woman softly.

"I met Helen not very long afterward. You know what it is like to be alone—to go walking alone, to read alone, to go to bed alone, to wake up in the morning and make your own breakfast and eat it in undisturbed solitude. To have none of the clothes of the other sex in your rooms, none of the smell or the voice sounds—nothing.

"Helen moved into my former apartment on the day after we met. It was springtime and I had been working hard. I took a month off—it was my second vacation after my wife's death. My first had been spent with her father and mother in Egypt and India and China and South America. Never mind. We went away—to California. Helen had always wanted to go there. I have thought of it all this time as celestial. Only in the last day or two have I remembered it correctly. When the places in which you've made love to a woman suddenly become anathema to you—" Finnley shrugged. "I remembered that the grass was green only where it was sprinkled daily and that the hills were crumbling, brown, treeless, and inhabited by dusty reptiles. I remembered the grotesque vulgarity of the thousands who have migrated there—the immense expanses of tawdry bungalows—the feeling of exile among acquaintances who had moved there—the thinness of the air, the coldness of the Pacific, the idiotic riot of the motion picture people at openings and at hotel ballrooms—do you understand?"

"I'd always thought California was marvelous."

"It's not. It's an irrigated hell, a hand-painted desert. It has the soul of a eunuch. It's the kind of place where aged farmers' wives sell dried, gilded horned toads and ice-cream cones from the porch of a maisonette built in the shape of a peach while an orchestra plays jazz over a radio and too much sun shines on the whole unplanned disarray. It's the soul of the middle class at leisure occupations. God!"

"You were talking about—that girl," Mrs. Ames said.

"And I still am. That's exactly what I was talking about. Helen's psyche and her spiritual entity. You see—well—let it pass. We came back from California and took an apartment and we were quite sure we were happy. I don't want to embarrass you—"

"Please go ahead."

"We imagined that we had solved the problem of marriage. We considered ourselves extremely modern. Helen was allowed to go out at any time she chose with any man she wished—to sleep with him if she liked—and I was allowed to do the same."

Marilyn Ames winced and said, "I've read about arrangements like that. They're stupid. They couldn't work."

Finnley paused. "But I think they could. In fact—they're essential to marriage. Fidelity's an addled notion. It flies in the face of nature—and anything that does that flies back with dire and natural consequences. We've been brought up stupidly. It's so simple. If we were brought up promiscuously, we'd go on living that way—and two things would happen: people's lives would remain glamorous; people would live with each other as man and wife for reasons of affection and family and companionship instead of for reasons of bondage. I don't mean to make you unhappy—or to criticize you. Perhaps better human beings will have to be born before married couples can be happy in such a system. But I think not. I think we'll have to change education. Anyway—that's the way we decided to behave. Now I've been thinking that if Hope—my first wife—had lived—she would some day have grown secretly tired of my ardent attentions and she and I would have worked out this scheme so perfectly that nothing could ever have separated us and that we would have enjoyed stimulating private lives nonetheless. I know that is true. Almost nobody can be faithful—and people must have a great love indeed to live happily together at all. A great love and what is called a community of interests. Children, for one thing.

"Finding that out—which I've just done—has made me very happy. You see—ever since Hope died I've been doubting that I would have gone on forever with no one but her—and I've felt it was treachery to her memory. Now I know that she, too, would have changed a little in the end."

Mrs. Ames, sitting in a chintz-upholstered chair, shook her head. "It sounds all right when you say it. But see how it worked out in my life."

"I was thinking"—his voice was lowered—"about myself. Only about myself. Talking about myself."

"I see. I didn't mean to interrupt—"

Finnley took a cigarette from a wooden box, lighted it, and crossed his legs. "I married her in what amounted to a frenzy. Helen, I mean. I wanted to have a strong woman—a capable woman—for a wife. I wanted to make my life stable and permanent. I wanted to hammer it to something solid. I wanted it to be intelligent and modern—and enduring. I closed my eyes to the fact that rarely does anything so intense last a lifetime. Helen knew the dimensions of that blind desire, and she fitted herself into them. Ricardo Jones and his wife Genevieve —the mother and father of Hope—begged me not to marry her." He grinned. "Ricardo threw a boxful of cigars, and his wife procured for me about twenty other girls to break the jinx. I'm a stubborn fool.

"What happened? Helen, with the license in a safety deposit box, lived as she pleased. I thought it was splendid—I think now that all the time I'd known the truth about her, and that I was glad to be relieved of the perpetual responsibility of her innumerable false emotions. Our arrangement often separated us in space—but I had to go on believing that we were inseparably united, because at that time there was nothing else for me to believe. Do you understand?"

"I think so."

"She was often away for a week at a time. But up to last Thursday I could make myself passionate by thinking about her and I believed that we were perfect mates. I thought one thing above all others: I thought that no matter what happened Helen would stand by me. I imagined her as infallible in any crisis. I believed that she had been through a number of small hells, that she was what I thought I also was—realistic, unawed, impossible to terrify.

"When, during this spring, she was away for a vacation with friends in North Carolina, and I met a very handsome Russian girl who was a dancer, I made love to her as casually as can be imagined. You see—by our system—I didn't suspect Helen of infidelity in North Carolina. I knew she would be unfaithful —and I didn't care or worry. That was the beauty of it." He rubbed his hand over his face. "God damn it! With Hope—" He shook impatiently. "Never mind. I know how it works.

You have to be in love—and being in love with our background is what makes the institution of it all so difficult. Anyway—I had a stunning good time with the Russian. But she fell in love with me some other way. She called me up, she wrote me letters, she came to my house, she stormed at my wife over the telephone—she acted, in other words, very badly. She had that insane possessive quality we've imbued ourselves with from childhood. By God, you can't own anybody. You can't possess a person—any more than you can actually possess property. It's there. You can enjoy it. But pick it up, carry it around, put it in your pocket—no. When you leave—property is there for others. When you die—it's still there. You can own nothing on this earth—least of all another human being.

"The Russian lady wanted to own me. She wanted to remove Helen from the picture and take me to bed and keep me there in a constant callid copulation, I guess. When I tried to talk to her she screamed like a police siren and bit her knuckles and kicked the furniture. I had a notion that if I clipped her in the chops, she'd quiet down and that she'd stay quiet if I occasionally broke in her door and raped her. But what the hell! I didn't want to any longer. She hadn't any more idea of how I felt or what I thought than I had intention of emulating her shocking behavior.

"A pretty dilemma. I explained it all to Helen—and she took it as I imagined she would and should; she sympathized and tried to help me plan how to mollify and eventually wean the Russian girl. That was rather a swell married experience—and that's the way marriage should be. I was elated. I didn't know that Helen wasn't until—Well—I had to see the Russian again occasionally. Once I had to make love to her—or thought I did—to keep her from losing her mind altogether. Then I stayed away and I heard that she had gone into a blue mood and finally I forgot about the whole thing—or very nearly.

"It was last Thursday night—"

Finnley was in his bare study, clicking from his typewriter an Epistle to the Corinthians.

His door was open and in the spacious living room the red-haired Helen perused a book while around her wove the strains of symphony music. The music floated from the wall, dulcet and accurate.

After a while Finnley came out and dropped into a chair. "It's about a man who dreamed he slept with an angel," he said, "and who woke up to find in his bed a pure white feather seven feet long. I'll read it to you—"

Helen put down her book. She seemed a little impatient with Finnley's enthusiasm for his recondite prose, but she did not let him see that.

" *'Horatio Tutbult suffered from insomnia,'* " he began.

The apartment bell rang.

"I'll go." Helen was glad of the interruption. She crossed the room—her long gray and green dress spreading and contracting with her steps. She came back with a package.

"The doorman brought it up," she said. "It's for me."

She unwrapped brown paper. Finnley's eyes dropped to his story, skipped ahead, and he chuckled. Then he looked at his wife again. She had undone the paper. Inside was an ornamental metal box.

"Candy!" said Helen.

"From whom?"

She lifted the lid. "No. It's something wrapped in oiled paper. There's a card."

He watched her read the card. Her color changed. Quickly she dipped her hands into the box and turned back the transparent paper.

Then she stood there.

She did not say anything. She swayed gently, swayed and stared into the box on the table.

"What is it?" Finnley said, a trace of agitation in his voice.

She looked at him. Her eyes were like stones. She swallowed, or tried to swallow—he could see muscles moving in her long neck.

"Good Lord, Helen, what's the matter?"

The stones glittered. Sparks lit up in their irises. They blazed. Her chest heaved. "You did this to me! You did this to me! You! You! Christ!"

Finnley jumped up, then, and looked into the box. Color left his face. He took the calling card from his wife's hand and read it. The Russian girl. He looked again at the hideous little object in the box. "I didn't even know she had been pregnant," he said slowly. "Listen, Helen. That's a filthy trick—obscene—but it's nothing. It was just a—and the girl's nuts. Surely—"

Helen stared at him with bright, glassy eyes. Then she hit him in the face with her fist as hard as she could. Then she spun around and ran upstairs.

His nose began to bleed.

He shut the box.

Helen came down with a coat on. She had a bundle of papers in her hand. She threw them at him. They fluttered in the air and fell all around him.

She opened the door.

"Hey!" he said. "That's nothing important. You understand that. Where are you going?"

The door slammed. There was a clatter outside.

Finnley stood in his tracks. One night at a party an ebullient guest had discovered that the high-backed chair in the vestibule could be dropped between the door from the living room and the door to the hall in such a way that it imprisoned anyone in the apartment.

Helen had knocked over the chair so that he could not follow her.

Something in that act stirred a place in Finnley's mind that had long been unconscious.

After a while he heard the elevator come for her.

He heard it go.

Then he saw the papers on the floor. He picked them up and as he inspected them a slow realization of their meaning came to him. They were copies of papers by which Helen was going to divorce him. The Russian girl was named as corespondent. There were affidavits from two people whose names he did not know who had hidden in Helen's closet one night when she had inveigled him into discussing his affaire with the Russian. She had been particularly sympathetic and understanding of his silly dilemma that night, he remembered. She was going to sue for thirty thousand dollars a year alimony. He put one of the papers—a letter to himself—in his pocket.

"That," said Finnley to Mrs. Ames, "is what happened. Night before last."

Mrs. Ames was taut and white. "The girl should be killed."

"My first impulse."

"Where is she now?"

"I went out for a drink and then I called on some of our mutual friends," Finnley said. "When they heard that Helen was divorcing me, they told me that she had had not affaires—but a particular lover. Name of Jean Delacroix. They told me a great many things that were different—from my notion of our relationship.

"I spent a bad night. It rained." Finnley halted for a full minute.

"In the morning I went over to our apartment. I forget why. Delacroix was there—packing up her clothes. I said

[267]

hello and he said hello and I sat down and smoked while he jumped around getting things together. He had a list. That's the way she is. And after he had gone, two very burly and uncouth men called for the trunks he had packed. She must have selected the men herself. But while Delacroix was there I merely sat. He was a shade embarrassed. I wasn't. Only Helen could get a man of his type to do what he was doing. I'd learned, also, that he'd given up his sister for Helen. She could manage such things as that."

"Given up his sister?" Mrs. Ames asked.

"He'd lived with her." Finnley's tone was noncommittal.

"Oh."

"Once, while he was bustling around packing, I had a notion I'd swing on him. He was a big, athletic, handsome bird. But I changed my mind. When he saw that nothing desperate was imminent, he became rather blithe. By and by he noticed the candy box as he rummaged around with his infernal list. 'Hers?' he asked. I wanted to say 'yes' and have him pack it neatly in a calfskin suitcase that was open on the divan. But I didn't. Finally he left."

"I feel almost sorry for him," Mrs. Ames said, surprised at her own reaction.

"I do also," Finnley replied.

"That girl should be killed."

He shook his head very slowly. "No. She's killing herself. A few months of cohabitation with Delacroix will fester her reputation. And I hazard the opinion that the sister will eventually reassume her place. That will be bad for Helen. I daresay their first hours together—they must be well into them now—will start hysterically, and the hysteria will increase." Finnley disturbed his posture. "Shocked—Helen might have been. But she wasn't. She was cold. She'd found an out. It was like her."

They had both forgotten the coffee. It was percolating furiously. Mrs. Ames rose and poured two cups of dark brown liquid. She brought cream and sugar in a small pitcher and bowl with gold edges and an iridescent glaze. "I never heard a story like that before," she said.

Finnley sipped from his cup. "I'm sure you have. People do millions of things like that. It's all in the telling. I've made it seem dramatic and unusual. It wasn't. It wasn't anything but a series of incidents. The kind that get tucked in the skeleton closet very quickly in most American homes."

"I suppose so."

"The point is—"

"The point is," she said, leaning forward, "that you wanted to tell me how to behave intelligently about marriage."

"Well—"

Mrs. Ames' spirits leaped as if they had been touched by a branding iron. "I see it all clearly! When Terry turned from the straight and narrow, I shouldn't have minded!"

"I think—"

"But it's not too late. Not even now. Our lives are our own!"

Her cheeks had become pink. She was tremulous. She leaned forward.

Finnley's soul said, "Oh, Jesus!" and he prepared to begin again—patiently. Nothing he did ever turned out properly. An agonizing weariness filled him. Life was a rich comedy, he whispered to himself. A rich comedy.

"I don't mean that in modern marriage one is always gadding about like a rabbit," he said helplessly.

She breathed. "But there are moments—a few—to be seized and remembered. One treasured hour is better than a century without ecstasy—"

She read that, Finnley thought, in some lousy book. Bruce Barton or Arthur Brisbane or Edgar Guest.

"You understand me," said Marilyn.

"Christ, yes," said Finnley's soul.

"I'll take this particular moment," she said. "I'll go to him—and forgive him."

Finnley's heart hooted at his head. He wondered if she had played some intricate feminine trick upon him—or upon herself. He choked and stuttered and felt that he was the greatest fool on earth.

"I've wanted him so—" she said.

He looked at her eyes.

He rejoiced to see them.

"I love him so!"

At the Dwyers' house I sat with most of the plaster fallen from my ego. A naked lull, in which other people moved about me. Violet had gone upstairs with Leslie. I didn't know his last name. He was a chemist.

chemistry, i reflected, had done vi a lot of good, and a *chemist* was a suitable man to consummate the benefit. i started thinking about hormones, which led to chlorophyl, and thence to the cosmic ray. i pondered the possible thought processes which might have guided mr. wilson to the invention of his crafty chamber in which electrical particles leave dewdrop trails and then i concentrated on aërodynamics and the stratosphere and piccard's haircut, which he had lost to america and for which no doubt he had been returned chewing gum. i saw flora romp amorously into the kitchen with paul and that gave me a side issue of meditation upon (a) bordellos and, (b) meditations in bordellos, which latter theme, i thought, would be more absorbing. then, turning back to science, i cogitated the changes in genes caused by a little judicious x-raying and the odd plants and flies that were produced thereby. i wondered how the human race would fare if its chromosomes were tampered with, and i thought that no doubt cosmic rays caused cancers. i ruminated the new hydrogen isotope which makes water that will sustain neither man nor beast, and, subsequently i went to the bathroom. it is fun to rock around in fine bathrooms as your bladder is drained of the major part of your drinks. i ran my eye over the medicines and the other accessories which had been mentioned by finnley and i had never seen a nicer assortment. the bathroom was mauve. a careful inspection of its contents carried me back once more to science, and i thought that in a few more decades the mass of available knowledge would certainly wreck the last barriers of prejudice and superstition and blockheaded credulity. the very existence of the discoveries that are soon to come will alter man and his systems and governments. for years we will annually learn something as important as the principle of the wheel, something as revolutionary as the discovery of electricity. a bald-headed man shaking a test tube is more powerful than all the woolly-haired orators in time. we would not have to decide to change. we would be changed.

Then, as I came from the bathroom, I saw the sad man.

"i am crying, he said, because of the horse. the horse is truc-
"ulent, stupid, dangerous and ugly. why do people ride upon
"him? why do they make pals of him if not of the oyster?
"he sweats and stinks and maims his tens of thousands. auto-
"mobiles are handsomer and more reliable and they leave at worst
"only oil in the spots where sane people step. i am an enemy of
"the horse.

"i am crying, he continued, because of crime. corruption,
"games of law, indifference—what a spectacle they give rise to!
"i sob and scream to find myself a citizen in a state in which red-
"handed riot and destruction sit smugly in the best clubs. i call
"for vigilantes. i call upon the president. i insist that an end
"be put to all crime, that all criminals be extirpated, slain,
"smothered, shot, chloroformed. shall we be tender to the
"maggots in our own bowels? who are the wet-bottomed
"christly fools who let our laws be made? away with them

"also! mow them down. a day is coming, sentimentalists.
"a day is coming, tough guys. we the people will castrate you
"both in the lobbies of the biggest hotels and we shall hang your
"bollocks on the chandeliers and shoot at them with rifles. i
"weep."

I beckoned to the gentleman, but he went away.

Violet had returned downstairs and she hammered from the
piano a mighty, exultant chord as I entered the living room.

She played

I cannot say how.

"I have a car outside," said Finnley. "We'll go at once."

In the speakeasy Finnley picked out the man instantly. But,
before speaking to him, he walked to the bar. "I'll have," he
said, "a double scotch."

He gulped the drink.

He saw himself walking past the long mirror—shot-looking,
bent; surprised to find his reflection wore an old coonskin coat.

He sat down beside the man.

Terry was alone. Everyone in the bar had heard the story
about a lady—everyone who wanted to hear. The rest—knew
stories about ladies.

Terry was not yet very drunk. Although it was Saturday,
they had been niggardly. Only beers. His own money was
gone: rent and a restaurant bill. It looked like a thin week-end.

"You're Terry Ames?"

He turned. His beard was raggedly shaven. He had cut
himself twice in his impatience to get to the speakeasy. Under
his beard was the gray of waste and hopelessness and oncoming
dissolution. "Yes. I don't think I know you."

"My name's Finnley Wren."

[272]

A deeper blue ran like dye into Terry's eyes. "You—you're the bird who married her."

"I am."

Terry laughed morbidly. "Have a drink?"

"Thanks."

"Wait a second. Have to rescind that. No money."

"One on me, then."

Terry drummed in the slops on the table. "Sure. Married her. Happy?"

"No."

"No."

"She left me," Finnley said.

Terry nodded without looking. The drinks came. "Here's to you," he said.

"To you," said Finnley.

"Now there'll be a pair of us sitting here every night."

"Maybe."

There was a pause. "She's easy to get over," Terry said.

"I hope so."

"A cinch. It's not losing a bitch that burns the blood—it's the bitchery she leaves behind."

"You'd been married." Finnley made it a statement of fact.

"I had."

"Why didn't you go back to your wife?"

"Why?" Terry nodded to the waiter. Still he did not respond. Two more glasses were brought. "She's through."

"No chance of her changing her mind?"

"None. I've written daily—almost."

"I didn't know that," Finnley said thoughtfully.

"How could you? Letters came back."

"I see. Well—here's to you."

Terry made a beer canal to drain the table. "How long do you think someone can go on drinking—as I do?"

"That depends. You were a husky guy."

"I was. Phi Beta Kappa. Four letter man. Funny."

"Would you go back—if she'd have you?"

"If," Terry whispered. "If. That's not very friendly of you. She won't—you see." He stared vacantly, his mind in other places. "I love that woman. She's not very bright, maybe. Not the most beautiful. But I love her. She's the mother of my two kids—my two—" he sighed. "I have two more I can't have. Did you?"

"Did I what?"

"Have my kids?"

"Yours and Helen's? No. A pair of nurses kept them in an apartment down the street. I've seen them. Frequently. They're elegant kids—Terry."

"Did she go to see them?'

"Never."

"Good."

"She wanted them adopted. I wouldn't let her do it."

"Why?"

"I don't know—yet."

"Thanks." Terry shook Finnley's hand.

Finnley drank the last of his whiskey. "Your wife, Terry," he said, "is at a hotel not far from here. I took her there. She's decided to forgive you."

The man grabbed his lapels and peered at his face.

"It's true," said Finnley. "I told her all about you and Helen —tonight. I hadn't known before. I'd thought that right was on Helen's side. I'd thought—never mind. Here's the address. Why don't you go to her?"

Terry rose and took his hat and coat from a shelf. "You mean that, don't you?"

"Yeah. I mean it."

He put on his coat. He stood beside Finnley immobile for a moment. At last he patted Finnley's shoulder.

Finnley took some bills from his pocket. "You'll be wanting a little supper, later on. It's a loan."

"Sure. Loan."

Terry abruptly ran out of the place.

Finnley sat at the table. Voices and smoke eddied around him. The waiter walked by. "Have another?"

"What? Oh. No. No more."

Eventually he fished in his pocket and found a nickel. There was a slotted box on the wall. He dropped the coin into it and a mechanical piano began to play, "Old Man River."

Finnley changed a half dollar into nickels and listened to the piano's repertoire. Then he put on the coonskin coat and left.

At four o'clock he turned the car into a side road between Milford and New Haven.

Overhead were trees.

It was cold.

He switched off the lights and a tunnel of branches vanished. Remote pin-points blinked in the distance.

He turned up the collar of his coat and fell instantly asleep.

PART VI

SUNDAY MORNING

I DROVE from the sixth tee, since it was my honor. Finnley followed me. My ball sliced into a wood, and his fell in almost precisely the same spot. I charged him with deliberation in the matter.

"I wanted to mope around in the leaves," he said.

"Did you really learn to play the way you do by being a caddy?"

"No. Ricardo Jones and I have a perpetual tournament."

"Oh."

Gray skies overhead preluded rain. Few were out on the course. The dead leaves made unnatural handicaps and in the low spots the ground was mushy.

Finnley had reached the Dwyers' house early. He had gone to bed for a few hours, bathed, shaved, and invited me to shoot a round of golf with him. In the first five holes of play he had sketched his actions on the previous night. But he had given me no glimpse of his internal condition.

I was glad to know why Helen had left him. Estelle had been responsible for part of my curiosity—although it is normal to wonder about the torments of any man who walks all night in the rain and begins a conversation with a reference to the bloody bowels of women. The portrait of Wren was filling out. And yet I could not decide whether he had lived an extraordinarily fantastic life or not, and I could not be sure of his feelings about himself.

There had been no caddies at the clubhouse on that opaque Sunday morning, so we dropped our bags at the edge of the rough and entered the woods. Each of us had taken a mashie, and we stirred the leaves ahead of our furrowing feet. Wren must have been tired—but perhaps he did not know it. His store of energy was more abundant than that of most men.

We didn't talk for a long time. Conversation was commenced by him. "What do you think of it?" he asked.

"Of what?"

"I mean—of all that I told Mrs. Ames. My views on marriage. Won't it complicate her new relationship with Terry?"

"She'll forget it. She's probably forgotten it by now. People don't remember precepts or plans of action. They can't even recall in the morning the important things they'd decided to do on the previous evening."

"That's right," Finnley said. "We forget everything."

"And especially systems of living."

"Sure." He laughed. "Once I tried to be a Buddhist. Once I tried to tell the exact truth every time I spoke. Once I undertook to make my manner romantic and colorful. For three weeks I was a hermit. And I remember that I used to be an Indian and a cowboy. She'll forget. It takes years to change the basis of a marriage. Years—and much thought. Marilyn can't think."

"No."

"But, God, I was exhausted. Here's your ball. I'll toss out a new one."

My shot ricocheted through the barren trees and eventually rolled out on the fairway. Finnley played neatly to the green.

"You're an understanding bastard," I said. "Most people wouldn't have attacked the problem at all. And very few—in that way."

"I was afraid." He stopped while I made my approach. "Estelle told me the story. Helen had also recounted it. In Helen's version she'd had no money, Terry had deliberately lied about his conduct with her and she had not known what made her feel so wretched until it was too late, he had put her out of sight in a New Jersey hell hole, and she had struggled ever since to support the twins. It seemed to me instantly that if Terry's wife could learn the facts, she'd relent. But I found her in no emotional condition to listen comprehendingly to them. That's why I told her about my own life with Helen instead. I decided that if she saw Helen Holbein—sharp as a bitch, she'd draw her own conclusions. Well—she did. Only—"

"Only—her private starvation cropped up between the yarn and the reasoning—stimulated by it and by you."

"That."

"But you were afraid that you'd upset the whole structure of your philanthropy."

"Why not?"

"Certainly." I putted and we walked to the next tee. "Why not? It must have been frightful."

"If people knew by what their lives were ordered," he said pensively—and then he drove with a fierce swing—"they'd never recover from the shock."

"That's wrong—and you know it."

"I know it. The capacity to perceive creates parallel to itself a capacity to tolerate. When you learn that—what else is there to discover?"

"Nothing."

"And so what do you do? Learn and bear?"

"Sure."

"O.K," said Finnley and he held his driver horizontally in both hands while I sent my ball skimming toward the drab horizon.

Between holes we dipped a chained cup into a spring and drank. Finnley and I sat down on the grass while a lone man who carried three clubs tucked under his arm quickly played through us. He went down the valley, leaving a wake of pipe

smoke. He had thanked us very cheerfully for the invitation
to go ahead, and he had said, before driving, "I've just preached
a sermon to three hundred dozing breakfast-digesters on abuse
of the Sabbath and now I'm here seeing about it for myself. I
never played on Sunday before. My game was never better.
What do you think of that?"

Finnley had answered, "I think I'd like to hear you preach
next Sunday."

The man had chuckled and smoked and followed a spectacular
drive into a vale below.

"If Tom had taken religion normally," Finnley said, "he
might have been that sort of a bird. What Tom eventually got
was weariness. He was tired of taking care of himself in a
civilization where the achievement of sound self-sustenance
requires so much energy. That fellow believes very earnestly
in God, but he's a damned good golfer, too. A monk! Jesus!"

"Bad."

"Prisons, paternosters, hoods and dongling bells. He'd make
a good Jesuit, though."

"Haven't you thought that he might become one?"

"By God, I haven't! He will, of course. And he'll discover
a new ocean current, or the secret of voodoo witchcraft, or the
explanation of cosmic energy—"

"He'll study, after a while, when he's ready."

Finnley clapped me on the back. He was much more cheerful. I reflected that on this morning he had been lost and without resources. He was leaning on me. Had he known, when
he spoke to me in the speakeasy, that within forty-eight hours,
he'd need consolation more than a confidant?

"Tom"—I spoke as if I knew him intimately—although in
my mind he was only a strapping youngster with sultry eyes
and a penchant for anfractuous conduct—"has taken the best
road for his condition. He belongs to the medieval scientists:
he's part mystic. He expects things to happen that never do.

But in the cloisters he'll get the illusion that they do—then he can work hard and think in peace."

"He will! Let's play. I'm sure that elegant preacher is far away by now. I bet he shoots a second round. Great! And I'm happy about Vi. I saw her this morning. She's happy about herself. Oh, willy-nilly and fiddle-faddle. Fuff, too, if I may quote the ineffable Flora. I don't believe there's a pattern, do you?"

"Pattern in life?"

"Exactly."

"A novelist," I said, somewhat sententiously, "invents patterns. He goes from here to there by way of a pattern. You can find some good Greek on the subject. And the Greeks believed that the emotional elements in an individual were the inalterable rudders of his trajectory through circumstance—on and on to secured symbolic tragedy. Most of our dandy modern authors must, I think, work out their horrors at the end of books and then go back to sow prognostic gloom—impregnating the spiritual mothers of their characters after their heroes' births—and, of course, deaths. Novels are written like detective stories, these days—and diaries are rewritten to correspond to detective stories, along with biographies, autobiographies, and tone poems, no doubt. I don't believe it. I've written a few by the system."

"Heredity, environment, the law of averages, the law of diminishing returns," said Wren, "are subordinate in the immediate now and in the broad aggregate to the great law of accident. You're perfectly right. Somebody ought to work out the incidence of accidents: how fleas in pages' eyes end dynasties; how a small boy's nail maces left in roadways delay by punctures directors' cars and bring new stars to the screen; how explosions in arsenals not only kill thirty-eight persons but spoil the breakfasts of direct descendants of the Huguenots by potting their cups of coffee with shell splinters—all that sort of thing. Since life insurance companies exclusively possess the nerve to contemplate them, and since even they do it by tables, nobody cares to reckon with fortune in his private life. Nobody cares to note it in writing. It doesn't make sense. Well —it doesn't make sense, but it makes life. Who is without his coincidence? Who is without his good and bad luck? Who has relatives to whom funny things have not happened? But who tries to fit the outré and preposterous into his scheme of order? We have no brains to think of such things. We do not think. When, at an early age and in the head, the fat and dust of common knowledge saponify we call the brain adult: there's the end to reason. Our preparedness goes no farther than to attach ambulances to hospitals—indeed—it can go no farther except in grooming the mind for the ungodly missiles of chance. A little groundwork of that nature might be done. Schoolchildren should doubtless be given foci for their endeavor, but they should also be taught an intellectual readiness—for comets, epidemics, exploding light fixtures, toxic hallucinations, falling manna, ghosts, bug plagues, booby traps, loose lamas and the like. There's no adjustment in the race—and the race needs that quality. Anything can happen. Suppose the Martians come? Suppose—suppose my brother Tom, while hunting for heathen to convert, runs across a race of people more handsome than human beings we know, who mature in six days, who are immune to venereal disease and cannot impregnate or be impregnated by any other race? Suppose he brings these folk to America and Europe as curiosities and in a year the world is overrun with perfect gigolos and whores? What then? Are our schoolchildren ready for it? Are our bankers prepared for it? Are our churches in shape to cope with it? They are not. God's round eyes! Our novelists would write about it after the fact, but how many would attack the problem in advance of its discovery? Ah—how few! Perhaps the mere idea has never occurred to a human being before. Think of

[284]

that as an example of mental destitution! How simple and logical a concept! Science may bring it about—next week— next century. Still—they won't be ready for it. What a pity!"

"A great pity," I agreed.

"An instance of the general vacuum. We don't know what we're about—and we don't even conceive of preparing for what is about us."

He drove.

I drove.

At the eighteenth hole, Finnley gazed across to the Sound. It was running coldly up on the beach and a rising tide slowly gorged small rivers and rusty marshes in the far distance.

"Night before last," he said, "I had the jitters. I thought— I believed—I was losing my mind. But now—I feel all right."

PART VII

SUNDAY AFTERNOON

PLAYED bridge.

PART VIII

SUNDAY NIGHT

NOT long before supper a girl named Sherry Wither-spoon arrived with a Saint Bernard dog.

Finnley and his sister had beaten Flora and myself in a half dozen rubbers. We pushed back our chairs and toured the house. People were playing ping-pong in the sun parlor and billiards in the den on the second floor. Outside it was raining. The Sunday-afternoon aspect of the demesne and the guests was relaxing and pleasant.

Sherry Witherspoon disrupted it minutely. Everyone had to meet her.

She was very handsome.

The Saint Bernard was handsomer still.

I went out of doors with him and we ran around the house until I was breathless, damp, exhilarated, and rid of my bridge-induced lethargy.

When I returned, Sherry and Mrs. Dwyer were sprawled in front of the fire. Both women had rosy cheeks from outdoor air, both were dressed in tweeds, both were drinking highballs. I made one for myself.

They were talking about Finnley.

"I never met a man," said Sherry, "who gave me such a feeling. What's he like? Where does he come from?"

Finnley walked into the room. Mrs. Dwyer saw him.

"Tell Sherry what you're like and where you come from," she said.

I handed my drink to Finnley and made another.

He looked at the girl placidly, sipped, and said, "I'm an ordinary man."

"Oh, you couldn't be!"

"I hate to disappoint you. But I am. If you insist on a résumé—I was born in North Dakota in nineteen hundred. My father was a doctor of the old school. He migrated to New Jersey when I was young and there he practices, badly but remuneratively, to this day. My mother died of cancer. I've been married twice. My first wife died. My second left me— last Thursday. I'm in the advertising business. I have a brother—younger—who leads a crazy life and is at the moment in a monastery. My sister is a fairly well-known pianist. I have a lot of acquaintances and a few close friends. Wylie, here, is one of them. Mrs. Dwyer is another. I've been around the world, but I haven't seen the Century of Progress. I've seen a forest fire, but I never saw a typhoon. I went to Yale. I didn't graduate. Once I was in a railroad wreck. I can speak fine French and I can also play the piano, mandolin, ukelele and the traps. I was on the college track team. I've shot moose. I never took dope. Nothing odd ever happened to me —no Yogis showed me the rope trick, none of my dreams has been an accurate prophecy, I've never been on bottom in a rammed submarine and I've never heard a banshee." A peculiar expression crossed his face. He hesitated and grinned. "An ordinary man."

"It sounds very ordinary," said Sherry.

"Believe me, it is. And I'm grateful for it. I've just realized it this very day, as a matter of fact—though I've modestly insisted on it all my life."

"Why don't you do something romantic, then?"

He laughed. "That's what I'm going to try not to do as long as I live. Something interesting or mildly amusing will be sufficient."

"That's senile."

"Exactly. And I embrace it with relief and comfort."

The larger and more bland of the Dwyers' two colored maids announced supper.

Afterward Finnley said, "More bridge?"

I assented—although I did not desire to play. There were a thousand questions I wanted to ask him. Our week-end relationship had given me an ambition toward the complete documentation and understanding of Wren. I thought that after the game he would talk to me again.

But he did not. At midnight he yawned. Violet, eager to keep a tryst with Les, who sat exasperatedly at another table, took advantage of her brother's act. She said, "Let's quit."

Finnley agreed at once. "I'm as sleepy as a goat," he said. And he went to bed.

Flora left for the one o'clock train in New Haven. "I've got to do a small operation at nine," she said.

She kissed me good-bye.

I had a feeling that the world was vaporizing and dissipating around me. Then I understood that it had been only a week-end—a somewhat drunken week-end, in the home of two broad-minded people.

Fantasies were fading.

The magic was magically causing itself to vanish.

Mrs. Dwyer closed the door on Flora. Outside, a motor started. "I feel thoroughly fin-de-semaine," she said.

I went to my room. In it stood the sad man.

"i have shed my last tear, he said."

"You son-of-a-bitch!" I muttered in an angry, despairing tone. I made a dive at the man. After all, he had been an embodiment of worries to me for long enough.

But there wasn't any man.

Nothing.

Just the worries.

I sat down on my bed with a headful of them. All the tribulations of the age.

"The world is nuts," I said. But, since the sad man had vanished, or had never been anything, I could not believe even that. I looked at the titles of about a thousand books and eventually determined not to read at all.

"I'd rather sleep," I said.

I undressed and lay down and thought about my wife in Bermuda. The blue, blue sea, the white clouds and houses, the green grass and the darkly green cedar trees, the clopping horses and the lassitude and peace.

On the very verge of a melodic coma I roused, remembering that I had not written to my wife for several days. After that my body could not excrete the drug of slumber. I turned on the lights and went to the desk. There was a ream of letter paper monogrammed "DD." I took a fountain pen from my coat pocket, pumped it full in a well of cobalt ink, and wrote,

Dear Sally,

The 'DD' doesn't stand for Doctor of Divinity or yet for dusty death, but for Donald Dwyer—a Yale professor at whose house I am spending the week-end. He and his wife live down the coast not far from our place and I think you'll enjoy the Dwyers when we migrate here in the spring. It's been the usual country week-end with perhaps a shade more libation pouring and gay debauchery than I am accustomed to.

But fun. I've met some rather amusing people—one I like very much—a bird named Finnley Wren who's in the advertising business. He's in a jam with his second wife and has reached the life-liberty-and-retention-of-a-modicum-of-individuality theorem which we maintain—although his second wife flubbed it. She was evidently a gross so-and-so. However, he's a grand guy who says such things as that all the evil in hell can't be purged with one suppository. Also many beautiful ladies and witty men.

I have a new idea for a novel I'll tell you about in detail when you come back which please God will be soon. If I were a European, the local boys might think it was a swell book. Maybe I can print on the frontispiece, "TRANS-LATED FROM THE FRENCH."

You'll be less interested in my bucolic follies than in the fact that I got all the tulips planted—Wren helped me—and that the moles haven't undermined the entire lawn—and that the laurel we moved is still verdant and vital.

In the morning I'll go back to town. Have fun. I love you.

PHIL.

I folded the stationery, sealed it in an envelope, stamped it, and put it in my pocket.

Then I lay down again, but for a long time my thoughts moved uneasily, like repetitive patterns on draperies.

PART IX

MONDAY MORNING

FINNLEY and I sat facing each other in the barbarous idiocy of a Pullman chair car. Grime, soot, thunder and discomfort.

We talked a little. We read. We tried to lean back and rest.

"I feel changed today," he said. "Thanks to you."

"Changed?"

He stared out at a flat blue bay. "The parade is past. The uproar is dim in the distance. Things will never again happen to me at the rate they once did—and the magnitude of their effect will be diminished.

"I'll be a bachelor now. Paying alimony. Playing the piano. Selling advertising. Writing fables. Loving a little—unable to love much. Funny." He sighed. "The mystery and the glamour become hard facts. Death isn't a mystery any more, and all the enigma left in life can be expressed in a few unsolved equations. Our deepest knowledge only defines our intellectual incompetence. We'll have to wait for the brain to evolve. And the maturing individual makes his conquest of agony at the expense of ecstasy. Flat and dull, Wylie. I've grown up, perhaps."

When I did not reply, he said, "All those people."

"What people?"

"The ones we talked about. Where are they now? What are they doing? Bitter fragments on the Lethe. Chips and gobbets. Human flug." He closed his eyes and murmured above the din of the wheels, "I could tell you what they are

doing.   I could tell you about them all. . . . .
. . . .
. . . .
. . . .

Monday morning.

Nine o'clock.

Dr. Gordon Wren, having finished his breakfast, pushed back his egg-yellowed plate, pushed back his chair, and removed from the socket of his right upper incisor a small corpuscle of matter which he deposited on the margin of the *Orange Park Register* and dissected with a toothpick.

The telephone rang.

"Good morning!" he boomed cheerily.

"How are you, doctor?"

"Splendid!   Never better.   Health always perfect!"

Dr. Wren told, perhaps, the truth.   Yet, as he talked, there crawled upon him and within him trillions of hideous parasites—

upon his skin—staphylococcus albus

around his teeth—bacillus fusiformus

in his bowels—colon bacilli, bacilli lactis aërogenes, and myriad entamœbæ coli

over his scalp—the bottle bacillus

around his mouth—streptococcus viridans and staphylococcus aureus together with unnumbered spirilla

down his throat—pneumococci

between his toes—trichophyton

a company of minute horrors which inhabit most of us, which compose perhaps a half of one per cent of our total weight—a mass greater than that of the ovaries or testes, for example—but one rarely given equivalent attention.

"I thought," said the voice on the telephone, "that since you were deserted by your family, you might take dinner with us."

Dr. Wren replied that he would be delighted. He would go to dinner—a walking host to germs, a chunk of infested meat—but not because he had been deserted by his family.

The fact that he was alone had no significance for him.

Think of Jessica, Finnley. Think of the girl who could not wait, think of the flower that opened on the mountain top in the vertiginous dawn. . . . .

Nine o'clock.

Jessica was nursing her fourth child. With her free hand she fumbled in a workbasket for a stocking that might match the one she had retrieved from a bureau drawer.

At the bottom of the basket, her fingers encountered an unfamiliar object and she took it out.

She began to cry.

No make-up on her face.

A torn kimono.

The child at her breast.

Tears fell upon the silk of his hair.

Tears for a dance program upon each dotted line of which in faint pencil marks was the immature autograph of Finnley Wren.

Her husband, Jeff, came half-shaved from the combination kitchen and bathroom. "My God," he said, "what is it now?"

But Jessica, who could no longer be identified with the rose, wept inconsolably for things lost and things that could never have been, for dreams and treasures and for youth.

And Libby—whose tumescence carried you to court, to disgrace—whose cloying hysteria sent you into the world—Libby. . . . .

Libby woke with a hangover.

Her head throbbed.
She had difficulty in seeing clearly.
She reached out for a gin bottle.

There were others in those mordant days. Alice Dunfelt who had been snatched into the family Buick by her mother when the newspapers began to lend malodorous publicity to your letch. Voluptuous Alice. Bill Davis, who had sworn to kill you if you mentioned his brother in the courts.

Where are they, Finnley? Where in this wide earth, and what are they doing?..

Alice Dunfelt lay on her death-bed.

"Water," she said.

A nurse brought a glass and lifted the woman.

"What kind of day is it?"

"Cold," said the nurse, "and clear."

"Sunny?"

"Sunny."

"That's nice." Alice, looking fat and middle-aged, smiled in an absent-minded fashion. "I had such a lovely dream. It was about a boy I used to know—long before I was married. I can't think of his name. He was tall and dark."

"Yes," said the nurse.

Alice budged the vast jelly of her person. "Lovely," she repeated.

In a languorous and unimportant way she bent herself toward the scythe as unreluctantly as she had bent toward the arms of nameless young men.

Bill Davis shuffled in a Minneapolis bread line, peered at the drab dawn, and whistled a song called "Ja-da" which had be-

longed to a time when he and Finnley had gone hunting together, when they had been happy, when the world was good.
The man ahead coughed steadily. The man behind chewed
tobacco. Bill was a dipsomaniac and he was engaged in per-
fecting a scheme for cadging drinks. He reasoned that if he
found a prospect, he could say confidentially that not long ago,
while very drunk, he had been told in detail the directions for
locating a buried hoard of jewels and money. He could further
explain that when he sobered up he could not remember the
directions so that he had set out to drink enough to bring them
again to mind. However—and this would be the master stroke
of the scheme—he had run out of cash in the endeavor. The
plan, Bill believed, would be good indefinitely. He could pan-
handle a quarter and buy a drink and sit over it looking sad
until someone spoke to him.

The line moved. Bill hugged himself inside his threadbare
coat and chuckled.

The pale and golden coil of Violet Wren's hair was all undone; she lay not half-awake, redemption in her eyes, a smile
upon her parted, breathing lips, and the morning bright around
her room, brighter on the sea, was beautiful as if by her com-
mand. Such smiles as hers are said to compensate the flesh for
tempest, toil and torment; it is too bad the negative necessities
of pain are naturally rendered more poignant than delight. Yet,
in one blissful hour that sad statistic can be ignored. She
turned. "My lord," she murmured and the young man at her
side awoke. Ah, God! Music, lost virginity, grapes and starlight are the poor substance of our happiness; faint benefits in
the nameless tragedy we share here together! Go out, now,
woman, and find some things that need not be acidly unremem-
bered, for it is morning and victory can make you strong!

And your brother, Finnley?..............................
Ave Maria.

Pater noster.

Dominus regit me.

The Lord is my Shepherd.   I shall not want.

Thomas Wren fed birds in the flagged courtyard of his monastery.

His mind was calm: the green grass of faith was already hiding the shambles life had made of it.   He thought of the goodness of God, and of the books he would read and the studying he would do.

The flight of one dusty creature wrenched from him an exultant whisper.

"Purpose!" said Thomas Wren.

Purpose.

Where is Hewitt, Finnley?   Where is the banker who brought ten thousand dollars to you and turned a supercilious mood to one of fire and vain endeavor?....................

He sat in a bed in a hotel in Washington.   Around him were the props of circumstance: leather suitcases with D.H. burned upon them, padded coat-hangers, silk pajamas, an opera hat, a breakfast tray, whiskey in a decanter, newspapers and a long white scarf, a wallet thick with new bills, a gold watch and a chain of gold.

His phone rang and presently a fat man stepped into his chamber.

Hewitt smiled.   "Good morning, senator."

The fat man sat anxiously upon the bed-edge and his voice was querulous.   "I don't see how you can lie here like a diva, eating—stuffing yourself—when you have an investigating committee to face.   Hell's loose.   They've turned up the fact that you didn't pay an income tax last year and the year before.   They're out to get you—"

Hewitt smiled with relish. "Let 'em—if they can. Life may be a bowl of cherries, senator. But it's not a game of marbles. My bank's as good as the dollar. And my character is my own handiwork. They make the laws. I operate within them. It'll be fun."

He chewed up a whole slice of toast and gustily washed it down in coffee.

And Hope's two splendid parents? Finnley surely knew what they were doing. Life gave them a fortune, took their daughter, taste and culture for a child.....................

Ricardo snorted at the morning *Times*.

Genevieve answered the phone.

She hung it up and smiled.

The maid disconnected it and took it away.

"God-damned lily-livered nitwits," Jones shouted. He shook the paper. "Look at this!"

"Ricardo," his wife said gently, "Helen's left Finnley. For good. That is—he won't go back, even if she will. Estelle just called me."

Jones flung his cigar through a Venetian blind.

Long ago—in school—Miss Busshussputts taught you and Doris and Beryl and Donald—ages ago—eons ago...........

Doris, sitting at her switchboard, connected Donald with Beryl and listened in; it was a hot conversation: they had been engaged for nineteen years now, and quarreling daily. At the same moment, Miss Busshussputt locked the great-great-great-grandson of Osiris in the privy and started to the New Building.

Estelle, having telephoned to Genevieve Jones, now lay in bed with her eyes closed. She thought about Bermuda. Odd that she had met someone whose wife was on the same boat with her husband. She bothered herself beyond sufferance with circuit reflections upon coincidence and related vicissitudes. She sat up at last, and yawned. Outside her window Park Avenue bumbled elegantly. She rang for her maid. "Irma," she said, "start my bath. And then phone the garage and tell them that I smashed my car all to pieces yesterday afternoon in Darien."

"Oh," said Irma. "Were you hurt?"

"Nobody was hurt," Estelle replied. "Not a scratch. I hit a truck. It was my fault, I think, because I wasn't looking."

"Oh, my," said Irma.

"I was looking at a monkey-man," Estelle continued placidly. "In a red coat, with a fine monkey which had a coat to match. There was a loud noise and I found part of the windshield in my lap. I removed it, bit by bit, and called on the Wallingfords while an estimate of the damage was made. You might start the radio before you start my bath. Peculiar things," she added, after a pause, "keep happening to people."

"Yes," said Irma. "Take my brother Pauley."

"Bath," Estelle replied firmly. "Pauley's sorrows seem irrelevant at the moment. I want to be alone with my thoughts, and damned skimpy they are this morning, too, in view of everything."

Remember Dingle, Finnley? Dingle who taught you so much? Dingle who suggested the possibility of other decorations than crosses for church steeples? . . . .

Incredibly old, fantastically energetic for his age, Dingle bounced out of his bed. He went to the head of the stairs and yelled, "Mrs. Fustian! Mrs. Fustian. My coffee, for God's sake!"

An antique voice replied in habit-worn tones, "A man your age shouldn't drink coffee!"

"A man my age," he yelled, "should commit suicide. My skin's all horn, my brain's a thin broth, little children run from me. Bring up a revolver with my coffee and, so help me, I'll do a job that God Almighty has overlooked for thirty years!"

"You're tempting the devil with words like that!"

"I wouldn't burn," Dingle roared. His nightgown flapped around his spindly legs. "I wouldn't sizzle. No juice in me. Worse luck!" He laughed. "I'd explode, like celluloid. Serve the devil right. Where's that coffee?"

"Coming."

Mrs. Fustian panted up the stairs. Dingle took the coffee, gulped some of it, and said, "Now go over next door and rout out that God-damned priest."

"You certainly don't want a priest at this hour."

"I don't want one at any hour. But yesterday I bet the old fool I'd beat him bowling at nine this morning."

"Bowling!"

"And tell him to put on a clean shirt—for the honor of Rome. Here. I'll send him a clean shirt." Dingle went back into his bedroom, guffawing.

Mrs. Fustian trailed behind, wringing her hands and enjoying her lot.

Helen lifted a cup of the coffee which Delacroix had made. "I can be late this morning—for you, darling," she said.

"Swell."

"You don't sound especially enthusiastic."

"It's Monday. I always feel low on Monday."

"Come here."

He walked from his bedroom.

Helen began to laugh. "Good heavens! Is this a joke?"

"Is what a joke?"

"Long underwear! You don't really mean that you wear it?"

"When it's cold. In the daytime. Habit I picked up in France."

"Well—you take it right off! Long underwear! Ye gods!"

Delacroix shrugged and unbuttoned the union suit.

"Come here," said Helen.

"Honestly—honey—"

"You don't love me—do you?"

"Why—of course—"

"What have you planned for today?"

He spread out his hands.

"Don't do that! It makes you look positively Jewish!"

"As a matter of fact," he said slowly, "I was going to see my sister."

"I thought that was all over. I thought you weren't—"

"Just to give her some money."

He sat on the bed beside her.

A long interval passed.

Suddenly she said, "See! You don't love me."

"But—Helen—"

"I knew it! I should never have left Finnley!"

"Listen—"

"Don't talk to me!"

"But—"

Helen picked up her coffee and threw it in his face. It was very hot. He shut his eyes and sat still until the first harsh burn had lessened.

Helen shuddered and was quiet.

She thought that he was going to hit her.

"Don't you dare strike me!" she shouted.

Delacroix turned back the bedclothes.

He grabbed a handful of her nightdress.

Helen began to scream for help.

He tore off the garment and wiped his face with it and threw it at her.

Then he walked to the window and stared out at the lewd architecture of Greenwich Village.

Helen stopped screaming and began to beg for forgiveness.

At the door of their nine-room three-bath South African Dutch Colonial house in Forest Hills, Terry Ames kissed Marilyn.

"I'm the happiest man on earth," he said gently and fervently. By an odd coincidence, and from celestial records, the statement could have been authenticated. Another man, in Moscow, would be slightly happier when he woke.

Marilyn had tears in her eyes. She said, "I've got to go in now and get the slip covers off of things."

What of Helen's other friends, Finnley? The squires of this modern day? The gentry of Gotham? How did they deport themselves? . . . .

Gordon Bannister started for the Stock Exchange, although his cold was worse. Nathaniel Kitteridge slept under six grains of luminal. Clive Rutledge poked in the wreck of a railroad train and found a child's shoe. Leonard Bellamy lay in jail, battered by a truck driver, but strangely bubbling with high spirits. David Tree sat in a scrofulous restaurant and pointed out Brooklyn Bridge to a homely female companion, saying, "I'd throw them off there. Millions of them!" Billy Vanderpole retched into a washbowl and then fumbled in a medicine chest for a hypodermic needle. Frank Newell clicked his cane on the pavement as he walked briskly to work—an attitude enhanced by the recollection of a quotation from Rousseau.

What, Finnley, of the farmers with whom Helen spent her months of pregnancy? . . . .

The Schlessengers one and all ran out into the yard to capture a pig which had strayed there from some neighboring sty.

What of the blond obstetrician?.....................
Flora scrubbed meticulously at a hospital basin. Her curls were concealed by a white headdress and a nurse held rubber gloves for her. Once, she giggled.

Of the gentleman who took you to Canada?.............
Briggs said grace and then continued a business conversation with his guest—a swarthy personage traveling under a forged passport to purchase lethal machinery for Central America.

Of the two boys you paddled away from the pyre that had been Rangadam?................................
Clarence and David Montgomery left their respective wives and started by a commuters' train for Chicago where they operated an air line. They were the youngest men in the business, but they were very able. If she had not hated them, their mother would have been proud of them. However, she had moved to California where she could despise them uninterruptedly, after having lost nine suits brought against her sons to take from them their father's money.

And what of your former secretary?..................
Miss Clerrindger, now traveling companion to a rich frump, was found on the sidewalk of the Boulevard des Capucines, in a dead faint, her right hand firmly clutching a batch of photographs she had kind-heartedly purchased from a passing vendor.

Martha and Don Dwyer sat at their breakfast table with Sherry Witherspoon, the chic and belated arrival at their week-end party.

"You just missed him," Mrs. Dwyer said.

Sherry blew smoke downward from her fragile nostrils. "I'll meet him again somewhere soon."

Martha looked at the girl with speculative eyes.

Don rumpled his newspaper. "He'd come out of it."

"Out of what?" Sherry asked.

"The heebie-jeebies."

"Oh. That."

"You seem to be pretty excited—for you," Martha said.

Sherry nodded. "I am. I'm going to marry him."

Don chuckled.

Nine o'clock.

The frost was vanishing from the fields.

The train thundered toward the City.

Coffee. Morning papers. Maids. Beds.

All was well.

Finnley opened his eyes and grinned at me. "Been thinking," he said.

"About what?"

"About my friends. I haven't many—real ones. And those I have make up what matters in this round little earth. I've had fun. But it's a silly business. Silly. Silly. Silly. What nitwits we all are!"

We walked along in the human serpent at Grand Central Station. Porters carried our bags.

I felt as if I were recovering from a wasting illness, as if my soul were slowly knitting. I had witnessed the last of the drama. Wren had grown up—before my eyes. There were no fears in him—but the magic was gone from him. People no longer looked at him and looked quickly again. He was adult and inscrutable now. He had stepped into all-time. Within him was the everlasting aloofness of self-conquest.

At the corner we shook hands. For a moment his eyes glowed with a lambent reminiscence—but the light was that of things seen remotely. He was thinking about his work, his office, his immediate future.

"Be seeing you," he said.

"Sure. Swell time. Thanks."

He walked away. I had an impulse to run after him. There were a thousand questions I wanted to ask. I wanted to know more about his childhood. I wanted to know what had happened to him at college. I wanted to read the rest of the story about the "greenies." But he had nothing more to say. He would regard such inquiries as rude curiosity.

I rode toward my apartment in a taxicab. I realized with a start that I could not remember how he had looked—although five minutes had not passed since I had seen him. I began to believe, in a sort of panic, that I would not recognize him if I met him again. The week-end became an hallucination. The moods encountered in it were dreamed hysterias. I had not been away. I had not planted my tulips. I had been riding around, drunk, for days and nights, alone.

I glanced anxiously at the meter of the cab, half-expecting to see a fabulous sum represented upon it.

I saw: thirty cents.

PART X

A DECEMBER NIGHT

M Y APARTMENT overlooks Washington Square. From the windows where I sit to write I can watch the traffic bend around the Arch. Hurdy-gurdies thump melodiously below me; abysmal bands snort in my street; the moon rises over the building at One Fifth Avenue; children yell and fall and roller skate all day; Italians squabble; lovers squeeze together on long benches, and the buses pause to renew themselves for their plunge uptown.

It is as atmospheric as the devil, although what energy the human mind is supposed to derive from pretty stage sets, I cannot imagine. Ventilation is vastly more important.

In any case, one evening before Christmas, when the town blazed with illuminated trees, and when drunks exhibited a uniform and grossly overtolerated tendency to sing "Hark, the Herald Angels" and "Silent Night," I sat staring at my typewriter, wondering why so impressive an affair was made of so easy a job as English composition, and why, with such arrogance to aid me, I could get off only the veriest trifles.

I had put a new sheet in my machine, blocked out of my ears the sound of several radios—some in cabs (a shocking graft of gadget upon gadget), and waited long for a golden thought to say in purple writing.

But since the more I pondered upon life the simpler it seemed and the less there appeared to be to say about it, I had gradually and unconsciously abandoned the process and sunk myself in retrospect.

How I came upon Wren, I do not know. I had neither seen nor heard of him since the blaring autumn morning when we parted. I had, however, told my wife many of the details of his examination of himself. I perceived him in my fancy with no especial intelligence but only as an interesting bird.

Then, the telephone rang. I dropped my mood and answered it reluctantly.

I recognized Finnley Wren's voice. He was excited.

"I've been in Brazil," he said. "I want to see you at once. For one thing, I'm in love. And for another, I've got a story to tell you about a countess and a dish of hash that

THE END.